R2S

HELL IS EMPTY

Also by Craig Johnson

The Cold Dish

Death Without Company

Kindness Goes Unpunished

Another Man's Moccasins

The Dark Horse

Junkyard Dogs

CRAIG JOHNSON

HELL IS EMPTY

VIKING

VIKING
Published by the Penguin Group
Penguin Group (USA) Inc., 375 Hudson Street,
New York, New York 10014, U.S.A.
Penguin Group (Canada), 90 Eglinton Avenue East, Suite 700,
Toronto, Ontario, Canada M4P 2Y3
(a division of Pearson Penguin Canada Inc.)
Penguin Books Ltd, 80 Strand, London WC2R 0RL, England
Penguin Ireland, 25 St. Stephen's Green, Dublin 2, Ireland
(a division of Penguin Books Ltd)
Penguin Books Australia Ltd, 250 Camberwell Road, Camberwell,
Victoria 3124, Australia
(a division of Pearson Australia Group Pty Ltd)
Penguin Books India Pvt Ltd, 11 Community Centre, Panchsheel Park,
New Delhi — 110 017, India
Penguin Group (NZ), 67 Apollo Drive, Rosedale, Auckland 0632,
New Zealand (a division of Pearson New Zealand Ltd)
Penguin Books (South Africa) (Pty) Ltd, 24 Sturdee Avenue,
Rosebank, Johannesburg 2196, South Africa

Penguin Books Ltd, Registered Offices:
80 Strand, London WC2R 0RL, England

First published in 2011 by Viking Penguin,
a member of Penguin Group (USA) Inc.

10   9   8   7   6   5   4   3   2   1

Publisher's Note
This is a work of fiction. Names, characters, places, and incidents either are the product of the author's imagination or are used fictitiously, and any resemblance to actual persons, living or dead, business establishments, events, or locales is entirely coincidental.

LIBRARY OF CONGRESS CATALOGING-IN-PUBLICATION DATA

Johnson, Craig,———
    Hell is empty : a Walt Longmire mystery / Craig Johnson.
        p. cm.
    ISBN 978-0-670-02277-9
    1. Longmire, Walt (Fictitious character)—Fiction.   2. Sheriffs—Fiction.   3. Wyoming—Fiction.
I. Title.
    PS3610.O325H45 2011
    813'.6—dc22   2010048021

Printed in the United States of America
Set in Dante MT
Designed by Alissa Amell

*For Joe Drabyak (1950–2010), who has died so many
literary deaths and continues to live on in so many well-read hearts.*

Hell is empty
And all the devils are here.

—William Shakespeare, *The Tempest*, act I, scene 2

*Ch'i' non averei creduto
che morte tanta n'avesse disfatta.*
I should not have thought
that death could ever have unmade so many.

—Dante Alighieri, *Inferno*, canto 3, lines 56–57

ACKNOWLEDGMENTS

Hell Is Empty could be the most challenging novel I've attempted so far and, like Dante, I would've found it difficult to make such an effort without my own guides into the nether regions. In my part of the country, the one thing you don't do is argue with your Indian scouts.

When I first signed with my agent, Gail Hochman, I didn't know what trustworthy hands I was placing myself in, but over the years it has become quite evident. The first person she delivered me to in the wilderness of the publishing world was Kathryn Court, my editor extraordinaire and president of Penguin USA. Second in command of my books, and the person to whom I must bid a fond farewell, is Alexis Washam, who has since moved on, but was a guiding hand in the writing of this book as well.

In the many rings of publishing, you hope for a head of publicity like Maureen Donnelly, a senior publicist such as Ben Petrone, a publicist like Gabrielle Gantz, and, of course, we all hope for an all-purpose angel who turned out to be Tara Singh.

My good friend and counsel, Susan Fain, continues to be an inspiration and assistant in the realms of higher literature, and without her help some of the more apocryphal and obscure aspects of *Inferno* might've escaped me.

Marcus Red Thunder has long been the influence for Henry Standing Bear and the guardian of all things Cheyenne and Crow in my books. Without him I would be the one lost.

Thanks to Bill Matteson for accompanying me on numerous trips into the Bighorn Mountains, including visits to the top of Cloud Peak, the only spot on the mountains with crystal clear cell phone reception.

A great big thanks to wilderness ranger Robert "Bob" Thuesen out of the Bighorn National Forest Powder River Ranger District for the times above tree line and my endless conversations that always started with, "What if...?"

These are my guardian angels, the people who enable me to do what it is that I do, but there's one who supersedes them all. Thank you, Judy, the one who shares my life and all my love.

1

"Didn't your mother ever tell you not to talk with your mouth full?"

I tried to focus on one of my favorite skies—the silver-dollar one with the peach-colored banding that seriates into a paler frosty blue the old-timers said was an omen of bad times ahead—as I stuffed a third of a bacon cheeseburger into Marcel Popp's mouth in an attempt to silence the most recent of his promises that he was, indeed, going to kill me.

At last count he'd made this statement twenty-seven times to me, eight to other members of the Absaroka County Sheriff's Department, and seventeen to Santiago "Sancho" Saizarbitoria, who was dragging a few french fries through his ketchup as his eyes stayed trained on a paperback in his left hand.

I looked at Sancho. "That was twenty-eight."

The sun reflected through the western window and struck my face like a ray gun. I was tempted to close my eyes and soak in the warmth of the early afternoon, but I couldn't afford the luxury. I hadn't allowed any silverware at the table and Marcel Popp was manacled, but I still warned him that if he bit either Sancho or me he'd go without food.

The Basquo tilted his head from the book. "Do dirty looks count?"

Popp glanced at Santiago, who was watching the other two convicts quietly eating their lunches, and we could only guess what his words would've been as he chewed.

"No." I placed the rest of the convict's burger on his plate and looked back out the window as the sunshine took another dying shot at my face.

Sancho and I had been amusing ourselves by keeping score, and even though the Basquo was down by eleven, he had made a fourth-quarter comeback with a tirade he'd received as we'd unloaded the transported prisoners at South Fork Lodge in the heart of the Bighorn Mountains. The Basquo'd apologized for handling Marcel's head into the top of the door while getting him out of the vehicle; I still wasn't sure if it had been entirely innocent.

I glanced at Santiago and then risked closing my eyes for just a second. Even with present company, I had enjoyed my own Absaroka burger and fries. South Fork was my favorite of the lodges, with the best menu and a river-stone fireplace in the dining room that owners Holli and Wayne Jones kept roaring when the temperature was under fifty degrees. It was a year-round, full-service lodge nestled away in one of the southside canyons, with snowmobiling, cross-country skiing, horseback riding, trout fishing, and hunting in season.

It was early May, and the summer crowds hadn't arrived yet. With the outside temperature in the high thirties not including windchill, I was afraid we still had a few shots of winter left.

Despite the weather, there was a comfortable, close quality to the lodge, and I fantasized about reserving one of the rustic cabins by the partially ice-covered creek and calling Victoria Moretti, another of my deputies, to see what she was up to this weekend. Vic had just bought a new house, and she'd invited me and my best friend, Henry Standing Bear, over for dinner tonight. I was still thinking about the cabin when Popp spoke again.

"I'm going to kill every single one of you motherfuckers."

It was a general statement, but he'd been looking at me. "Twenty-nine."

Currently, Marcel wasn't a happy camper. I hadn't released either him or the other two murderers from their traveling chains in order to eat. Marcel had already killed two Winnemucca, Nevada, city policemen and a South Dakota highway patrolman in an attempt to escape a year back. That and his limited vocabulary had endeared him to the entire Absaroka County staff. We would be just as happy to be rid of him when we met up with the Big Horn and Washakie counties' sheriff's departments, the FBI, and the Ameri-Trans van near Meadowlark Lodge in less than an hour.

Ameri-Trans was a private firm that contracted with law enforcement to transport prisoners, but they had no contract with us; I didn't like the fact that they had a record high percentage of escapees and wouldn't allow them in my jurisdiction, so we'd made a little jaunt into the mountains this afternoon with the prisoners.

I'd asked the FBI agent in charge over the phone what all this was about but had been told that the details would be made clear when we delivered the convicts to the multiagency task force that awaited us a little farther up the road. I didn't like his answer, but for now that was my problem.

I glanced at Raynaud Shade, the prisoner who worried me most, the one who continued to look at his plate as he chewed. I didn't know why the Crow-adopted Canadian Indian was being transported but would be just as glad when he was no longer my responsibility. He hardly ever spoke, but in my estimation it was the quiet ones you really had to worry about. I'd been distracted by my thoughts for only a second, but when I paid attention again his pale eyes were studying me from under the dark hair. He had this unnerving ability that whenever you refocused your eyes on him, he was there with you—like a cat in a cage.

"I'm going to kill you, you little Basque prick. I'm gonna kill your big boss here—I'm gonna fuckin' kill all of you."

I picked up the rest of the burger and pushed another third into Marcel's mouth.

Sancho stuffed the paperback under his arm, looked at the stack of books at his elbow, and smiled a wayward, electric smile that made the women in the county give him that second look, or even a third. "That was a triple."

"Almost an in-the-park home run." I frowned at him. "That was one for you, one for me, and a general score we can share."

"C'mon."

I tallied it up. "Thirty to nineteen."

He sighed and resumed reading Dante's *Inferno* as I reached over and slid *Les Misérables* off the top of the pile to reveal *Les Trois Mousquetaires*—both in the original French. The Basquo, regretting a stint in higher education devoted almost exclusively to criminal justice, was attempting to fill in some of the literary gaps. We had all made lists for him, including *Bury My Heart at Wounded Knee* from Henry and, of all things, *Concrete Charlie: The Story of Philadelphia Football Legend*

Chuck Bednarik from Vic, but my dispatcher Ruby's list, which included *Crime and Punishment* and *The Pilgrim's Progress* as well as the *Inferno*, had been the most daunting, so the Basquo had started with it. I, taking pity on the poor kid, had included *To Kill a Mockingbird*, *The Grapes of Wrath*, and the aforesaid *Musketeers*.

"How's it going, troop?"

He peeled a thumb against the sides of the prodigious paperbacks, especially *Inferno*. "Slow."

"Hey, I am God-damned starving here."

Popp was a monster, just the kind of obstacle you didn't want to meet in a dark or otherwise illuminated alley. Roughly my size, he was already in shape when he'd gone into the South Dakota Maximum Security Facility in Sioux Falls, and four hours of weight lifting a day over the last year hadn't allowed him to exactly winnow away.

"And fucking dying of thirst, you assholes."

Or improved his vocabulary.

Hector Otero, the third of our terrible trio, smiled at the latest of Popp's outbursts, and I wondered what wrong turns had resulted in the scam artist killing two people on Houston's south side. The ever-smiling Latino had been shocked when Santiago had spoken to him in fluent Spanish. I'd understood only a percentage of the conversation, but the Basquo had rolled his eyes afterward, putting the street hood's intelligence in question. "Who wrote that anyway?"

Sancho regarded the Latino with one eye. "What?"

The gangbanger seemed actually interested, his eyes like drips of crude oil flicking between Sancho and me. "That book, that Dante's *Inferno*; who wrote that?"

The Basquo and I traded a look, and I waited to see how my deputy was going to play it.

"Hector, do you know who's buried in Grant's Tomb?"

"Nope."

Saizarbitoria went back to his Penguin Classic. "Didn't think so. Just be glad we're letting you eat at the big-person table."

Otero, aware that he was being made the butt of a joke, clicked his eyes to me so I'd know that he wasn't up to anything and then raised in his chair just enough to see the other titles in Saizarbitoria's pile. "Yeah, well, at least I'm not reading a book by Alexander Dumb-ass."

Hector was grinning when Raynaud Shade sucked the air out of the room.

"Shut up, Hector."

If anybody had ever said that to Hector Otero in the outside world, they might've gotten more than a couple of ounces of lead in response, but not Shade. The smaller man looked at the Indian but said nothing.

When I looked at Shade, he was staring at me again.

His features were flat, his nose spread across his face like a battering ram had been used one time too many, the bones of his brow and cheeks prominent. He was an average height, but his chest, shoulders, and bull neck let you know that if something were to start, Raynaud Shade would get his share. You wouldn't have thought him capable at twenty-seven of the rap sheet he carried—but when you looked into his outlandish eyes, it was all there. His irises were the same washed-out blue as the winter Wyoming sky and just as cold.

At least one was. Raynaud's left eye was a replacement, and whoever had done the work had failed to capture the exact color. The shade, no pun intended, was an elusive one reflecting an altitude where humanity could not survive.

I'd read about him—he must have been the one the Feds were really interested in. He was on the express back to Draper, Utah, to either a lethal injection or a firing squad, which meant that he was a dead man walking and, as long as he walked in my county, he would walk in chains.

He looked at me through the hood his dark hair formed and spoke in an empty, halting voice. "Thank you."

It was the sixth time he'd communicated since we'd been responsible for him, coming up on seventy-two hours. "For?"

His eye stayed with mine for a second—it was as if he was half paying attention—then panned around the café like a searchlight. "For allowing us to eat in a restaurant." He smiled as though he didn't know how, and I figured it was the only one he had—the one with a lot of teeth and no warmth. "I imagine this will be my last time to do something normal."

He spoke in the cadence of the Yukon Territory where he'd been born, and his voice carried—one of those you could hear from a hundred feet away even when he was whispering. His eye went back to his plate, and his hair fell forward, again covering his face. "I gotta go to the john."

I studied him. "In a minute."

He nodded and raised his cuffed hands, putting the fingertips on the table at its edge, his thumbs underneath. I watched as the fingers bent backward with the pressure of his grip.

"Me too, I gotta take a fucking piss."

Popp made a clicking noise as he spoke, and I could tell he was thinking of spitting again. He'd spit on Sancho as we were unloading him, at which point I'd grabbed him by the back of the neck and pulled his face in close to mine, making it clear that if he spat again he'd go without lunch. My fingerprints were still on his neck; I was feeling bad about that.

"I've been here before."

I turned back to Shade. "Excuse me?"

"First kill outside of my family."

He said it like they didn't count.

"I gave one of his bones to two other men who sent it back to me in the mail in an attempt to get some money I have put away—that's why they're meeting us."

He had finished his meal and carefully pushed his plate back a couple of inches, his thumbs still under the table, his hair still covering his face. "There is an FBI psychologist that I've been seeing; her name is Pfaff. I told her about where the body is buried." He was suddenly silent, aware that everyone had been listening to him, but then stared directly at me. "I just thought you might be curious."

The waitress interrupted the little breakthrough and squelched my hopes of extending Shade's confession. "Would you like some more coffee, Sheriff?"

It took me a second to come back; Shade's dead eye was like that—it drew you into the cold.

"Yes, ma'am."

I caught her looking at the convicts and figured it was to be expected. If they're lucky, most people in the private sector never get to meet someone like Marcel Popp, Hector Otero, or especially Raynaud Shade, but with our little road show of recidivism, prurient curiosity was to be expected.

She poured in a distracted manner. "Do you get the check?"

"Yes, ma'am." I looked at her. "I don't know you, do I?"

Her eyes slid away. "No, I'm new."

"Hi, New. I'm Walt Longmire."

I held out my hand, and she took it as she held the coffee urn out of the way. "Beatrice, Beatrice Linwood."

I listened to the way she rounded her vowels. "Minnesota?"

She nodded without enthusiasm and took a second to respond. "Yah, Wacouta."

I smiled. "Well, you don't have to be ashamed about it. What's that near?"

"Red Wing."

"Where they make the work boots?"

"Yah."

I sipped my coffee in appreciation and studied her for a moment; midforties, she was too thin and a little mousy, but it was a nice smile. Something else there, though, something that reminded me of my late wife. Her hair was thin, and she looked like she might've undergone some form of chemotherapy recently.

"What brings you out this way this time of year?"

She shrugged and pushed her glasses back onto the bridge of her nose, and I noticed her rubbing her finger where a wedding ring might've once been.

"Snowmobiles."

I should've figured. Most of the flatlanders got tired of doing a hundred miles an hour on the ice of the ten thousand lakes and eventually wanted to try their hand at the mountain trails. A lot of them ended up buried in the snow or running into trees. I'd tried the power sport once with the Ferg, my part-time deputy, but didn't like the noise or the sensation that my crotch was on fire.

"Holli and Wayne treating you well?"

She glanced toward the opening where the smiling head of flamboyant chef Alfredo Coda had appeared from the kitchen, and then turned back to me. "Yah, they've all been great."

"I don't mean to break up old home week, but could I get something to fucking eat and drink?"

I tipped my fawn-colored hat back and looked at Marcel, but Saizarbitoria was faster. Holding a portion of *The Divine Comedy* in one hand and picking up the remainder of the prisoner's burger in the other, he gave him the last bite. I noticed Sancho was even less gentle than I'd been, and his voice was a little irritated. "Anything to shut you up."

I reached over to take the coffeepot from Beatrice so that she wouldn't have to get in arm's reach of the prisoners. "Here, I'll take that."

She pulled away, just slightly. "No, I'll get it."

I took the coffeepot anyway and tested the temperature. "That's all right." To a desperate man, anything was a weapon. I poured a round for the chain gang and one for the Basquo. "Can't be too careful."

She smiled up at me. "They don't look all that dangerous."

"Well." I stood and returned the pot to her. "I'll take that check now."

She put it facedown alongside my empty plate.

"Shade? Let's go." I glanced at Sancho, making sure we made eye contact, and left him with the other two.

The convict stood and then rounded the table toward me. I glanced at Saizarbitoria one more time. He rested the paperback on the table and nodded. I took Shade's arm, and he began a shuffling, manacled gait past the front counter, through the gift shop, and around the corner to the communal sink and the two doors that led to the bathrooms.

Shade paused. "Do you need to come in with me?"

I glanced into the small stall that said BUCKS and noted the only egress was a seven-inch vent in the ceiling. "Not unless you're planning on turning into a field mouse and crawling up that pipe."

"No." He stared at me. "Not a mouse."

"Leave the door ajar."

He did as I asked, and as he busied himself I remembered how he had stumbled in the dining room as we'd gone past the last table where they had been rolling silverware, bumping it with his hip and pausing for only an instant.

There were small alarms going off in my head as he came out a few moments later, turned his back to me, and began washing his hands. After a few seconds he raised his head, and the eye studied me in the mirror. "I'm sorry if I seem preoccupied, but it is difficult to see you."

Aware of his disability, I nodded as he lifted his cuffed hands with the traveling chains that led to the manacles at his feet and tore a paper towel from the dispenser. "It's the snow." He tossed the towel into a trash can in the corner and stepped toward me. "It's difficult to see you because of the snow; surely I'm not the first one to tell you that?"

I stared back at him and dropped my hand to the Colt at my hip. "Snow."

His face was impassive, and he gestured with one hand, the other along for the ride. "There is the outline of you, but inside is only snow—like an old TV."

I watched as the one hand dragged the other over his shoulder. "You mean static?"

"Yes, but not exactly like that. It's as if you carry the snow within you." The pupil in the live eye stretched open while the dead one remained still. "When did this happen?"

I stood there for a long moment, studying him and trying to get a read on whether it was an act or if he was truly insane. I'd been around crazy people before, but none with the dedicated malice that this man seemed to exude. "We should get back to the others."

He leaned in and whispered as his hands dropped and shifted to his side. "I didn't have to go to the bathroom but wanted to speak to you alone about the snow and the voices."

I didn't say anything, and he stepped in closer.

"You see them and hear them, too."

I countered and casually brought the large-frame Colt up, holding it loose at my hip. "Shade, you wouldn't have palmed the steak knife from that table in the dining room?"

He said nothing, but the one eye slit. There was a slight twitch as his motor response was to try for it, but then he smiled with his wide, even-set teeth and brought the knife out, wrapped inside a fist.

I turned so that he could see that the Colt was cocked and the safety was off. "Give it to me."

He held back and regarded me for a long moment, letting the words settle between us like ash. "You don't believe that they are near, do you?"

I didn't move, didn't even breathe. "Give me the knife."

His other hand folded around it in a two-fisted grip, the

blade pointed directly toward me. "The Seldom Seen; they are with you, but you pretend that they aren't."

I still didn't move.

"When did they first become known to you?" I could feel my breath becoming short as he continued. "They spoke to me infrequently after my first kill, but now it's constant—they talk to me night and day, many voices as one." He shifted his shoulders the way you would if you were preparing to move. "Many voices as one."

I raised the Colt and pointed it at the center of his chest.

"You have also killed, and they speak with you—we have something in common, Sheriff."

I raised the sight to his head. "The knife."

"We are pawns to these spirits, souls they play with for their own satisfaction like hand games." He didn't move, and we both knew that the next threatening shift, no matter how slight, would result in his death. He continued to show me his teeth. "It will be interesting to see how they respond to your disbelief, who it is that they will send for you."

The tension went out of his body as he lowered the knife, and he drew back. Keeping the .45 trained on his face, I reached over with my other hand and took the knife, handle out.

Handle out—I'd never seen him flip it.

I got my breath back and thought about the ghosts slamming about in the particular machine in front of me as I reholstered my sidearm and put the knife in my back pocket. "Let's go."

I guided him back through the gift shop, past the counter where Beatrice Linwood watched us.

Shade said nothing more as I seated him at the table, but he looked back up at me and stared as if we had shared something important. I stood there thinking about what he had said, then straightened and found my deputy studying me.

"You all right?"

It took a second for me to respond. "Yep." I glanced back at Shade and shot another look at Sancho, who closed his book again, gave me an almost imperceptible nod, and turned to look at the prisoners like a red-tailed hawk regarded field mice. I picked up the check and crossed the twelve steps back to the cash register, peeled off three twenties, and asked Beatrice for a receipt.

She held the money and glanced back as Holli entered behind her through the swinging door that led from the kitchen. The owner/operator paused at the register and looked past me toward the seated men. "What did they do?"

I thought about whether I really wanted to tell her, finally deciding that if she didn't want to know, she wouldn't have asked. "They're murderers, all of them." I waited a moment to see if the two women wanted me to continue, and they did. "The little guy with all the tattoos, his name is Hector Otero. He's a credit card hustler and gangbanger from Houston. The big guy with the mouth is Marcel Popp, a methadonian who . . ."

Holli looked puzzled. "A Methodist?"

I cleared my throat. "Sorry, it's kind of an inside joke— heroin users who use methadone clinics to get high."

Beatrice stiffened a little. "I don't think that's very funny."

I thought of telling her about the dead officers and Popp's girlfriend, whom he'd strangled to death with an electrical cord, and how none of them had thought their situation very humorous, either.

I looked at the woman behind the counter. "Yes, ma'am."

As I turned to go, her whisper came after me. "And that one?"

I stopped and stuffed a portion of the change into a tip jar and the receipt into my wallet without looking back at her. "Beatrice, you don't want to know."

2

Our combined breath billowed like steam in a rail yard as our little group made its way out the door and onto the porch of South Fork Lodge. A familiar custom Suburban had parked beside the borrowed Department of Corrections van, and a dapper-looking individual in a full-length lambskin coat with intricate Lakota beading and a 20X black hat with a sterling silver band bearing chunks of turquoise that must've taken wheelbarrows to get out of the mines of New Mexico looked up and grinned through his blond Vandyke. But for his height you would've thought it was George Armstrong Custer.

"Hey, if it ain't the long arm of the law." He glanced at the prisoners in their orange jumpsuits. "You fellas providing taxi service?"

Saizarbitoria held Marcel by the arm as I motioned for Hector and Raynaud to stand by the van. I unlocked it with a chirp from the remote. "Hey, Omar."

The millionaire big-game hunter rounded the front of his SUV and leaned on the hood. "What're you doin' up here, Sheriff?"

I gestured toward the prisoners as they complained about the cold and climbed in. "Federal deal at the county line. What about you?"

He smiled an ingratiating smile and, straightening his collar as if he were in court, glanced up at the colorful sky. "Hoping to get snowed in. I've got a few commissioned pieces that I've got to get done, and I'm doing the work up at my cabin."

Omar Rhoades sometimes deigned to do taxidermy for struggling concerns like the Museum of Natural History, the Smithsonian, and the Autry. I nodded and took my gloves from my coat pocket and pulled them on. "You've got a cabin up here?" I could only imagine what Omar would classify as a cabin.

He threw a thumb over his shoulder. "Up on West Tensleep, past 24, near Bear Lake." I nodded and waited; evidently he had something on his mind. "Hey, I heard Jules Beldon got twenty-one days of community service for that thing at the Rainbow Bar over in Sheridan."

That thing at the Rainbow Bar that Omar was referring to was an incident in which the jackleg carpenter and cowboy Jules Beldon had tried to climb through the bathroom window in an attempt to evade his tab and had kicked the sink loose, which had then flooded the area near the pool table. Judge Stu "Hang-'em-High" Healy had ordered Beldon to repair the damage and then had sentenced him to three weeks of community service.

"Yep. Why?"

"Well, he was going to do some work for me out at the ranch."

I looked at my boots, smiled, and looked up at Omar—the condensation from his breath had begun to freeze in his mustache.

"I'm going to need somebody to do some landscaping,

Walt, and with the methane stuff, nobody wants to handle a mattock and a shovel around here anymore."

I thought about it. "You're not going to do that till June, right?"

He stepped in a little closer. "Yeah, but I want to get somebody lined out to . . ."

"You're not just trying to get Jules out of his community service, are you?" Omar and Jules were cowboys, and the locals had their own mafia.

"No. No, no."

I folded my arms and waited as Saizarbitoria finished loading the prisoners and stood on the other side of the passenger door.

The millionaire smoothed his mustache and wiped his gloves on his black jeans. "All right, you got me." He took another breath. "He's seventy-four years old, and you know what it means if he's doin' his community service in May; he'll be out there shoveling every parking lot in town with that cheap, plastic snow shovel he's got."

"Well, he was spry enough to try and climb out the bathroom window of the Rainbow Bar."

"He didn't make it."

"It wasn't for lack of trying." We stood there looking at each other, and I thawed a little, knowing the big-game hunter was right. "Throw Stu a letter and mention my name—say I said it'd be all right to suspend Jules's sentence till the end of May so that he can help you out at your place."

He offered his hand, and I took it. "Thanks, Walt."

"Keep him out of those bars in Sheridan; they aren't as forgiving as we are."

"I'll try."

Omar mounted the steps, and I assisted Sancho in securing the ankle manacles on Hector, Shade, and Marcel Popp to the floor of the van. The three knew the drill and leaned forward as I made sure the chains going through the iron floor loops were secure and the padlock was shut. Next I attached the handcuffs to the locks on the seat, but as I started to stand, Shade leaned forward and murmured in my ear, "Who will they send for you, Sheriff?"

I stood up the rest of the way, my hand on the sliding door as Saizarbitoria started around to the driver's side. I inclined my head to get a clear look into the prisoner's eye. "Raynaud, you do know that anything you say to me is admissible evidence?"

"Yes, I understand that, but do you understand me?" His lips compressed, but he spoke through them, his powerful hands firmly clasped, his neck muscles bunched. "They have spoken to me since the first one, which is how I knew my mission was the only way to stop them."

I started to slide the door closed. "Uh huh."

His voice stopped me. "Do you think you're a good man, Sheriff?"

I wasn't quite sure what to say to that, especially within context, so I just nodded and fell back on the lessons my mother had taught me. "I hope so."

He grew still, and his eyes looked like nails driven into his face.

I stood there studying him for a second. "Don't test me again."

"But I will, Sheriff—I will." He continued to regard me

with the one eye, and his breath traced across a corner of his mouth like a wisp of steam escaping from a kettle.

I closed the door. Normally I drove, but the Basquo got bored riding, so I had given him the option when we'd left Durant and he'd taken it. As I got in the passenger side, I remembered I'd put Shade's stolen blade in my pocket.

Sancho started the used van and glanced at me. "Route 422 toward Baby Wagon?"

I pulled the errant steak knife from my jeans and threw it onto the dash. "Yep." The Basquo, more than a little curious, looked at the knife and then me. I pointed toward the road ahead. "Good thing this piece of crap is full-time two-wheel drive . . ."

Twenty miles down the road there was a gravel cutoff that led to the right and a slight upgrade. There were two black Chevy Suburbans with government plates, what looked to be about a half-dozen Feds, a heavily armored Ameri-Trans van with two men seated inside, one uniformed man on the outside, a Big Horn County Sheriff's Department truck, and another from Washakie County—it was a regular cop convention. Sancho wheeled the van in among the parked vehicles next to the large cluster of men.

Before I could get my seat belt off, Joseph Iron Cloud, the Arapaho sheriff of Washakie County, banged on my door. "Hey, hey, we got too many cops out here; you got any bad guys in there?"

Joe was newly elected in the county west of us. A handsome veteran from the first Gulf War, he had model good looks only slightly reduced by a scar that ran from the corner of his mouth to his hairline. He was about Saizarbitoria's age and cut quite a swath at the Wyoming Sheriff's Association meetings.

He hung a couple of fingers on the handle as I cracked the door open. "We got three; is that going to be enough?"

He grinned, revealing the small space between his two front teeth as he kicked his chewing gum to the other side of his mouth. "I don't know. How bad are they?"

I buttoned my sheepskin jacket and flipped up my collar. "Pretty bad."

Sancho joined us at the door and shook hands with Joe. They were a lot alike, and I had a feeling I was getting a glimpse of the future of Wyoming law enforcement. Saizarbitoria gripped Iron Cloud's shoulder in his gloved hand as Troy Old Man, another Arapaho and one of Joe's deputies, joined us.

Sancho smiled. "Jesus, Indians."

Joe nodded in faux seriousness—he was still working his gum. "Yeah, they brought us in to counterbalance the influx of ETA terrorists from the other side of the mountain." He turned the grin on me. "Hey, how come you didn't bring that other deputy, the good-looking one?"

Joe was smitten by my undersheriff, Vic. "I left the womenfolk behind. We heard there were Indians."

The three younger men followed me over to the larger group that leaned against one of the Suburbans as Joe continued to have fun introducing us to the assembled manpower. I stuck a hand out to Tommy Wayman, who was Rosey's cousin and the sheriff of Big Horn County, as Joe kept talking. "You guys know Grumpy." Vic had tagged him with the nickname, and everyone used it, but only she and Joe used it to his face.

Wayman shook my hand, but his heart wasn't in it. "Walt."

I'd heard that he had planned to retire last cycle, but then I'd also heard that about myself. He was a rough cob and most of the state didn't care for his my-way-or-the-highway style of management, but he was one of the few sheriffs as old as I was, so I liked keeping him around—if for nothing more than comparative purposes. "Tommy."

I shook hands with Wayman's deputy, but his name escaped me in the gusts of wind. I figured it didn't matter since we would be parting company soon.

The next couple of individuals were probably the reason for the sheriff of Big Horn County's bad mood. They were Feds, and a number of years back Tommy had accidentally become a national figure when he'd challenged, in court, the rights of federal agents to operate within the confines of his county without proper authorization from him.

It must've been a pretty important deal for these two organizations to come together, and I had a feeling it had to do with our proximity to the Bighorn National Forest.

A crew-cut man in Ray-Bans and black insulated coveralls extended his hand. "Special Agent in Charge Mike McGroder, Salt Lake Division."

I nodded as a few more gusts buffeted against us. "Enjoying the weather?"

"I hear this is classified as a fine spring afternoon in Wyoming." He turned to the young woman standing beside him. "This is Special Agent Pfaff out of DC." The lean blonde with the athletic build and direct chambray-colored eyes shook my hand and then Saizarbitoria's. "And Tom Benton from the Federal Marshal's office in Denver."

Benton was a tall redhead, with a black ball cap to match his own noir ensemble, including the tactical shotgun slung to his chest. He smiled but only as a professional courtesy. "Hello."

"Howdy."

There were a few other men in coveralls who were holding close-range weapons and who approached and shook hands, introducing themselves as Marshal Jon Mooney and Agent Bob Belmont. There were three more men in the transport company's uniforms, but I supposed they weren't worthy of introduction.

I glanced at the two individuals in the back of the Ameri-Trans van just to make sure they were, indeed, prisoners. One was studying his hands and rocking back and forth with more energy than remaining seated and manacled would allow. The other man pasted his nose against the back window like a child. He had long hair that covered most of his face but, unlike his friend, he had taken the time to stare at us newcomers.

"You know, there's gotta be a reason why all the good guys are standing out here in the cold and all the bad guys are in the vans with the heaters running."

McGroder smiled. "You'd think, wouldn't you?" He folded his arms over his chest, and I wondered at the perfection of his government-issue, close-cropped crew cut; with no cap, it must have been a little breezy for the current temperature. "Sheriff, do you mind if we transfer two of your prisoners and talk with the other?"

"Be my guest." I nodded at Saizarbitoria and handed him the keys to the prisoners' shackles and watched as he, two of the armed federal men, two of the Ameri-Trans men, and Troy Old Man headed over. "Do you really want to talk to him in our van?"

McGroder looked at Pfaff, and she was the one to speak. "Yes, but I'll wait till the other two have been transferred so that I can speak with him alone."

I looked at the assembled group. "It's your party."

McGroder glanced at Tommy Wayman and then back at me. "Thank you, Sheriff."

We stood there a few minutes more and then watched as Marcel Popp and Hector Otero were switched into the Ameri-Trans van. Once this was accomplished, the Salt Lake agent nodded and moved toward the vehicle with Pfaff and Benton in tow. Saizarbitoria passed them on the way, but they said nothing to him.

We local boys stood there and looked at one another, none of us aware of what the others knew. I didn't know much of anything other than what was in the reports I'd read, so I asked, "What the heck is going on?"

Tommy sighed. "Oh, the usual horseshit."

Joe laughed and stared at his insulated boots, making patterned footsteps in the compacted snow with short, fancy dance steps. "They haven't told us anything, Walt. I guess we're just the transport."

"Three counties' worth?"

The Arapaho spit his gum out into a wrapper and tucked it into his coat pocket. "Yeah, but I gotta tell you that knowing what I know about this Shade fellow, I'd just as soon drag him out, shoot him in the head, and charge the Feds for my time and ammo."

I glanced at the agents in the van and the three standing between the two vehicles. "Well, correct me if I'm wrong, but within a half mile of this location we can be in Big Horn, Washakie, and Absaroka counties, not to mention the national forest."

"Oh, it's got to be a jurisdictional deal. It's just that they don't know where they are or what the hell they're doing—per usual." Tommy sighed deeply again.

Joe's dark eyes shifted, and his edgy features reminded me of my buddy, Northern Cheyenne Henry Standing Bear. Tonight he and I were going to discuss the planning of my daughter's wedding to Michael, who was Vic's younger brother. Cady wanted to have the ceremony performed up on the Rez this summer, and the Cheyenne Nation was my go-to guy.

Joe's voice broke up my thoughts as we all turned toward the van. "Maybe that's what they're finding out."

We were about to adjourn the meeting and climb in somebody's vehicle when McGroder and Pfaff exited, leaving Benton seated behind Shade.

The Salt Lake City agent immediately approached Joe. "Thank you, Sheriff Iron Cloud. We won't be needing you."

Joe kicked his face sideways with a grin. "Excuse me?"

McGroder repeated himself.

Iron Cloud stood there for a minute more, then shrugged and turned toward the rest of us. "Hey, hey, must be north of here, boys. But then again, these federal agents have a long-standing dislike of us Indians since Pine Ridge."

Knowing better than to hang around when he wasn't needed, Joe shook all hands and started off toward his vehicle with his deputy. As he passed Saizarbitoria, he pulled out a pack of gum and offered the Basquo a piece, which he took. Joe spoke in my deputy's ear.

Sancho laughed and then unwrapped the gum, stuffed it in his mouth, and began chewing.

McGroder stuck his hands in his coveralls as the Washakie County truck pulled away and then considered me. "I'm sorry, Sheriff Longmire. It's Longmire, right?"

"Yep."

He continued to study me like a multiple-choice question. "You'll have to come with us, Sheriff—it appears that our plans have changed."

It was a short distance on a snow-covered gravel road until we reached the corrals at the junction of 422 and the spur of 419 that straddled the line between Tommy Wayman's county and mine; both portions were overlapped by the Bighorn National Forest.

Raynaud Shade sat in the middle seat of our van with McGroder on one side, Pfaff on the other, Benton still behind him; the agents were talking in low voices as Saizarbitoria drove.

When we got to the corner, the prisoner spoke. "Here."

The Basquo slowed and even went so far as to put on his turn signal for the Suburban that followed us; the other federal vehicles and the Ameri-Trans transport with Otero and Popp had gone ahead to Meadowlark Lodge.

Pfaff was talking to Raynaud Shade with the familiarity that a doctor had with a patient. "You're sure? It was a while ago."

I could see the reflection of his one eye getting the lay of the land. "I'm sure."

The road got bumpier as we left the loop and headed north toward Baby Wagon Creek. We got to a turn where I'd remembered a Basque sheep wagon being parked during a fly-fishing trip with Henry and the Ferg. It was going to get a lot rougher from here on in, and I was relieved when Shade spoke again.

"Here."

Saizarbitoria eased the van to a stop, and it shifted a little down the incline toward the creek.

I turned in my seat. Agent Pfaff stared at the side of the prisoner's face, and McGroder, holding a plastic-sealed quad sheet for comparison, read the LED display on a handheld global tracking device. "It's within a hundred yards of where he said."

Shade looked past me through the windshield. "We can walk from here."

I turned to look up the creek bed and could see a number of rock outcroppings sticking up through the snow before the dark shadows of the fir trees blocked everything out. It was getting late, and up this high the shadows were long.

We unlocked Shade from the floor, threw a blanket over him, and he walked with one of the Feds on either side. Pfaff followed, and McGroder, Saizarbitoria, Sheriff Wayman, Marshal Benton, and another of the field agents pulled up the drags.

McGroder continued to read the GPS with the assistance of the map but surprised me by speaking as we trudged through the snow. "So, did he say anything while he was in your custody, Sheriff?"

I thought about the things Shade had uttered over the last day, most of it indiscernible. "He said that two men had sent him a bone in the mail—about wanting the money."

The agent's eyes slipped up to mine. "Is that all he said?"

I thought about it some more. "He also said something about voices and testing me, but I think that was mostly guff."

McGroder nodded.

Up ahead, Shade turned, the heavy wool blanket forming a makeshift hood that shadowed his dark face and, like a malevolent monk, he looked directly at me. "Here."

The group assembled around a slab of moss rock about the size of a door. "I buried him here."

McGroder checked the GPS one last time and looked at his map before turning to look at Tommy. "Thank you for your help, Sheriff Wayman. I'll have one of my men drive you back down to your vehicle."

He turned to me.

"Not your lucky day, Longmire."

3

The temperature had shifted to slightly above forty degrees, and the booming in the distant, dark clouds promised a freezing rain if we weren't lucky. We continued to watch as the younger agents and Saizarbitoria, under the attentive eye of Special Agent Pfaff, excavated the snow from around the boulder.

McGroder and I were too old for that kind of foolishness and were sharing a thermos of really good coffee in the cab of one of the Suburbans. "And those're the two other convicts who were in the Ameri-Trans van?"

"Yes." He blew into his stainless travel mug—even it was black. "I'm sorry about all the cloak-and-dagger stuff, but we're on a need-to-know basis and, until I could verify which county we were dealing with, I had to keep my cards close to the vest."

I nodded.

He drank from his mug. "I was just as happy to not have it be Sheriff Iron Cloud's jurisdiction."

"Because?"

"The victim is Native American." I looked at him as he continued to sip his coffee. "Crow, to be exact; taken from a vehicle parked at a bar/bait shop near Hardin, Montana. Shade

ID'd the victim, even though the child was never reported missing."

There was a long pause, and while I thought that one over, I heard a few frigid drops of sleet, sounding like pebbles, hit the top of the Chevrolet. I gestured toward the other Suburban.

"And those two?"

"Just your garden variety psychotic scumbags; Calvin 'Fingers' Moser is the one with the stringy hair, and Freddie 'Junk-food Junkie' Borland is the one who can't keep still. A couple of fun-loving drug abusers from Arizona who liked to get high, kill people, and then sell the body parts."

"Charming."

"Isn't it though? Through Shade they had a medical connection in Mexico to which they gave a running supply of kidneys, livers, lungs, hearts, and eyes. Years back, on some PCP-induced binge, they killed an elderly couple near Sedona and buried their bodies out in the desert. Borland was working at a livestock dismemberment plant when Shade turned them on to the guys in Central America. They pretty much drove around killing people and selling the parts." He sipped his coffee some more and then waxed financial. "You can get forty to fifty thousand dollars for a healthy kidney on the open market. Some guy had one for sale on eBay."

I interrupted, mostly so that I wouldn't have to hear more. "Is that your specialty, organ trafficking?"

"No." We continued to watch as the working class finished shoveling around the boulder, and we were faced with the eventuality of getting out of the SUV. "Pfaff's the specialist—psychotic schizophrenia—and Ray 'No' Shade is the textbook for psy-schiz. No-Shade's first American homicide was

this Native American child abduction across state lines; then
there's the supposed missing 1.4 million dollars . . ." He grew
silent but finally spoke again. "You pull up the file?"

"Only part of it. What I did read sounds like a horror
movie."

He finished off his coffee and placed the travel mug back in
the holder. "That it does."

I swallowed the rest from my thermos top and did the
same, closing the doors behind us and tromping across the
trampled snow to where the crew was working. They had produced a pry bar, were laboring around the edges of the rock
to unfreeze it from its surroundings, and had connected a tow
strap to the back of one of the Suburbans as well. There was a
nudging sound, and with one more spot of leverage the boulder broke free and shifted a few inches.

"That's enough." McGroder produced a Maglite from his
breast pocket and, shining the beam behind the rock, slipped
between the other men. "Difficult to see; we're going to have
to move it further."

A large man in one of the tactical uniforms moved to one
side of the rock while another went to the opposite side. They
braced themselves and heaved mightily as the tires of the Suburban spun and the distant thunder echoed off the surrounding peaks.

Nothing happened.

With a quick estimation, I figured the boulder weighed
close to five thousand pounds.

They tried again but with the same results.

I glanced at McGroder. "Shade supposedly moved this by
himself?" I spoke to the nearest agent. "Climb up on top and

push with your legs, and I'll try this side." I stepped past the Fed on the left, planted a foot against the embankment, and worked my hands behind the cold surface of the rock as the agent braced his boots against it. "On three. One. Two. Three."

Same result.

I looked up at McGroder's arched eyebrow. "Well, even Atlas shrugged."

I worked my hands in deeper than before, and on the count of three the rock shifted and revealed its egglike shape, with the more narrow portion being the part we'd been pushing on. We hadn't so much moved the boulder as repositioned it, and if we were planning on doing any more, we were going to have to break out a hydraulic jack and pray we got it done before the sleet began in earnest.

McGroder leaned over the boulder with the flashlight. "That's all we need for now."

"They mailed him part of the jawbone in prison to get him to tell them where the money was?"

McGroder looked out at what would have been the panoramic view from Meadowlark Lodge as the sleet pounded the plate-glass windows. "Shade had given the boy's bone to them—who knows why? Maybe as a gift, maybe as a warning, but Moser and Borland still wanted their part of the 1.4 million the three of them had supposedly extorted from the organ-donor business. The bone arrived in a brown paper wrapper at the Draper, Utah, prison where Shade was being housed, with a post office box return address in Bisbee, Arizona. That's where we apprehended the two. These guys are not exactly destined for Mensa."

The agent mentioned Shade's residence in Draper like the killer was renting an apartment rather than being housed in the maximum security prison for only the most violent and escape-prone prisoners in the country. "What was his name?"

"Who?"

"The boy."

"He said it was Owen White Buffalo."

There are moments in your life when you hear that first click of the dominoes, and you know that whatever happens from that point, it's all going to be bad. I sat there in that moment listening to the noises inside me—my heart, the blood surging through my veins, the unwanted adrenaline that was now causing my hands to grow still and my face to become cool.

"Jesus, Sheriff. I haven't seen a response like that in quite a while. You knew this kid?"

My mouth was dry, and I suddenly wanted more coffee. "No, but I know the family, and up until now I thought I was conversant with all their miseries." I fought the weight in my chest by asking more questions, unsure if I was going to like the answers. "From what you've told me, it doesn't fit Moser and Borland's MO. Can you even take organs from a child that young for transplant purposes?"

"The boy was before they partnered. That's why the other two are so quick to give Shade up—they had nothing to do with this one. Personally, I don't think there is any money, but it got the other two to surface and that's good enough for me. We were just going to use Shade to find the body, but I needed confirmation and that's where the other two come in."

The conversation we were having was only made worse by the immediate surroundings. The lodge at Meadowlark Lake had been closed for a couple of years and Holli and Wayne had not planned on renovating it until they finished with South Fork and Deer Haven, which was a couple of miles west. We sat in the empty café and listened to the coolers cooling nothing and the sleet hissing on the tin roof, an accompanying wind skiff kicking up snow devils across the icy surface of the lake. By all rights it was spring, but every year somebody forgot to tell the mountains.

Most of the FBI agents except McGroder were still at Baby Wagon Creek; the agent and I had elected to retreat to Meadowlark in the wake of the prisoners.

"Raynaud's something of an opportunist. You noticed his eye?"

I tried to focus on something other than the name White Buffalo and watched the lightning strike in chains across the big lake. "I did."

"Plucked it out himself."

I wasn't quite sure what to say to that and was saved by a melodramatic clap of thunder.

"During the stint in Draper. There was an altercation between Shade and another prisoner over a female correspondent."

I still wished we had more of the good coffee, but supplies were slow coming from South Fork Lodge, where we'd had lunch. My stomach gnawed on itself, reminding me that it was coming up on six o'clock at night. It was a Friday, which also reminded me that I hadn't called to cancel dinner with Vic and Henry. "Shade killed him?"

"Yeah, Raynaud had a postal affair going on with the woman, and this other guy made some remarks which cost him his life. Carved him up with a homemade knife, but at the time it appeared as if he'd lost an eye in the fight, which got him sent to the medical unit, where he escaped. They consequently discovered that he'd plucked the eye out himself and cut it loose with the same shank. Shows a specific type of determination, doesn't it?"

I looked out the window to see Saizarbitoria rushing by the parked but still running vehicles with a couple of sacks containing what I assumed was the first round of supplies from South Fork Lodge.

I wasn't sure if I was still hungry.

My eyes stalled on the fogged windshield of our borrowed WYDOC van, where Raynaud Shade sat chained in the center with Marshal Benton sitting behind him and another marshal seated in the driver's seat. The other prisoners, all four of them, were awaiting departure in the Ameri-Trans van under the careful eye of yet another marshal and the three Ameri-Trans employees.

The Basquo booted open the front door of the lodge with his foot. He glanced back to where Beatrice was pulling more bags from the passenger seat of her Blazer, which she had parked under the overhang of the building. "We've got more, but I'm not sure how you want to feed the prisoners."

McGroder, a little daunted by the deluge outside, stood and picked up his satellite phone from the table. "In the vans and locked down. I'll go get things coordinated with my guys." He paused as Sancho pulled out a waxed-paper-wrapped club sandwich. "Save one of those for me, will you?"

The Basquo smiled and pulled out two more. "You bet."

Beatrice entered with more sacks and rested them on the

table. "Boy, the roads are bad from the lodge to here. This is the last of it." She glanced at me. "Are you paying again, Sheriff?"

I gestured toward McGroder. "The federal government will be picking up the tab this time."

The Fed took the receipt from the woman. "Don't we always."

He proceeded out the door with her to implement "Operation Dinner" as Saizarbitoria, still dripping from the thawed sleet, handed me a sandwich and a Styrofoam cup of coffee. "I called in and Marie said she could put Antonio down on her own. She also said that NOAA reports we've got a heller of an ice storm coming in—going to last the entire weekend. Any time now, it's supposed to turn from sleet to frozen rain and then snow by morning." He folded the wrapper down and placed his paperback on the table. There was a red, cellophane-flagged toothpick in his sandwich that he extracted and pointed toward me. "By the way, you're in trouble."

I broke my reverie of White Buffalos and thought about my more personal problems. "Henry or Vic?"

"Both."

"I am in trouble." I considered. "Can I borrow your cell phone?"

He handed the device over, and I watched as he began devouring his food—he spoke through the bacon, lettuce, and tomatoes: "Just hit SEND; they're at her house."

I punched the green button, held the phone to my ear, and waited.

There was an immediate answer. "Fucker."

I sighed. "It's not my fault." She remained silent. "Did Saizarbitoria explain?" I glanced up, and the Basquo nodded.

"I made my Uncle Al's lasagna rustica; do you know how long that takes?"

"I'm sorry."

"The Cheyenne Nation, your dog, and I are all drinking wine and talking about what a shit you are."

"Dog is drinking wine?"

She exhaled audibly. "Well, I poured him some; so far he's just looking at it." There was a long pause on the line. "Sancho said it was something to do with the Feds—a body?"

"Yep, and we caught the jurisdiction." I sighed again. "Seven-year-old boy, almost a decade deceased, but there's a very big twist. The victim's name is Owen White Buffalo."

I glanced up and could see the Basquo's dark eyes grow enormous, and he stopped chewing. I nodded to him briefly and then listened to the phone. It was, by far, the longest pause yet, and her voice sounded strained. "You're shitting me."

"I wish I was."

Her pitch softened a little with the wonder of our predicament. "What does this have to do with the prisoner transport?"

"One of them may have been involved with the murder in a primary way."

I listened as she readjusted the phone. "The Shade guy?"

"Yep."

"Figures. The voices in that fucker's head are singing barbershop." It was quiet, and I listened to her breathe. "Here's Henry—you better talk to him."

I could hear her hand him the phone, and my lifelong buddy came on the line, a man with whom I'd endured the Wyoming public school system and Vietnam. "You are in trouble."

"More than you'll ever know." I explained the situation.

"Do you have any idea if any of the White Buffalos had any children who might've disappeared about nine years ago?" I waited as he absorbed it all. I tried not to mention the four-hundred-pound Indian in the room. "Can you make some phone calls?"

"Yes."

"Do you still have Eli's number over in Hot Springs?"

"I do."

"Could you check with him and then call me back here on Sancho's cell?"

There was talk in the background, and Henry spoke again. "She wants to know if you have eaten."

I stared at the sandwich that was still wrapped on the table in front of me. "Not yet, so tell her to save me some lasagna." There was more talk, but I interrupted. "Hey, Henry?"

"Yes."

"Have you had any contact with Virgil since last summer?"

"I will ask Vic to save you some lasagna."

"Virgil White Buffalo was briefly a suspect in a homicide case we had last August."

McGroder, trying to get a read on why I was telling him all this, studied me as he ate his turkey sandwich. "Uh huh."

"He wasn't guilty, but he did display a number of antisocial characteristics and is . . . at large."

The Basquo stated flatly, "In more ways than one."

McGroder glanced at Sancho and then back at me. "What the hell does that mean?"

"He's a very big man."

The Utah agent studied me. "Bigger than you?"

"Much." I took my hat off and balanced it on my knee. "In our part of the world, he's what some people refer to as an FBI."

Sancho provided the translation: "Fucking Big Indian."

McGroder stopped chewing. "Dangerous?"

"He has had his moments."

The agency man set his sandwich down. "Let me get this straight. You've got a giant Indian sociopath running around in these mountains who may be related to our victim?"

I noticed he'd lost the politically correct sobriquet. "I'm checking on that, and besides, he may not be anywhere near here. All we have are rumors. The Cloud Peak Wilderness Area alone is 189,039 acres and it's completely surrounded by the Bighorn National Forest, so the chances of running into him or of him knowing anything about your investigation are slim." I drank some of my coffee and listened to my stomach complain about waiting for the lasagna. "We didn't know about the investigation until a few hours ago."

McGroder sat there looking at his half-eaten sandwich, his appetite having just taken a hit. "I don't like coincidences."

"I'm not too fond of them myself, but I thought it was information you should have."

"Thank you." His hand came up and covered most of his face.

"There's another concern."

He looked at me through his fingers. "There is?"

"Have you guys checked the weather recently?"

The agent glanced out the window with a glum expression. "It's shitty. Why?"

We both watched as the waitress pulled her aged SUV from the lot and turned left, driving carefully onto Route 16. I assumed she was done for the night and heading home the twenty miles to Ten Sleep where she probably lived.

"It may get worse. The temperature is dropping and in an hour or so this whole mountain range is going to be encased in a couple of inches of ice."

McGroder sighed, and I continued. "There aren't any working facilities open in any of the lodges around here, so you're going to have to haul your people back to South Fork Lodge. I think you should secure the scene and get the rest of these prisoners off the mountain."

He plucked the Motorola from his hip and clicked the mic. "AT, when can you be ready to go?"

After a moment, a strong signal came back from the van in the parking lot.

Static. "Can we eat first?"

He glanced at me, and I spread my hands.

McGroder clicked the mic again. "As soon as you're done, get out of here." He rested the radio on the table and looked at me. "Six hundred and some miles back to Salt Lake?"

"Six hundred fifty miles from Durant, about eight hours in good weather." We both looked out the windows again. "Which you are not going to have until you descend a couple thousand feet." My eyes stayed on the DOC van holding Raynaud Shade. One of the marshals was proffering bags of food to Benton, who divided it and handed some to the prisoner. "What about him?"

"He stays." McGroder sipped his coffee. "But there's no reason that you have to. If I had a warm bed and hot lasagna an hour away, I'd be leaving skid marks."

I glanced at my deputy, who was making a pretense of reading and probably anxious to get home to his wife and young son. "You're sure you don't need us?"

"In about twenty minutes, I'm going to have a mobile task force of two field agents and four marshals to guard only one man." He stood and extended his hand. "I think we can handle it. Would you mind borrowing one of our vehicles so that we can keep him in yours?"

I placed my hat back on my head and reared up into a standing position. I could see the relief on Sancho's face as McGroder handed me a set of keys. It was nice that I hadn't had to remind him that even though it was his investigation, it was still my county. "When do you want us back at the scene?"

"Weather permitting, probably early in the morning—say 0800."

We shook hands, and I stared at his crew cut again. "Semper Fi?"

He grinned. "Yeah, you?"

I picked up my coffee and put the lid back on. "First Division."

Wearing a pasted-on smile, he slapped me on the shoulder. "Get some sleep, Sheriff. I'll see you at South Fork in the morning." He stretched a hand toward Saizarbitoria but looked at the both of us. "Thanks for your help, Deputy. If I don't see you again and you're ever over Salt Lake way, look me up. I'll get you over to The Pie for a good pizza." As we got ready to go, he picked up my wrapped sandwich and tossed it to me. "Something for the road?"

"Class act."

"Yep." I was contemplating the sandwich in my lap and wondering if I could eat it now and the lasagna later. The Basquo momentarily slid the borrowed Suburban into a turn, then carefully corrected and straightened. "Slick?"

He nodded but kept his concentration on the road. "Like greased goose shit."

"Better slow down."

He heeded my unneeded advice, and we rolled/slid along the road at forty-five. "You think the Shade guy did it?"

"Well, he all but admitted to it when I took him to the bathroom." I thought about the adopted Crow Indian we'd passed on our way to the borrowed federal vehicle. He had been eating while Benton, still holding the shotgun, watched. The marshal had nodded to us as we'd walked by in the freezing sleet, but it was Raynaud Shade's eye, the glass one, that seemed to track along with us as we passed. The thing was wayward at best and it was probably just another reflection, but it was as if the dead eye was watching me.

"What?"

I turned to look at the Basquo. "Hmm?"

He continued to study me. "You were thinking of something?"

I fiddled with the waxed paper. "Did you read the file on Shade?"

"No."

"He was one of the last of the Tukkuthkutchin tribe up in Canada—Northwest Territories." I refolded the sandwich and stared out the window. "Transferred from one of the residential boarding schools to a private orphanage when he was eight. They tested him, and his IQ was off the chart. Raynaud ran away to live with his non-Indian father, who took responsibility for him. Two years later a social worker stopped in to check on the boy and discovered that the father had died eight months earlier."

Sancho stared ahead. "What'd you do, commit the file to memory?"

I thought about it, about the parts I wasn't telling. "That ten-year-old boy had been living in a cabin with his dead father in the bedroom for eight months. He got kicked around to a number of foster homes before being adopted by a couple in Lodge Grass. The woman was Cree; her husband, Crow. She was related to Shade's mother, but there were problems, behavioral and otherwise; he ended up dropping out of school. That must've been the period when he killed Owen White Buffalo, and who knows who else. He returned to Canada and joined the army up there—Dwyer Hill Training Center outside Ontario."

Sancho reached down and turned the defrosters to full, and I watched the already-ice-encased tree line as we passed, the conifers looking like some gigantic army standing at attention along both sides of the road.

"He was married, and his wife disappeared during a camping trip. There was a provincial hunt in Ontario, but she never turned up—must've killed her, too. A year later one of Shade's buddies went missing, and the Ottawa Police Department started asking some questions. The military stonewalled it, but Shade was drummed out. He turned up as a suspect again in Factory Island Reservation, Ontario, in a search for an outfitting business partner a couple of years later. He was arrested, and when they searched his apartment they discovered blood trace from the guy he killed."

"Jesus."

I pulled my cup from the holder and sipped my coffee. "They stuck him in Kingston Penitentiary, but he got transported to a psychiatric prison for observation and, after three months there, he escaped into the U.S., hid out up in Lodge Grass, and killed the old couple that had taken him in when he was a child."

Saizarbitoria shook his head as we slid around another sweeping corner.

"He's supposedly a very interesting case, a specific form of psychotic schizophrenic where the subject is overcome by a culture-bound syndrome and hears voices—sees . . ." I couldn't help but pause. "Sees apparitions. He refers to them as the 'Seldom Seen' and believes that he's actually possessed by evil spirits that force him to sacrifice others."

"Sounds like the old Basque priest at the Catholic Church who believes in fairies."

I nodded. "The versions vary from tribe to tribe, but these spirits are purported to be malicious, supernatural beings. The people they inhabit supposedly have malevolent spiritual powers but are shunned by their own people."

There was some chatter on the Feds' radio about the mobile unit coming down from Baby Wagon, and I was glad to hear it. The Basquo slowed for another curve, and I could feel the Chevrolet fishtail. He glanced at me. "You believe that stuff?"

I was just as glad that he hadn't been privy to my experiences in this very area of the mountains more than a year ago, when I had seen and heard my share of strange things. "I believe there were spiritual signposts that these tribes put into place so that no matter how dire the situation, the members would never be tempted to do things the tribe considered absolutely taboo." I felt tired and slouched into the seat. "Imagine beginning to see people, things that no one else can see, and in punishment the real people around you begin drawing away—leaving you to these . . . spirits."

"Isn't that kind of like pitting the monsters of your imagination against the monsters of human nature?"

I smiled. "You have been reading your Dante." I stared out the side window and wasn't smiling when I made the next statement. "Wonder who would win."

At the next bend, I could see a few dusk-to-dawn lights over the cabins that comprised South Fork. "I want you to drop me off at the main lodge; I'll just stay up here tonight."

He hunched his shoulders. "You're going to be in even more trouble."

"I know." I looked down at my lap. "Could you call and tell them I won't be coming to dinner after all?"

He glanced at me again as we gently slowed, listening to the sleet being thrown by the tires. "Why do you want to stay?"

"I just don't feel good about leaving those guys up here by themselves in this weather."

He nodded and turned in the drive. "I'll stay, too."

I looked at the headstrong Basquo, at the same time thinking about the promise I'd made his wife a couple of months back about keeping him out of harm's way—even if harm was just keeping him up on the mountain for a night. "No, you won't. Go home."

He pulled the Suburban up to the porch at the front of the lodge, and we both peered through the windshield into the darkened windows—there were only a few lights on. "Looks like you might have to go down, too."

After a moment, though, Holli emerged from the kitchen, passed the counter to the glass doors, and squinted in our headlights. She pulled on a coat, pushed open the door with an arm over her eyes, and shouted. "Can I help you?"

I rolled down the window of the SUV and hung my head through. "Holli, it's me, Walt Longmire."

She approached, wiping her hands on her jeans. "Hey, Sheriff."

I shifted my hat back; the sleet smacked the ground around us like shrapnel. "The Feds call you?"

"About the food?"

"No, they're going to need beds up here for the night."

"Nope."

That was odd.

She stuffed her hands in her pockets only to bring them out a moment later. "How many?"

"About a half dozen, and one for a prisoner."

She zipped her fleece over her stained apron and pulled up

the collar. "Unfortunately, I have rooms. A lot of my guests couldn't make it in."

"You have seven plus one?"

"Who else?"

"Me."

She looked past the hood of the Suburban to the cabin nearest the lodge. "I can stick you in the hired hand's bunk. It's small, but it's got a single in it."

"That'll do. Thanks." I pushed open the door and stepped out with the sandwich in my hands. "Kitchen closed?"

She looked sheepish. "I'm afraid so. Good thing you brought your own."

I began unwrapping it. "I'll wait up for the Feds."

"That's okay, Walt. You get some sleep. I'll get Beatrice to do that, wherever she's gone off to."

Holli flipped a few fingers at Saizarbitoria as I closed the door, and the Basquo waved back but he still sat there, parked.

I thought about how I'd seen the waitress turning left as she got back on the main route. "Last time we saw her, she was headed toward Ten Sleep." I took a bite of my moveable feast.

"Well, damn it, I guess she decided to go home."

The club sandwich was good, and I was starved. I swallowed a bite and reached in the open window to retrieve my cup of lukewarm coffee from the holder on the dash. "Maybe she misunderstood or got scared of the roads."

The lodge owner nodded, not very happy with the situation.

Sancho called out from the driver's seat, "You sure you don't want me to stay?"

"I'm sure." I took another bite of my sandwich and backed

away from the truck to allow the Basquo to escape. I had taken a step back when I felt something in my mouth other than bread, turkey, bacon, lettuce, and tomato. I handed Holli my cup of coffee.

"Something wrong, Sheriff?"

I reached into my mouth and pulled out what I thought might've been one of the little, flagged toothpicks that held the sandwich together but instead found a bobby pin with one of the small, cellophane flags attached.

I held it up for both of us to see.

"Jeez, Walt, I'm sorry." Holli ran a hand through her thick hair. "Not mine."

We both laughed, but the laughter died as I held the thin piece of metal up and could see that the protective tip had been removed from one end and that it had been bent into two opposite-facing right angles near the head—so that it looked like a key.

4

It had taken us only a few minutes to get going once we discovered the makeshift handcuff key, but it was taking an agonizingly long time to get back to Meadowlark Lodge—we'd run off the road three times already.

I held the mic from the Feds' radio close to my mouth. "Come in, unit one, this is unit two; Agent McGroder, this is Sheriff Longmire. Over?"

Static.

Sancho risked a look. "This isn't good."

"No, it's not."

I braced a hand against the dash as we made the turn at Powder River Pass on the Cloud Peak Skyway, almost ten thousand feet above sea level. The storm had gotten serious, and the sleet now pounded the top of the Feds' Suburban like a snare drum. Sancho was doing his best, but the puddles of slush that pooled in the tread swales of the mountainous road made every turn feel as if we were attempting to corner an overloaded rowboat.

I pulled out the Basquo's cell phone, but there were no available bars. He glanced at me. "Anything?"

"Nope." I'd had Holli make the 911 call down the mountain

with the landline she had in the lodge, but we weren't likely to get cell reception again until we got back to Meadowlark.

"Line of sight, or it could just be interference from the storm."

"Yeah, but they've also got those satellite phones, so somebody ought to be able to get through to them." I pressed the button on the mic again. "Unit one, this is unit two. How 'bout it, McGroder? Over." I waited a second and then depressed the button again. "Anybody?"

Static.

Sancho gained a little speed on the straightaway as we sluiced past the cutoff to county roads 422 and 419 where Shade had buried the remains of the boy. After a few minutes we could see the lights of something in the gloom of the darkened sleet up ahead. "Are those headlights?"

"No, it's something else."

As we got closer, we could see that the gas pumps at Meadowlark Lodge had exploded, billowing black smoke and flames into the sodden night. The Basquo slowed and reverted to his mother tongue. "Kixmi."

We turned and continued down the sloped parking lot and could see the reflection of the chemical bonfire in the lodge windows, and the melted sheen of the parking lot glowed in triplicate in the freezing fog. I kept thinking that if I looked at the images long enough, perhaps what they mirrored wouldn't be real.

The Feds' other Suburban was lodged sideways into the pump island at a crazy angle, and we could see the still-burning bodies slumped in the driver and passenger seats. I drew the .45 from my holster, held on to the door handle, and nodded to the left of the Suburban. "Over there."

The Basquo steered our vehicle toward the building, but a safe distance from the heat and flames. "What if the tank on that thing goes?"

"It already has."

We slid to a stop, and I lurched from the SUV. Glancing at the flaming T-boned Suburban, I extended my firing arm as I rushed toward the front door of the lodge, where I could see a body.

The tactical yellow lettering across his shoulders bore the three letters. I was careful to walk around the blowback of what must have been the original shot and the trail of blood that he had made while trying to get to the main building. The blood was already frozen in the spot where he'd been gunned down, and it was probably the heat from the fire that had kept his body from freezing to the surface of the parking lot. He was still dragging himself toward the door.

I could feel the pressure of the air moving toward the fire, creating a vortex that pulled the sleeting snow along the ground and back up into the flames before disappearing into the conflagration. I glanced toward the lodge windows, but it was only cursory; with the DOC van missing, it was obvious where they—or, more important, Raynaud Shade—had gone.

I placed a hand on McGroder's shoulder, and he stilled. Some of the air went out of him as I pulled him over: double-ought buck, his thigh and the oblique muscles torn to shreds. His eyes didn't focus, and his lips hung open, but he was breathing. "Michael?"

He gargled, and his throat pulled and constricted as the blood drained from the side of his mouth. His face contorted, and it took a moment for me to realize that he was trying to speak.

"Michael?"

With the surging noise of the fire and the continuing wind, I bent lower to hear his voice.

"Where—do . . ." He coughed, and more of the coagulated blood pushed out of his mouth. "Oh, hell . . ."

"Lie still and stop talking." I had to get him inside. With the lack of blood pressure and the cold, he would soon go into shock if he hadn't already; I had to get him stabilized. I glanced at the Basquo, who had approached the burning vehicle, braving the blown-out heat of the fire to check for survivors. "Sancho!"

McGroder's eyes wandered but then settled on me. "Who?"

"Walt Longmire, the sheriff. Remember?" It was textbook shock from blood loss. "Sancho!"

A moment later, he was beside me. "They're all dead."

McGroder's eyes remained unfocused, and the pupils began clicking back and forth like a metronome. He jolted at the statement. "Oh, God . . ."

"Help me with him." We lifted the FBI agent as carefully as we could, with me taking his shoulders and Santiago his legs. I butted the glass door open with my back and we laid McGroder on the bar to our left. I unzipped his jacket and pulled aside his shirt and thermal. The wound was gaping, but it didn't look as if it'd gotten any of his organs, so we were just battling blood loss.

There was a stack of bar towels under the counter, and I packed them into the wound in an attempt to stanch the bleeding, hepatitis C be damned. The Basquo returned from the back with a pile of wool army surplus blankets, folding one to place under the agent's head and then covering him with another three.

Sancho tapped numbers into his cell phone then snapped it shut in disgust and grabbed McGroder's satellite phone from the floor, where it had fallen from the table. The weather conditions must have screwed up the cell service. I lowered my face to the wounded man. "Michael, can you hear me?"

I supported the side of his head with my hand.

He swallowed. "Procedure perfect."

"I'm sure."

"Don't know what happened."

I nodded. "They took our van?"

"Killed Benton and the other marshal, Jon Mooney, right off, shot me before I could even get my . . . Took my sidearm."

I nodded. "Was it Shade alone?"

"Yes." He swallowed. "He got Benton and Moody in your DOC van. I heard the report and ran out, but he was already standing there and he shot me with the marshal's shotgun. He took my Sig, went inside, and got the keys from the table." He tried to swallow again. "Can I have something to drink?"

"Can do, buddy. The EMTs are on the way." I leaned in closer—his eyes were clearing a little, and the focus was returning. "When did your other vehicle show?"

"Just as he was taking off in your van. He slammed into them and then unloaded on the driver, then the passenger—Pfaff was in there." He sighed a rattling gasp. "Set the whole thing on fire with the pumps . . ."

Saizarbitoria appeared on the other side of the wounded man with the satellite phone still in his hands. "Need to talk to you, boss."

I glanced back at McGroder. "You're going to be okay, just rest easy and we'll get you something to drink." I stepped around the bar toward the windows that still reflected the collective bonfires. "East slope?"

"Everybody's coming, but it's going to take forever. They've closed off the road; the whole east side at Powder River Pass is covered in ice and they can only go maybe fifteen miles an hour. I've alerted the DOJ and marshal's offices. Henry and Vic are on their way with the EMTs and HPs."

"West slope?"

"Joe Iron Cloud's got 16 blocked along with 47 and 434. He's on his way up with Tommy Wayman, but it's already turned to snow west of here. We're going to get buried."

I ran a quick topographic in my head; we were close to the spine that made up the Bighorn Mountains, and the majority of the precipitation would fall here before heading onto the plains. "Yep, we are." There was another surge of flame from the gas pumps, and even if the damn things were empty, they were liable to cause a continuing hazard. "Get him something to drink. I'm going to go out to the side of the building and find the cutoff to those pumps."

Snow was just starting to mix with the sleet, and it was cold outside, colder than it had been when we'd arrived.

Around the corner, there was a lath fence beside the mudroom that housed a compressor and stacks of old tires, but in front of that there was an emergency kill switch. It was possible that, even empty, the pumps were still pushing gas vapor through the lines. After I threw the switch, the fire died down.

Still keeping my distance, I returned to the front of the building and studied the burning Suburban. I could go in and try and find a fire extinguisher but figured that wouldn't be the best utilization of my time, considering the circumstances. My eyes remained on the Chevy—the back access door and the rear passenger side hung partially ajar, and I could see where Shade had run the van into the SUV, forcing it onto the pump island. One of the gas handles lay on the melted asphalt, the hose burned and gone.

I stepped in closer and carefully counted the bodies and then walked around the vehicle and searched the surrounding area, just to be sure.

Back inside, Saizarbitoria was talking to McGroder, and the agent's color was a little better. Sancho broke off when he saw the look on my face. "What?"

"Mike, how many of your people were in the other Suburban?"

His head shook, but his eyes were steady. "Two of mine and a marshal. Three."

Sancho glanced back at McGroder as I bundled up, and we watched the fire bank itself and dwindle even further in the face of the sleet/snow and cold. The Basquo's voice was tight. "I think he's gonna make it."

"He's tough, but you need to keep him talking."

"Yeah, I know." Sancho's dark eyes reflected the waning fire as he spoke. "What're you going to do?"

I sighed. "I'll take a sweep between here and Boulder Park to make sure the convicts are not in a ditch. If they aren't, Iron Cloud will have a better chance of seeing them on his way up. No word from Joe or Tommy on the Ameri-Trans van?"

"No."

"What about Beatrice Linwood's Blazer."

The Basquo looked grim and then tried to put a good face on a situation that had none. "They didn't say anything, but if this Beatrice Linwood lives in Ten Sleep, wouldn't they have seen her?"

"Call them back and ask them to check it."

"I will." He bit the inside of his lip, a habit he'd picked up from me. "What are you thinking?"

I pulled out my pocket watch and read the time: creeping up on ten o'clock. "I'm thinking that an awful lot of our bad eggs just got out of the basket, and I'm afraid they've got one of ours with them."

"What do you mean?"

"There are only two bodies out there, and the cargo door was open. I think he took whatever was behind the seats and the woman agent, Pfaff."

"Why in the hell would he do that?"

"She's the one he's been talking to, and he's going to need insurance." I hustled back to the bar and placed a hand on McGroder's shoulder; he was definitely looking better. I glanced at the can of root beer Sancho had found on the shelves. "You want another sip?"

The agent grinned. "Only if you've got something stiffer."

"No such luck." I cleared my throat. "I've got bad news; it looks like you're going to make it."

He laughed slightly. "So, what's the good news?"

"I think he's got one of your agents."

The grin faded. "Kasey Pfaff?"

I nodded. "All the roads are blocked on both sides of the mountains, but I'm going to make a quick loop a little west of here. I'm hoping they're in a ditch, so I might be able to round things up quick."

"He'll kill you." He said it like taxes.

I patted his shoulder. "I'm kinda hard to kill."

"Yeah, I know. I talked to a buddy of yours who's in the Bureau—guy by the name of Cliff Cly. But still . . ."

My turn to grin. "Let me guess: Cly was reassigned to the licensing office in Nome, Alaska?"

"Something like that; he says you punch like a mule kicks."

I shrugged. "He's overly kind. Look, McGroder, I've got to get out there."

His voice took a different tone, and his sable eyes focused on me unlike they had before, as his hand grasped my sleeve. "I'm not screwing around here, Sheriff. Listen to me. If you go after him alone, he'll kill you. Wait for backup and . . ."

I took a breath and leaned in. "I'm just going up the road a bit."

His face remained immobile. "You'll never come back."

I smiled at him, but it was one of those moments when everything freezes in time. I could hear the coolers laboring away, the sleet on the roof, and the last few dying sounds of the fire outside. You know those moments are a signpost, something telling you that you shouldn't go any farther—the ones you try and ignore.

As I hurried toward the door, the Basquo intercepted me. "Hey, are you sure you want to do this alone?"

"Yep, I'm sure. I'm sure I don't, but there isn't anybody else for the job." He started to interrupt, but I cut him off before he could get going. "With your experience in corrections, you have a lot more medical training; if he goes into cardiac arrest, you might actually be able to do something about saving him."

He studied me, knowing full well I wasn't telling him everything, including the promise I'd made to his wife.

He was holding something out to me.

"What's this?"

"It's my daypack with supplies. I found some stuff behind the counter—candy, granola bars, a couple of cans of pop, some chips, chewing gum . . ."

I took the bag and slung one of the straps onto my shoulder. "Well, at least my breath will be kissing-sweet." He stared at me. I swear Vic was the only one who got my jokes. "I'll be right back."

"They took all the satellite phones that the Feds had except this one that they must have missed; they're these Motorola Iridiums, high-end Fed stuff that might have about thirty hours of power left in them, so take this one."

I didn't take it. "Then you have no phone."

He glanced at McGroder. "They know where we are."

I still didn't take it.

He handed me his cell phone that he had carefully wrapped

in a Ziploc bag. "Well, at least take this—maybe you'll find a signal."

I took the phone but balked when he tried to hand me his Beretta. I patted the .45 on my hip. "I've got a weapon. Anyway, in this weather they might come back." I took a deep breath of the warm air. "Do me a favor—call Ruby and report in. Tell her what's going on but don't make it sound too dramatic. Also, have her see what she can come up with on Beatrice Linwood's record."

"Got it." I didn't move, so he shoved the .40 back in his holster. "Look, when Benton was moving their stuff into our van, he put a gun case in the back section. It wasn't long enough to be a full-fledged rifle, but it looked longer than the Mossbergs they were carrying, so I asked him. He said it was one of those Armalites with laser sights."

I snorted a laugh. "Great." I nodded and put a hand on the metal bar that stretched across the door. "If I find the vehicle, I'll get it and a satellite phone. Keys?"

He nodded toward the Suburban. "They're in it."

"How trusting of you." I smiled, but he didn't smile back.

It was, as the Basquo had said, like driving on greased goose shit, and now it was really dark with a skim of snow on the road that made it even slicker. The Suburban was heavy, and I started slowing before Willow Park but still locked the wheels in a left-hand turn that resulted in my sliding into the crusty snow at the side of the road and knocking over one of the ten-foot reflector poles.

"Well, hell."

I threw the Chevy into reverse and easily backed off the roadside onto the snow-covered asphalt. I hit the brakes and could feel the whole truck slide backward an extra four feet.

"Wonderful. At this rate I'll be in Ten Sleep by Memorial Day."

I dropped the gear selector down into *D* and pulled back into the flow of things, slowed a little, and was able to keep the Suburban on the road as my mind raced ahead. All the signs pointed to Beatrice Linwood and Shade being in cahoots—the bobby-pin keys in the sandwiches, her turning west instead of east, the fact that she hadn't been able to keep her eyes off of him at the lodge—but the Ameri-Trans van was another story. Why hadn't it arrived at Joe Iron Cloud's or Tommy Wayman's roadblocks at the base of the mountain? The snow continued to collect on the conifers, and they began looking like rib cages in the contrast of light and dark as I thought about all the loose strings.

It was after I'd made the last curve before hitting the downslope that I saw lights shooting up at an angle. It was a steep embankment alongside a relative straightaway, but there was something odd about the reflection. As I got closer, I could see that it was not one vehicle in the barrow ditch but two.

I crept the Suburban to a stop about thirty yards away, cut the motor, and put on the flashers along with the Lite-Brite—the name my daughter Cady had given the emergency bars on the roofs of my assorted cruisers. I directed the spotlight at the vent window—a term from my own youth—and illuminated the wreckage.

It was Beatrice Linwood's Blazer and the Ameri-Trans convict transport van. From the slush marks and the point where the two vehicles had crashed their way through the snow piled by the road, I was pretty sure that she had driven into their vehicle at the front driver's side. With her greater velocity, she'd been able to push the much heavier step van into the ditch, where it had partially rolled over and now lay on its side.

Drawing my Colt, I stepped from the Suburban, careful to take a wide stance, which resulted in my sliding a good nine inches on the glassy surface of the road. I let out a breath, and it sounded like a rattler uncoiling in my lungs, the condensation blowing back in my face with the smell of snakes. I minced a few steps toward the front of the Chevy and could see the body of another one of the federal marshals, lightly covered with splatters of the wet snow, lying beside the ditch.

"Damn."

I eased past the grillwork and crouched by the man's outstretched hand. There's nothing quite so still as the dead—an otherworldly stillness. His flesh was frozen, and there was no movement in him. His coat was missing along with his boots and weapons—the sidearm and the shotgun.

Crouching a little, I pulled my hat on tighter, just to keep it from sailing off with the wind, and started down the slope. The lights were still on inside both vehicles, but the ones from the old Blazer were starting to dim to a sickly yellow. The main cargo doors of the reinforced van were open—I couldn't see anyone inside but could see the restraints that had attached the convicts lying in the doorway.

Slipping my Maglite from my belt, I focused the beam into the cavernous space where the prisoners should have been but weren't. I played the light over the cab of the Blazer, but no one was there either. The tracks led back up the hillside and onto the road—a lot of tracks.

If I was to make an assumption, it would be that Shade had picked up all of the survivors in our DOC van.

I scanned the surrounding area again and then continued to the front of the transport. The driver was there, leaning against his seat belt, and he was painfully and obviously dead, as was the man in the passenger seat. They'd both been shot at close range with one of the .40 pistols. I rested an elbow on the cracked windshield and listened to something in the distance, something unnatural.

It was a whining noise that rose and fell and then stopped.

I listened some more but could hear nothing except the wind. The collar of my sheepskin jacket was providing little protection, but I improved the odds by pulling it up higher and buttoning the top button. I took a second to think about the numbers: that meant six fugitives including Beatrice Linwood and two hostages—Pfaff and the other Ameri-Trans guard.

Just to make sure no one was hanging around, I checked the front of the Blazer at closer quarters, but it was indeed empty. Slogging my way back up the hillside, I remembered Santiago's cell phone and pulled it out of the Ziploc. I flipped open the face of the device and watched as it searched for service. After about a minute, I decided it was another opportunity to wait for Memorial Day and pocketed the useless thing.

I pulled the federal marshal completely from the road and covered his face with his hat. It was all I could do for now.

The Suburban started up easily, and I punched off the emergency lights and flashers; if I ran into the DOC van farther down the highway, they weren't likely to pull over. I kept the spotlight pointed in the general direction of the roadside and pulled out.

I'd gone about a quarter of a mile when something caught my eye, and I stood on the brakes. It was the main entrance to Deer Haven, another of the shuttered lodges in the throes of renovation. The Chevrolet slid sideways but finally stayed on the road. I refocused the spotlight and could see a clear set of tire tracks leading into the deep snow.

"Gotcha."

I wheeled the SUV into the entranceway, careful to avoid the deeper drifts to the left and the remnants of the broken swing gate where they had crashed through; the padlock was still hanging on the post to the right.

There was a single, dusk-to-dawn fixture about thirty feet above the ground, with a bulb that created a giant, illuminated halo that lit up the blowing snow but didn't shed a lot light on too much else. I repositioned the Suburban's spotlight into the gloom. Up ahead, there was a forest service bridge with a large drift blocking the road, and it looked as if they'd attempted to head up West Tensleep but had been turned back. The tracks showed that they had reversed and then swung around just ahead of me and plunged into the area where the parking lot would've been.

This was when a smart man would've parked the Suburban at the head of the road and waited for backup, and I thought about it. It was going to take hours for my reinforcements to get here, if they ever did, and I had a federal agent and a transport officer being held hostage. I applied the simple rule that allowed me to make stupid decisions in these types of situations: if I was down there, would I want someone coming after me?

Yep.

I swept the spotlight to the left and could see the complex of low-slung, dark log cabins—but no van. The tracks led straight across the flat area in front of them and then turned to the right, away from the main lodge. I drove slowly in their path and finally saw the van parked between two of the log structures that sat in a row.

The place was a bushwhacker's wet dream, with an assortment of cabins surrounding the seventy-five-yard open area, which I'd just crossed. They'd had enough time so that they could be anywhere.

I followed the path the van had cut in the parking lot and saw that the DOC vehicle had gone off the edge of the gravel and buried itself in the drift between the cabins. The noise I'd heard back on the side of the road must've been them trying to spin their way out in two-wheel drive.

There didn't seem to be anybody in the van, so at least I knew one place they weren't.

Figuring there was no reason to give them a very clear target, I shut off the headlights on the Suburban. Also figuring that for my purposes it was just as good to have things be as quiet as possible, I went ahead and killed the engine. I pulled out my Colt and slammed it into the light in the Suburban's overhead console. Bits of plastic fell onto the passenger seat, but I thought not giving them another target as I opened the door was a terrific option.

Let the government bill me.

I pulled the keys, opened the door, and stepped into the snow, the surface crusty from sleet. Something fell out along with me. When I looked down I could see it was Saizarbitoria's pack that now lay on the snow-dappled steps leading to the porch of one of the cabins. I kicked it aside and figured I'd pick it up when I got back to the vehicle.

There were no windows on the sides of the two structures that faced each other, only small ones in the fronts along with glass panels in the two doors. There was no movement that I could detect inside either cabin. I'd check them again after I searched the van.

I eased the door shut and started toward the back of the DOC vehicle. I was pleasantly surprised to see that the occupants had all gotten out through the sliding door at the side and continued on past the cabins to the left.

As far as I could tell, the only electricity that worked was the dawn-to-dusk at the entrance of the parking lot. There probably was no heat either, and huddled in one of the cabins or the main lodge, the group was most likely breaking up furniture to burn in one of the small fireplaces in an attempt not to freeze to death.

The bodies of the two marshals were still lying on the floorboard of the van, both of them, as McGroder had indicated, having been dispatched with one of the appropriated shotguns and at close range. Benton was the nearest, so I reached out and closed his eyes—once again, there was little else I could do. The convicts had taken everything including the steak knife that I had left on the dash. I started to return to the rear cargo door where Santiago said that Benton had stored the enhanced Armalite; I figured I'd feel a lot better if I could get a proper rifle in my hands.

Something moved above me.

I scrambled back against the cabin wall and raised the big Colt.

My back thumped into the dark brown logs, and I stood there in a two-handed grip, trying to get my blood pressure under control. There was a loud snarl like the kind you hear in the movies, but this one was up close and real. I figured it was going to take a couple of hours to get the hair on the back of my neck to lie back down.

As Lonnie Little Bird would say, she was a big one, but she was thin, and I was lucky she didn't have cubs or I might've been dead. She snarled down at me and backed her haunches into the cove section of the twin-peaked roof of the cabin on the other side of the van. Her eyes were the only things I could see.

I'd never been this close to a mountain lion, and I had to admit that—even snarling with a ferocity that vibrated my own lungs—she was a beauty.

Evidently, she'd taken advantage of the shelter provided by the overhang that gave her the ability to stay covered yet capable. I guess she hadn't moved when the van had pulled in, but when I'd driven up and started poking around, she'd decided enough was enough.

I waved my sidearm at her, and I'll be damned if she didn't slam a paw as big as Dog's into the roof of the cabin in order to back me off. I stood there, a little surprised. The big cats usually aren't so tenacious when confronted with human beings.

I guess she figured there was nowhere better to go, and she'd been there first.

"C'mon, get out of here. I'll be damned if I'm going to march around waiting for you to hurdle off onto me. Scat!"

I waved the pistol again, but she pushed herself deeper into the alcove. We were at a standoff, and there wasn't much more I could do to make her move.

With one more glance, I eased around the van and shot a breath from my nose, pulling the handle on one of the rear doors. Just as the Basquo had said, there was a Hardigg polyethylene deployment case lying there—olive drab, my favorite color, or so the Marine Corps had taught me.

I gave another look to the roof of the cabin where I hoped the cougar was still crouched, stuffed my fingertip into my mouth, and yanked the glove off with my teeth. I slipped my naked hand into the plastic handle and pulled the case toward me. I was always amazed at how light the M-series rifles were—they had always felt like plastic toys.

I flipped open the antishear latches and opened the case, revealing the foam cavities for a full cleaning kit and extra magazines and the laser sight. There was a cutout for an M203 grenade launcher with accessories, which had been filled in with foam. The attachment had obviously not been in there—the problem was, neither was the short-barreled rifle.

It was about then that I noticed, for just an instant, a tiny green dot reflected in the van's rear window.

5

I threw myself sideways, multiplying the speed of my descent by slipping on the ice.

The report of the .223 was very loud. I hit the ground with a grunt immediately following the sharp *spak* of the bullet going through the back window of the closed half of the van where I'd been standing.

I rolled over and looked at the bullet hole in the glass, small shards and snow still floating down on me as I reconsidered what an intelligent man would've done in this situation. I had an image of my smarter self, munching on a year-old Snickers bar, seated in the relative warmth of the Suburban, which I would have parked at the road head.

It's a maxim that in these situations the first person to move is the first person to die. It was possible that the shooter thought he'd hit me and I could wait to see if he'd show, but that meant lying in the snow, exposed for longer than I really cared to be.

If I wanted a clear view, I was going to have to crawl out from between the two vehicles, which meant really showing myself, something I was loath to do. I reached over and picked up my hat, dusting it off and placing it back on my head.

Small comforts, but I always felt better with my hat on.

There were noises coming from the other side of the parking lot and then some voices. I couldn't make out what any of them were saying, but they said a few things to one another and then it was silent again.

I waited for a few moments more and then looked around the passenger-side fender. With the blowing snow, it was almost like playing tag in a river. There was someone outside, and I just caught the fleeting image of a man darting past the windows on the porch of the main lodge.

It looked to me as if he were carrying one of the shotguns, which meant that someone else was probably still out there with the .223 and that the runner was going to try and flank me from the cabins at my rear.

I had to move, but I wasn't going to attempt crossing the lot—not with the Armalite waiting for the possibility of another lucky shot in the current conditions. If I squeezed past the DOC van and right, I'd probably meet the shooter somewhere out there. I leveraged up on my elbows and knees and glanced back to see if I could triangulate the rifle fire. It looked like it had come from slightly to my right—the same basic area where I'd seen somebody moving at the main lodge.

I crouched and moved, picking up the Basquo's backpack as I went, sliding between the van and the cabin where the cougar had been. The snow slid off the van and landed on my hat and shoulders. I didn't wipe it off this time, in hopes that it might provide some cover from the scope, but when I turned my head, there was a SIG SAUER P226 muzzle pointed up and under my chin.

"Move back."

With the shadows, it was difficult to see who was holding the semiautomatic, but hearing the Latino accent, I had a good idea. I retreated with my .45 held above my head. "Hey, Hector."

"Raise your arms and shut up." As he stepped into the minimal light afforded by the parking lot lamppost, I could see the pant leg of his orange jumpsuit and the tactical boots that he must've taken from the dead marshal. He also wore a three-quarter-length parka, which he must've appropriated from the convict transport. He motioned for me to move to my right. "Step over there."

I did as instructed and, knowing that a little cover was better than none, was careful to place myself between the DOC van and the Suburban.

Hector stepped around as well, carefully holding McGroder's Sig at an angle—gangsta style. He raised a hand to his face and yelled back toward the main lodge. "Got him!" I shifted, with my hands still above my head, and his eyes darted back to me. "I said don't move."

"Actually, you didn't."

"Shut up!" He paused and turned slightly as we heard noises coming from the big building. "And gimme your gun."

I thought about my situation, how I was soon to be surrounded by some very desperate and well-armed individuals. I thought about how the odds of one-on-one were a hell of a lot better than five-on-one.

With my hands still raised, I tossed the Colt up onto the roof of the van.

Otero looked at me. "What the fuck?"

I shrugged. "You said to get rid of the gun."

He studied me from the depths of his acrylic-lined hood. "What, you don't think I can get up there or what?"

"Well, you are kind of short."

He gestured with the .40 for me to back up, which I did with my hands still raised, as he placed a foot on the doorsill of the van and pulled himself up by the gutter rail. "Fuck you, Alexander Dumb-ass." He really was kind of short and had to reach across the top of the snow-covered van with one hand while keeping his pistol pointed at me. It was quite a balancing act.

I retreated another step.

"I said don't move!"

The wind blew another gust from the roof of the cabins and pushed the hood of Hector's parka against his face; he kept yanking it back, but it continued blowing forward.

I was beginning to wonder how much movement it was going to take.

To give her credit, she didn't make a sound until she moved and when she did it was something to behold. She bounced once to contain her speed and swiped out with a massive paw at Hector's hooded head. He jumped when the sound and fury came out of the alcove, and his foot slipped on the wet sill. The cougar's lethal claws raked the cloth on the top of his head, his face was pushed forward by the force of her swipe, and he flipped backward to land at my feet. The Sig should've gone off, but it didn't.

I landed all two hundred and fifty pounds on his chest with a knee and listened to the air go out of him, which for a moment stopped the screaming, and then the semiautomatic popped from his hand.

It was a calculated risk, turning my back to the cougar, but I figured Hector was the moment's primary threat. I snatched the .40 from the snow and then whirled to face the mountain lion, but she'd stayed on the roof of the van and was snarling and spitting.

"Shoot! Shoot the motherfucker! Shoot!"

Evidently, Hector had gotten his wind back.

"Shoot!"

She slapped the roof of the van again with her big paws, and I guess she was waiting to see who, between Hector and me, was going to come out on top. I figured she was planning on eating the loser. I flicked off the safety lever near the slide action, something you might not know to do if you were unfamiliar with the weapon, and kept the semiautomatic on the cougar.

"Shoot!"

Leaning on the grill of the Suburban next to Hector, I kept the sidearm trained on the mountain lion but glanced at the Latino. Trickles of blood were running down his face from where the lion's claws had gotten him. "I think you're annoying her." The wind blew more gusts of snow, and I could hear footsteps along with a few shouts. "I think you better tell your friends you haven't got me anymore." He looked at me questioningly. "Go ahead—yell." He paused for a second, but I gestured with the gun toward the angry cougar. "You don't yell, I'm going to let her have you."

The mountain lion continued to snarl and again slapped the roof of the van.

"Hey, he's got my gun—and there's a fuckin' tiger over here!"

I could still hear them moving closer and figured it was time to take action. I might regret the loss of ammunition later, but I needed to back everybody, including the cougar, off. I raised the P226 and fired off a couple of shots.

There was more cursing, but I could hear them scrambling back toward the lodge.

When I glanced up again, the mountain lion had disappeared.

I wedged my shoulder against the grill of the Suburban and peeked over the hood. There wasn't anyone there.

When I realized I hadn't breathed in a while, I took a deep one and slowly exhaled, feeling like a portion of my soul was escaping along with the vapor from my nostrils.

Hector was feeling his head and wiping the blood off his face. "That thing bit me!"

I pushed the barrel of the P226 in his ear. "New rules— stop complaining."

My Colt was still on the top of the van. I figured the big cat was gone, but I still wasn't too hep on the prospect of climbing up there and getting a .223 in my spine. I could always make Hector do it, but I wasn't sure that they wouldn't shoot him, too.

I glanced back at the main lodge. "Hey Hector, do you want to go up there and get my gun?"

His eyes looked like ping-pong balls with pupils. "Fuck that."

"That's what I figured." I glanced at him. "So they're all holing up in the lodge?" He didn't say anything, so I nudged his ear with the Sig, reinforcing the rules.

"Yeah, yeah . . . they're in the lodge thing."

"They've got the FBI agent, the blonde woman?"

"Yeah, they got her."

I made some quick calculations and took the barrel of the gun away from his head. "What about the other Ameri-Trans guy?"

He looked at me for a moment. "Yeah, they got him, too."

I wondered briefly why they hadn't simply killed him, but it was possible that they were smart enough to realize that they should hang on to all potential hostages. "What about Beatrice Linwood?"

"Who?"

"I need you to pay attention, Hector." I sighed. "The waitress from South Fork Lodge, the one that served us lunch."

"Oh, Shade's bitch . . . Yeah, hey that dude's crazy. He says there are ghosts all over these mountains and that they talk to him."

I stared at him, and fortunately he misinterpreted.

"I'm not kidding. He says there are hundreds of them all around watching us." He wiped the blood out of his eyes. "He's fuckin' crazy, man."

I looked down at the top of his head and could see the four grooves where the big cat had gotten him. It was a good thing he had had that hood or it would have been worse. I figured I'd play on it. "You might need some stitches."

"Hey, no shit. I'm bleeding to death here."

I looked around at our situation and wasn't overcome with confidence. The only positive thing I could think of was that I had all the modes of transportation and a pretty good vantage point. Of course, there was also the opportunity to freeze to death before the sun came up in the morning.

The gangbanger looked up at me. "Hey, you know I wasn't going to shoot you, right?"

I kept my eyes on the porch of the lodge but couldn't see anything amidst the streaking snow. "Well, I appreciate that, Hector."

"Yeah, I mean I was just supposed to slow you down till they got that thing going."

I studied him. "What thing?"

"The tank thing."

"Hector, what are you talking about?"

He wiped more blood off his face with his sleeve. "When we got the van stuck, Shade said you'd be the one that would come after us; that the dead Indians told him." He tapped the front of the Suburban with a hand. "When you got here we'd take your truck. But then one of the other guys, the guy they call Fingers, he found the tank thing in the shed behind the lodge and said he could get it going if we gave him enough time."

I seemed to remember an old surplus Thiokol Model 601 Spryte snowcat that had been brought up from the Air Force Academy in Colorado Springs back in the midseventies for use at the ski resort near Meadowlark Lake. So much for keeping them penned, but how far and how fast did they think they were going to go in a snowcat? If I were them, I'd still try for the Fed Suburban.

I stood and checked for the keys to the SUV, which were still in my pocket, and then tapped Hector on the shoulder. "C'mon."

He looked up at me but didn't move. "What?"

Slitting my eyes to guard against the snow, I glanced across the hood. "We're gonna go break up the party."

He settled into the parka, which was a good two sizes too big for him. "Fuck that."

I looked down at him and snorted, losing a little more of my soul through my nose. I raised my eyes and tried to sound indifferent. "Suit yourself, but with you bleeding like you are and alone, I'll bet that hungry mountain lion comes back."

There wasn't much cover between the cabins and the lodge, and I was going to have to hustle between them in open view of whoever was shooting the assault rifle. Occupying myself by thinking about how many wrong career choices I'd made to lead me to this lovely pass, I stood at the front of the van, shrugged the strap of Sancho's pack onto my shoulder, and took a few deep breaths.

I jolted forward and to the right, postholing only one step in the open. I slammed against the notched corner of the other cabin but didn't hear anything. I was tempted to wave my hat but figured I'd already pressed my luck—and anyway, I liked my hat.

I motioned for Hector to follow me. I'd cuffed him but figured his legs should still work fine.

He shook his head and brought his hands together in a praying gesture.

I'd given him the option of going first, but he'd said he'd rather follow. I guess he was having second thoughts now.

I yelled above the wind. "C'mon." Say what you want about the small man, he was agile and fast. He ran into my shoulder and stood there panting. "You do that again, and I'll leave you out here."

His eyes circled the immediate vicinity, and I could only guess how many phantom cougars he was seeing.

I stayed close to the cabin, careful to slip under the window, and continued to my right. If I remembered correctly, there was a straight shot to the lodge up ahead, but we had to go through another opening between the next two cabins before we could get there.

I waited at the corner and hoped that when I made my mad dash, somebody wouldn't be waiting on the other side with a riot gun. I stood there awhile just to break up the rhythm. I thought of Santiago's cell phone in my pocket but didn't want to open it out here in the dark—it'd be like a beacon for bullets.

I shrugged the strap of the pack farther up on my shoulder and launched across.

My back flattened against the logs of the next cabin about halfway down the row, and I looked back at Hector. He was still panting and held up a finger. After a moment, he threw himself into the opening, slipped in the snow, and fell to his knees, finally scrambling across on all fours.

I grabbed him by his collar and stood him up beside me. "I think after that epic display of catlike grace, we can safely say that they're not keeping too close a watch on us."

"Fuck you, man." He trapped his struggling mustache in his lower lip. "That shit's slippery."

"Stay here until I motion for you."

He nodded. "I'm good with that."

I continued around the cabin and peered past the corner— it was a straight shot of about thirty yards to the side of the main lodge, but with the oblique angle of the lodge windows, I had a reasonable chance of taking them by surprise. There was a large lean-to shed behind the building with a set of steps that probably led to the kitchen. I was thinking that that might be just the opening I needed.

The wind continued to pick up, and I imagined it was blowing at a thirty-mile-an-hour clip. The snow on the road-way between us and the lodge was a little over ankle deep, but after watching Hector's Ice Capades, I wasn't so sure we could make it before being discovered.

I leaned back against the logs and waved for him.

"Hey, Sheriff, are there more of you true blues coming?"

"Lots of them."

"Are they bringing food and stuff?"

I glanced at him. "What, are you hungry again?"

"Yeah, an' that bitch only brought that freeze-dried shit."

"Beatrice brought supplies?"

"Uh huh, food packs—even snowshoes."

Well, double-hell. Why would she go to the trouble of bring-ing freeze-dried food? Packs and snowshoes? Where were they going that they needed these kinds of provisions? All things con-sidered, the sooner they were stopped the better.

I turned to look at Hector. "We're going to hustle across to the lodge, and my advice to you is to keep up. If they even think they see people moving around out here, they're just the type to shoot first and identify the bodies later. Got me?"

He didn't look enthused with the elegant simplicity of my plan. "Yeah."

"Ready?"

He shook his head. "No."

"All right then, let's go."

I rushed forward, the wet snow sticking to my right side

like plaster of Paris. All of a sudden the whiteout was so thick you could've cut sheep out of the air with a sharp knife. I stumbled once and could hear Hector's breath at my back.

The drifts got deep toward the lodge where the snow had whistled against the building and had settled in a steep upgrade that wasn't there anymore. I stopped at the base of the steps and clung to the railing, the air in my lungs feeling like battery acid.

Hector stumbled onto the first step. "Hey, we're not going to stay out here, are we?"

I swallowed and grabbed my breath by the tail ends. "No."

I listened—something didn't sound right. The noise was coming from my right, and I'd just about made up my mind that it was just the wind striking the corner of the building when the keening increased its pitch.

I grabbed Hector as the padlocked barn door of the shed blew apart, with the majority of the nearest twelve-foot door tumbling on top of us. The metal bars of the railings, which were set in the concrete steps, held the weight of the thing above us, but it shifted when something very big rolled over the wooden planks, first raising them and then slapping them down on us again. The wood splintered this time, but the railings held, and Hector and I crawled toward the building, toward the only opening afforded us.

I was the first to get clear of the shattered remains of the shed and slid up at the corner of the lodge in time to see the big, weathered blue shoebox of a 601 Spryte snowcat pivot a few times as the driver attempted to get a feel for the thing. He finally got the thirty-two-inch tracks going in the direction he wanted, which happened to be into the parked Suburban.

The Thiokol thundered into the side of the Chevrolet, pushing it onto the porch of one of the cabins; the porch collapsed and the SUV was buried in the rubble. The 601 pivoted again, and I could see the primer patches on it—the U.S. AIR FORCE 6385 443 designation was still painted on the back, along with, scripted below, FOR OFFICIAL USE ONLY.

I raised the .40 and aimed at the small windows in the thing, but what was I going to shoot and whom? I allowed the Sig to slip to my side as the snowcat pivoted once again, climbed the small embankment, and turned left on West Tensleep Road.

Left.

I ducked my head down and peered into the gloom and blowing snow just to make sure I'd seen what I'd seen. They weren't heading for the paved road to the south but north, up the snow-covered, dead-end road toward West Tensleep Lake.

Left.

I watched as they continued toward the bridge, easily maneuvering over the drift that had stopped me flat, the motor accelerating in the distance until the noise mingled with the wind and was gone.

"This ain't fair." As if to demonstrate the cruelty of my act, Hector yanked at the handcuffs that secured him to the water pipes. "What if that fucking tiger comes back?"

I finished patching his head with the available medical supplies in the first-aid kit under the counter. He looked like he was wearing a gauze beanie, but at least the bleeding had stopped for good. I stuffed a few of the water bottles I'd found into the Basquo's pack and tossed one to Hector. "Here."

He caught the bottle with his free hand and sat back on the chair I'd provided for him behind the counter beside the cash register next to the pay phone. "What am I supposed to do?"

I needed to make more room in the pack, so I emptied it and arranged the items on the round table in the dining area of Deer Haven Lodge. Saizarbitoria had scrounged up a pretty good amount of candy bars, a bag of Funyuns, and a few cans of Coke. I axed the pop—the water was what I was going to need. "Around these parts, we drink it."

"I mean about the tiger!"

I pulled the cell phone out of my pocket and from the plastic bag. I planned to place it in the nifty, little pouch on the outside of the pack so that I could find it later. First, though, I flipped it open and looked at the battery indicator, which read about three-quarters, and then at the signal indicator, which read nothing. There was no service; it was just as well, since I was going to feel pretty silly telling everybody about how I'd found the escaped convicts but, after being shot at and pretty much hit with a barn door, had allowed them to escape.

On a whim, I went over to the pay phone next to Hector, picked up the receiver, and clicked the toggle—there was a dial tone. I dialed 911.

"Absaroka County Sheriff's Department."

"I'd like to report a storm in Maybruary."

She practically screamed. "Where are you!?"

"Nestled in the heart of the Bighorn Mountains."

Ruby calmed a little but was adamant. "Where exactly?"

"Deer Haven Lodge at the cutoff to West Tensleep Lake."

"What are you doing there?"

"Hell is empty, and all the devils are here."

"Have you found them?"

"One down, four to go." I held the phone out. "Say hello, Hector."

He lurched forward, the handcuffs rattling against the pipe. "Hey, this guy's crazy, and there's a fucking tiger up here!"

I returned the phone to my ear and lodged it against my shoulder as I buckled up the main cavity of the pack. "Hector's a little excitable, but he'll be at the main lodge when they get here. Speaking of which, where's my backup?"

"They're on their way from both sides of the mountain. Joe Iron Cloud, Tommy Wayman, and about a division of Highway Patrol and search and rescue are on their way from the west, but the switchbacks in Tensleep Canyon are filled with drifts. Henry and Vic with an even larger contingency are on their way up from our side, but I haven't heard anything from them in over an hour. I'd imagine they're encountering the same conditions."

"Maybe worse. Hey, you didn't say *over*."

She sighed, but I could still tell my dispatcher was slightly amused. "It's a phone, Walter. You don't use radio procedures on a phone."

"Ruby, the remaining convicts stole a snowcat from the lodge here and are headed up West Tensleep Road; give a call to everybody and let them know what's going on."

"They went up the trailhead road?"

"Yep. Maybe they think it comes out somewhere. Boy, are they going to be surprised when all they find is a parking lot and some Porta Potties." I shifted the receiver to my other ear as Hector watched. "Sancho loaned me his cell, but there's no service." I read her the number in case she didn't have it handy. "He says that if I get one of the Fed satellite phones, it should work; I would imagine they're sequential, so just add a digit to the end of the one he called you on, and you'll probably have the number. Read me his, and I'll put it in Sancho's mobile." I leaned against the wall and shared a look with Otero as I repeated the number she read to me, "Sancho's still back at Meadowlark with McGroder; the convicts took Pfaff and one of the Ameri-Trans personnel. All the rest of the federal agents and marshals are dead."

There was a long pause as I waited for the lecture that was coming. "Walter, if they've gone north on that road, there's no way for them to escape. You should wait until someone gets there."

I thought about the private cabins up here and the hostages. "I think it's better to keep close to them and know where they are."

"Alone?"

"Yep, well . . . Manpower seems to be pretty much at a shortage up here."

There was an even longer pause. "Do you have your radio with you?"

It would only be helpful if there was line of sight, and if they got within thirty miles of me, sans weather conditions, but I figured I'd keep that little nugget of information to myself. "Yes, ma'am."

"It'll only be good if they get within thirty miles, but it makes me feel better knowing that you've got it."

"Uh huh."

"I'll give the cell and the potential satellite number to everyone."

I listened to her breathing on the other end. "I gotta head out . . ."

"You do realize it's two o'clock in the morning?"

"That's okay—it's a weekend, and I'm becoming something of a night owl."

Ruby, aware of the Northern Cheyenne belief that owls were messengers from the great beyond, didn't take mention of them lightly. "Don't talk about owls."

"What, you're starting to believe the heathen-red-man's sorcery?"

"Let's just say I'm playing it safe."

"Good night, Ruby." I hung up the pay phone and then palmed open Saizarbitoria's cell to check again—still nothing. I looked at the screen saver of Sancho's wife Marie holding their son Antonio. I sighed, turned it off, and slipped the device into the Ziploc. Then I tried to put it into the outside compartment of the Basquo's pack, but it wouldn't fit. I unzipped the compartment, pulled out a paperback, and turned it over.

The cover art was a detail, *The Damned of the Last Judgement*, from the fourteenth-century cupola mosaic in the Baptistery in Florence. A very large blue devil appeared to be munching on the unfortunate next to a sticker that proclaimed a "New Translation" by Robin Kirkpatrick. I peeled through the pages, Italian on the left, English translation on the right.

That Basquo.

The first page caught my eye:

At one point midway on our path in life,
I came around and found myself now searching
through a dark wood, the right way blurred and lost.

Boy howdy. I walked over and stood there looking out the windows for a second, then closed the Penguin Classic and popped it back in the pack. I picked up the Sig semiautomatic from the table, palming the clip and thumbing the remaining rounds into my pocket—body and soul, crime and punishment, law and order.

"How 'bout you give me that gun."

I'd all but forgotten about him. I turned and gave my attention to Hector as I buttoned my sheepskin coat and slapped the mag back in the grip. "I'm not sure how they do things down Texas way, but we try to keep guns out of the hands of convicted killers up here in Wyoming."

I came back over, sat in one of the chairs, and tossed the Sig onto the counter between us. He immediately snatched it up and pointed it at me.

"Besides, it's empty."

He pulled the action and then dropped the clip just to make sure. He tossed it back onto the counter. "What if that tiger comes back?"

I rubbed my face with my hands. "Hector, I don't think a mountain lion is going to be bold enough to break down the door to get in here even if she feels like a little Mexican."

"Fuck you." He looked past me toward the fireplace. "Hey, give me that stick from over there, huh?"

I glanced behind me, and sure enough there was a walking staff with a leather loop on one end and tacked on the shaft a number of tiny, metal plates commending the places the stick and its owner had gone. I walked over and took it from the freestanding coat rack, behind which were hung an old pair of strung-gut willow snowshoes. There was also the outline of something that must have been hanging next to them, like a rug, maybe, or a skin of some sort.

"There was a buffalo thing or something hanging up there. Shade took it with him."

Now, why would he do that? I looked at the bear-paw-pattern snowshoes again: waste not, want not. I pulled them off the wall and stuffed them under my arm, walked back, and handed the stick to Hector. "There you go."

He slapped the thicker end of the five-foot staff against the flattened palm of his cuffed hand to test the weight and seemed satisfied. "Cool." His eyes came back up to the antique snowshoes under my arm. "Are you really going after them in this friggin' blizzard?"

"Yep."

He paused but then blurted out. "You should wait for some help. I'm jus' sayin'."

I pulled the brim of my hat down to set it against the wind and started examining the buckles and leather straps on the snowshoes. "That seems to be the consensus."

His voice became flat. "No, really. I seen some guys in my life, Sheriff, but that Shade—he's crazy bad."

I nodded and sat in the chair in an attempt to get the straps over my boots. As I rested my chest against one of my knees, I thought about just staying there like that and maybe taking a nap. Who was I kidding? I wasn't in any shape to head out into a blizzard in the middle of the night after a bunch of homicidal maniacs. Then the other voice in my head got me to thinking that they wouldn't make it very far, probably would choose to hole up in one of the cabins farther up the road or possibly at the Tyrell Ranger Station. I'd try not to be as conspicuous as I had been. I'd just keep an eye on them till the troops arrived, just keep an eye on them—at least that's what I was telling myself.

I got up, smiling at his concern. "Thanks, Hector."

Just for laughs, I hit the remote on the Suburban—the horn tooted and the lights flashed from under the collapsed porch. The left rear tire was flat, and the quarter panel had been pushed up into the wheel well. I could probably get it going if I had the Jaws of Life, parts, and a day to work on it.

I loped along on the surface of the snow against the blowing wind. It was a little tough, but I got the front of the snowshoe in the open back doorway of the DOC van and pulled myself up, glancing more than once at the alcove on the adjacent cabin where the cougar had appeared.

Nothing, just more snow.

I scrambled my hand around on the top of the Dodge till I found my 1911 and pulled it toward me, banging the collected snow off and returning it to my holster as I hung on to the back drip rail. My eyes clung to the mountain lion print closest to me, and I was reminded of just how big she was.

I was glad now that I'd moved one of the benches from the porch in front of the door of the lodge.

The sound of my snowshoes landing was muffled by the snow, and I turned toward Tensleep Road but froze. The big cat hadn't gone far and stood in plain view underneath the lone light on the power pole, her eight-foot-long body pale in the halo of the falling snow. She looked at me from over her shoulder, and I was beginning to think that this was extremely odd behavior.

It was possible that she was just angry with Hector and me for driving her from her temporary lair, but it didn't seem that way. It was almost as if she was saddened and, even with the reception I'd given her, unhappy to leave.

It was probably warmer in the little corner of the roof she'd found.

Pulling the .45 from my holster, I waved it at her, but she just stood there looking at me.

A gust of snow blew from the collapsed roof, striking my face like sand and, ducking slightly away, I closed my eyes.

When I reopened them she was gone, and the flakes continued to float down in the circle of light like the spotlight on an empty stage, and it was as if she hadn't been there at all.

6

They'd blown through the piled-up berm at the bridge. The dual tracks of the Thiokol Spryte were almost three feet wide leading up West Tensleep Road, but it was easier to just walk between the tread marks in my borrowed snowshoes.

That wasn't why I was standing there, unmoving.

After they'd busted through, they had stopped. You could see where the snowcat had steered slightly to the right. I pulled my Maglite from my duty belt and shined it on the tracks, hoping I'd see an oil or fuel leak. There were a few drops, but nothing that was going to slow the behemoth. My eyes were drawn to something leading to the snowbank, what looked like a different kind of leak—possibly antifreeze.

I stood there looking at what was illuminated by my flashlight, which, like the light in the parking lot, provided a center stage spot for a curtain call or maybe a prologue.

Pissed in the snowbank was a single word.

ABANDON.

Raynaud Shade had pretty good handwriting, considering the instrument.

ABANDON.

He'd seen the Basquo reading the *Inferno*. He'd left the message for me and evidently hadn't had the bladder capacity to finish the stanza: ". . . hope all ye who enter here"—the warning above the gates of hell in Dante's opus.

Maybe he'd seen a similarity between our situation and that of the Italian poet. The wind pressed at my back and the flakes swirled around, but the impromptu calling card stayed there as if he'd written it in molten lead.

It was about a mile up to the Battle Park cutoff, where I assumed they'd turn west and try for the Hyattville Road that led toward the tiny town and eventually to Manderson, which was situated alongside the Big Horn River. Then what—north to Basin or south to Worland? Try as I might, I couldn't see what they were gaining by going off-road. They, and by they I meant Shade, had to know that there would be an entire law enforcement army waiting for them when they got off the mountain in either direction.

There were no roads that connected the north side of the Bighorns with the south side, and the only substantial trail that led east was over Florence Pass near Bomber Mountain and Cloud Peak toward the Hunter Corrals. Florence Pass was more than eleven thousand feet, and if they tried that they were likely to solve society's problems on their own, which was fine for the convicts but not for the two hostages.

A lot of people made the mistake of heading up West Tensleep in the hopes that it led somewhere besides Cloud Peak, a 13,167-foot glaciated monolith, seventh largest in Wyoming, with a vertical mass of one minor and three major cirques that supported its own weather pattern. The Crow, Cheyenne, and Lakota venerated Cloud Peak as a place to bestow gifts of redemption and to retrieve *Eewakee*, or the mud-that-heals. In 1887, U.S. Engineer W. S. Stanton, the white mountaineer who claimed to have conquered the mountain's west slope first, discovered medicine bundles and a bivouac that the Indians had left behind.

So much for being first.

ABANDON.

The message pissed in the snow kept invading my thoughts as I trudged on, my snowshoes keeping me on the surface of the snow, the history of Wyoming alpinism unable to wipe the urinated message from my mind.

The trees on either side of the road had sheltered the way so far and I appreciated the protection, but the weight of the snow was already taking its toll, and I could hear heavy branches cracking and falling like severed limbs.

There was a consistent wind, and I ducked my hat against the gusts as the snow continued to dart down at a thirty-degree angle—at least it wasn't adhering itself to me like it had in the open spaces back at Deer Haven—but I could tell that the temperature was dropping.

I figured there wasn't much need to be concerned about being ambushed, just the steady slog of working my way higher into the range and staying between the wide tracks of the surplus snowcat. If I fell into one of the troughs, I knew I was off course.

The collar of my sheepskin coat had attached itself to the left side of my face, and the narrow V-shaped aperture that I looked through allowed me only a limited view of the road ahead, so I was more than a little surprised when suddenly there was the glare of a lot of lights and the thrum of internal combustion from a fast-moving, highly lifted 4×4.

I bounced off the Jeep's grill and threw myself to the right—the vehicle had slowed and missed rolling over my legs by about a foot as it slid to a stop. I lay there for a moment and then started getting up. The snowshoes were cumbersome, and it took me a while to stand and make my way to the lee side of the Jeep, which was shaking from some kind of thunderous music being played on its stereo. I paused for a second and remembered another time on the mountain when I'd been assaulted by a different kind of music—drums, specifically.

I waited patiently as the driver rolled down the window about four inches and looked out at me. His voice was agitated. "What the hell are you doing walking in the middle of the damn road?!"

I breathed a laugh and had a coughing fit from the cold of the high-altitude air. "What the hell are you doing speeding down a mountain in this weather?"

He was middle-aged, a little chubby, and in his early fifties, with black hair and a black goatee, a Hollywood smile, and a black down jacket with a black Greek fisherman's hat. On closer inspection, even the Jeep was black, black being the new black. I glanced at the Wrangler—it probably had about thirty thousand dollars' worth of modifications, and from the decibel level, they were mostly in the stereo.

"You mind turning your music down?" I hung an arm over his side mirror and took a few breaths as he did as I requested. He seemed a little worried, and I guess I would've been too if

I'd found somebody traipsing up West Tensleep Road in the middle of a high-altitude blizzard. "I'm Sheriff . . ." I cleared my throat.

He rolled the window down a little farther. "What?"

"Sheriff . . . I'm Sheriff Walt Longmire."

"Oh." He seemed uncertain as to what to do with that information. "Are you okay?"

"Yep. You haven't seen a Thiokol Spryte go by here, have you?"

He looked at me, blank like a freshly wiped chalkboard. "A what?"

I pointed toward the tracks in which he was driving. "Big snowcat; square like a very large lunchbox."

He shook his head. "Nope, we pulled onto the main road from our cabin and started driving out. Haven't seen anything except you."

I shifted the knapsack farther up on my shoulder, crouched against the Jeep for cover, and could see a blonde-haired woman in the passenger seat. "How far up is your cabin?"

He paused and glanced at the woman before resting his eyes on me again. "Look, Sheriff—if you are a sheriff—I don't want any trouble . . ."

I fumbled with the opening of my coat and tried to unbutton the top button so that I could show him my badge, but my gloves made it slow going. I finally got my jacket open enough so that he could see it. "There."

He stretched out the next words. "All right."

"I need your help."

He really looked worried now. "To do what?"

"Give me a ride back up this road."

He looked around, as if to emphasize the point. "You're kidding, right?"

"No, I'm not."

He sighed and placed the palms of his gloves on the steering wheel. "Sheriff, we've been listening to the radio and they say that they're . . . that you guys are going to close the roads."

"They're already closed, in both directions on 16. Once you get out of here you're only going to get as far as Tensleep Canyon to the west and Meadowlark Lodge to the east. If you've got food, supplies, and heat, I'd advise you to go back to your cabin till the WYDOT guys can break through."

He glanced at the woman again, and she folded her arms and looked out the other window. He tipped his hat back and looked at me. "Actually, the electricity went out about an hour ago."

I thought about all the cabins I knew of on the mountain. "Don't you have a secondary heating source?"

"A what?"

"A fireplace or a stove?"

He nodded. "Yeah, there's a fireplace."

"Firewood?"

"Yeah." He sat there without looking at me and then spoke. "We think we'd rather take our chances."

I stared at the side of his face. "You're not listening. The roads are closed, and I've got three sheriff's departments, search and rescue, a couple of detachments of HPs, and the majority of WYDOT shoveling their way up here. If you go on, you're going to end up sitting on the roadway waiting for them to clear it, and if they don't do that before you run out of gas, you're going to get very cold. My advice is that you go back to your cabin and let me borrow your Jeep."

He set his jaw and stared at the instrument panel with a disinterested nonchalance. "We'd rather go ahead."

I thought about how I could just commandeer the Wrangler, but how far would that get me and how much time would it take?

I took my arm off his mirror. "When you get down to Deer Lodge, don't go in—there's a guy cuffed to a water pipe in the main building. My advice is to head east. You'll get as far as Meadowlark; one of my deputies is in charge, and they had power the last time I was there—that's probably your best bet."

His mood suddenly brightened. "Great. Thanks!"

I felt like smacking him but instead rebuttoned my coat and started past; it would appear that no matter the price, the boatman was not going to ferry me across.

Not losing any time, he gunned the motor, and the shiny, black vehicle leapt forward, the rear fender extension clipping my hip and bumping me. I watched after the retreating vehicle as he squirreled it in an attempt to get away. The music surged back up, and I'd swear they were laughing.

"Happy motoring."

I made the mile to the Battle Park cutoff in pretty good time—but the Thiokol hadn't cut off.

I shined the Maglite up the pathway, but the calf-deep snow on the road was pristine. I reached up and banged the tin sign, loosening the snow that revealed the large black numbers on the yellow background—24. I wanted to make sure, knowing how easy it was to mistake distances and directions in these conditions.

The tread tracks continued on the main road toward West Tensleep Lake—maybe they'd missed the turn and had taken the one from the north. I tucked my head down into my jacket and continued on another couple of hundred yards, but the arching entrance onto 24 from that direction was also vanilla-cake smooth. The tracks continued on 24 toward the inescapable, highest point in the Bighorn range.

Once again I stood there, dumbstruck. Where the hell were they going?

There was only one way to find out. I kicked off and after another mile could see where the Jeep had pulled out near the Island Park campground. I looked down the short road that must've led to the Jeep driver's cabin and thought about the firewood and the fireplace.

My legs were unused to the added exertion of walking in snowshoes and were tired. I could get a fire started and warm my feet and hands—the parts of me that were approaching numb. My Sorels and snowshoes stamped in the tread tracks, anxious for me to make up my mind. "Well, hell."

I trudged on, but I didn't get far. The snowcat had stopped again, and this time it was only another quarter of a mile up the road. They had pulled to the side, and then it looked as if they had sat there for a while before moving on.

I scanned the area with the Maglite and looked for another message. I could see where at least two individuals had gotten out of the thing, and that one of them was big, with shoes as large as mine. He had walked on the side of the one access road that led off to the left and then disappeared into the trees. The other had followed. The Thiokol, on the other hand, with five remaining occupants, had continued north.

It was possible that they'd dropped off the two women and that one of them was wearing the boots of the Ameri-Trans guard. It was also possible, as Vic would say, that flying monkeys were soon to appear out of my ass.

I clicked off the flashlight and changed direction, remembering that Omar had said something about having a cabin on West Tensleep, past 24, and up near Bear Lake.

I followed the footprints to a rise leading to a hanging shelf from which I could see a large, old house. Through the blowing snow I could make out the shape, but there were no lights on. According to the couple in the Jeep, the power was out, and it certainly looked as if that was the case here as well.

The road continued along the tree line until it ended at the side of what only Omar would call a cabin. As I got closer I could see that it was a log-and-stone affair and something any of the rest of us mere mortals would've called a house, a very large and extravagant house, which overlooked the frozen, snow-covered, and partially visible expanse of Bear Lake.

The Forest Service was pretty strict about remodeling any of the historic cabins in the Bighorns, especially the ones not only in the national forest but adjacent to the wilderness area. You were not allowed to change or expand the original footprint of the structure, but Omar seemed to have overcome that hurdle by simply going up.

The front of the cabin was oriented toward the lake with an overhang supported by huge, burlwood logs. The extended deck stuck out from a massive set of archways below, with an overhanging shingled roof above. Even in the limited visibility, I could make out the four sliding glass doors that led to the deck, but other than a diffused light deep within the recesses, possibly from a fireplace, I couldn't see anything inside.

I continued to follow the boot prints and stuck close to the tree line with the flashlight still off; if they were looking, there wasn't any sense in advertising like a used-car lot.

The wind was carrying the smoke from a fire in the other direction, but I could still smell it. I was reassured by any aspect of normalcy and came up on the garage-door side of the building. The doors were closed, but there was a walkway to the right that must've led inside; the prints, however, led to the left and around the building next to a rock retainer wall where the drifting snow had piled up.

All I really wanted to do was get inside, so I decided to try the nearest door. It was unlocked, so I pushed it open and stepped through into a lengthy mudroom with a washer and dryer.

I quietly closed the door and then stood there for a moment, just orienting myself from being outside. I still leaned to the left as I'd done all the way up the road and drifted forward, countering the effects of the wind and the movement of the snow. I slowed my breathing, stood up straight, and looked down the oblong room at another door, one step up.

There was still no noise, but as I'd expected, the flicker of some fire fractured a warm light on the glass panel. I slid the flashlight into the retainer loop on my belt, took off my gloves, stuffed them in my coat pockets, and unbuckled the snowshoes. I unsnapped the safety strap from my holster and drew the large-frame Colt.

I took another deep breath, carefully stepped across the mudroom, and peered through the corner of the glass pane. There was, indeed, a fire in the fireplace and, to my relief, Omar Rhoades was standing at the center island of the kitchen, his back to me, a dish towel over one shoulder. It looked like he was eating a very large sandwich.

I turned the knob and held it as I stepped up onto the hardwood floor, which was partially covered with what looked to be a vintage Navajo rug; the hardened snow sloughed off the sides of my Sorels onto its red and black wool. I glanced around the timbered structure, which was illuminated by a few candles that flickered from the draft.

In one swift movement, the big-game hunter swung around and leveled the business end of a Model 29 .44 Magnum at the bridge of my nose. It took quite a bit to not counterraise my Colt, but I was assisted in not moving to action by the twisted wire-loop handle of a cleaning rod that stuck comically from the barrel of the big revolver.

I just froze there, first making the strongest eye contact with him that I'd ever made, and then looked around the rest of the room.

By the time my eyes got back to him, he'd lowered the Smith & Wesson, and the cleaning rod fell from the barrel to the floor between us. He was leaning against the butcher-block counter with one elbow, exposing the blood-soaked surface of his shirt beneath the towel wrapped around his armpit. He tossed the blued and engraved revolver onto the island amid the other cleaning supplies—the heavy weapon made a frightening clatter. Omar's voice was thick with drink, fatigue, and possible blood loss. "Took you long enough."

From all appearances, there was no one else in the room. "Are we clear?"

He breathed a whistling laugh and stretched his eyes to keep them open. "Clear as the noonday sun." He picked up his Dagwood sandwich.

"You cleaning that Smith?"

He glanced at the detritus on the counter, which included a tumbler and an ancient, half-empty bottle of Laphroaig. He bit into the sandwich and mumbled, "Yeah."

I knew from experience that he cleaned his guns only when he was upset. "Settling your nerves?"

It took forever, but he smiled at my knowledge of him. "Yeah."   ·

"You're hurt."

"A little; bullet went into the refrigerator. Took out the ice-maker." He gestured toward the massive, stainless steel appliance behind him. "Better it than me." His voice trailed off with the crackling of the fire.

"You got visitors?"

He breathed the same laugh, smaller this time, and then looked up at me as if surprised that I was there. "Wasn't the Girl Scouts."

"Where are they?"

"Um . . ." He paused, as if trying to remember. "One . . . one's in the bathroom, the other one's over by the door."

I took a few steps toward him, but he turned a hard shoulder toward me and held a hand out. "I'm good, I'm good . . . but you better go check him."

I nodded and directed my .45 toward the entryway across a sitting room in the back. I stepped over the head of a massive

Kodiak bear rug and could see something lodged against the front door. The stained glass of the door panel was shattered, and the blowout from an exit wound had sprayed in a spot a foot wide with foreign material embedded in the wood. The liquid pattern narrowed in a sliding path to a solidifying pool of dark blood and the slumped and inert body of Marcel Popp.

There was one of the Sig .40s in his lap, and I used my boot to flip it from between his outstretched legs. His head had lolled forward, and the back of it was pretty much gone.

As a formality, I lowered a hand and placed two fingers along his neck but could feel the unnatural coolness of the postmortem flesh and no pulse. I stooped a little more and looked at the side of the big convict's face. There was a jagged hole at the left cheekbone from which thickening blood slowly dripped, his still eyes following the path to where his life had drained.

I fought the urge that my legs telegraphed to collapse under me and take a rest. I stood and looked out the shattered door. The shot had fittingly exited through the middle of a rose-red triangle, and the insidious cold pulsed through the hole as if the wilderness was attempting to give back the bullet and the death that it carried.

I wavered there for a moment, then turned and looked at Omar, who was intently studying the crystal in his hands. He reached behind him for the bottle, poured a full four fingers, took a slow sip, and returned it and the bottle to the counter. "Happened fast. They knocked on the door, and I don't answer the door at three in the morning up here without accompaniment."

I crossed back toward the kitchen but stood a little away

from him. The bullet he'd taken must've clipped him below the main tendons in his shoulder and above the clavicle, but it still must've hurt like hell.

"Said their car was stuck. I let 'em in, but when I turned from the door he raised up that automatic and got a shot off. I guess maybe he saw the Mag in my hand, and it spooked him." He breathed heavily, and I could hear a faint whistling sound. "Got me in the shoulder, but I don't think it hit anything important—still works." To emphasize the point, he raised the arm a little. "Rolled to the side when he fired again, and I put one in his head."

I found myself nodding. "Are you sure you're all right?"

He breathed some more. "Yeah." He picked up the tumbler with a sickly smile. "Sterilizing from the inside." He took a large swallow. "Funny, I'm hungry as hell." He took another bite of the sandwich and chewed. "You want half of this?"

"Maybe later."

"I'm horny, too."

I took a while to respond to that one. "I don't think I want to help you out with that, either." He laughed, and the timbre of it was a little higher than I remembered and a little unnerving as well. I gestured toward his sandwich. "It's a normal, life-reaffirming process. Kicks in when you really think you're going to die and don't—the urge to reproduce, eat . . . It's when you almost lose your life that you really start appreciating it." Omar was staring at the counter again, so I switched to another topic, a more urgent one. "The woman's in the bathroom?"

He glanced up. "Huh?"

"He had a woman with him. She's in the bathroom?"

"Yeah."

"Where's that?"

He used his good arm to gesture after picking up the scotch. "Down the hall."

I began to turn but stopped when he started to go for the scotch bottle again. "Omar?"

"Yeah?"

"Stop drinking."

He didn't move. "Right."

We stood there like that, neither of us so much as twitching. "I mean it; I may need you."

He set the glass down, and I made my way into the hall. There were three doors—the nearest was closed, so I knocked on it. There was no answer, so I knocked again. Someone whimpered, and it didn't sound the way an FBI agent would whimper. "Beatrice?"

There was more keening, and I leaned in closer to the door. "Beatrice, it's Walt Longmire, the sheriff from the lodge. Is it okay if I open the door and see if you're all right?"

There were no more sounds, and I did what I had to do, turning the knob and carefully opening the door. It was dark in there, but I could see a body wrapped around itself and wedged between the bathtub and the toilet.

"Beatrice?" She started when I spoke again. I slipped in sideways and holstered my Colt. "Are you okay?" It was a stupid question, but I had to open with something. "Do you remember me?" Another stupid question. I started thinking I should try some statements. "Beatrice, you're not hurt."

She mewled into the crossed arms that covered her face above her drawn knees.

"You're going to be okay." Nothing. "Are you hurt?"

I kneeled down and leaned against the side of the tub, the burning in my legs attempting to overtake me. She didn't appear to be physically damaged but continued to huddle against the wall. I carefully reached a hand out to her. "I'm here to help, Beatrice. I need to know if you're okay."

The moment my fingers grazed the sleeve of her jacket, she yanked back and screamed and didn't stop. Her eyes were wide, and she stared at me with the fierceness that only cornered animals have, animals like the one I'd encountered on the roof of the cabin at Deer Haven Lodge.

I didn't move at first but finally allowed the leg under me to collapse, and I slid against the far wall, my hat falling into my lap. I sat there looking into the ferocity of her eyes and took all they could give.

7

She sat on the sofa near the fire and was wrapped in a rust- and ivory-striped wool blanket that had a band of Lakota ghost ponies woven on the edge as I attempted to bandage Omar's wound. I placed the affected limb in a sling made from a couple of monogrammed linen napkins from William the Samoan, as Lucian Connally referred to the purveyor of fine tableware.

Omar looked up at me, and I could see that his eyes were starting to clear a little at the pupils. "You'll help me bury the body, right? I mean, that's what friends are for."

I had finished my own ham and cheese and tried not to watch the pot of water on the propane range for philosophical purposes. He was still drunk, but I'd found a French coffee press, unsure who needed the caffeine more, him or me. I had gotten him to sit on one of the fringed leather barstools and retrieved the finally whistling kettle. Carefully pouring the boiling water over the grinds in the glass contraption, I stood there for a few moments thinking about all the things I was going to have to do before heading out after the remaining escaped convicts. Henry had a French press, and from the many times I'd seen my friend go through the procedure at his house, I probably should've waited longer for the coffee to brew, but I had work to do. I depressed the strainer to compress the grinds and poured three of the O bar R Buffalo China cups to the brim.

I turned and sat one of the heavy mugs in front of him. "Drink that."

He nodded, and I picked up the other two mugs and moved toward the sofa. "Beatrice, how 'bout a little coffee?"

She stayed crouched in the Pendleton blanket with her legs curled under her. I had found her glasses, and they reflected the flames of the fireplace; it was as if I were looking into two miniature hatches of a firestorm.

"You want anything in it?" I stood there for a minute more and then crossed the rest of the way and sat on the edge of the cushion beside her. I could see that she was shaking. "If you drink a little something you might feel better."

The eyes shifted behind the mirrored blaze but didn't make it all the way to me. I took a chance and held the mug out in her sightline, between her and the roiling fire.

She finally looked at me, and I smiled. "Coffee?"

She took a deep breath, letting it out in a shuddering release that seemed like an exorcism, and the words that came from her were barely audible. "I like tea."

I felt like laughing but couldn't risk the energy. "Would you like me to make you some tea?"

She nodded, just barely.

I'm not sure if she really wanted tea or if it was a way of insulating herself for just a little bit longer. I refilled Omar's coffee with the contents from Beatrice's cup and, with his help, found a box of Earl Grey bags and submerged one into what was left of the boiling water.

I lifted the edge of my improvised sling to check the patch job I'd done on the big-game hunter—it looked like the bleeding from his shoulder wound was subsiding. "How are you doing?"

"Fuzzy, but I'll get there." He yawned, which emphasized the leonine aspects of his features. "He was—I tried to . . ." He stopped speaking, and the only noise was the popping of the pine logs in the fire.

I studied him. "What?"

He took a deep breath. "Nothing."

I clamped my jaws shut to keep from yawning in sympathy, thinking about how much further I had to go, wondering how far that was and what I'd find there. I thought about my plan, or lack of one. They were mobile, and unless Omar assisted me, I was not. They were many and well-armed, I was not. The only thing I had going for me was the topography— the simple fact that they would soon have nowhere to go. They didn't know it, but they had bottled themselves up, and other than Tyrell Ranger Station, the concrete, not-so-portable potties were the only indoors in all the great outdoors.

They would have to stay in the Thiokol for the night, so I could grab a few hours of sleep and maybe that would help me clear my head.

I looked at the shine in my friend's eyes and thought about how many creatures Omar had killed and in how many exotic locales, only to slay his first human being literally on his own doorstep. I lowered my voice. "There's a conversation we're going to have to have, but not in front of her."

He nodded and slowly sipped his coffee.

When I got back to the sofa, Beatrice was still hypnotized by the fire. I stood there feeling the heat radiating against my back, pulling at my sore muscles, and prickling my skin. The waves of exhaustion washed against me like an ebb tide, causing me to waver a little. I forced the air from my lungs and blinked to clear my eyes to find Beatrice's looking up at me.

She took the tea and held it in front of her face in clasped hands. "Thank you."

I waited, but she didn't say anything else.

"Um, I have some questions."

"I bet you do." She looked away from me and back to the fire. "'The heart has its reasons that reason knows nothing of.'"

"Pascal."

She looked at me again.

I tipped my hat back. "I've been thinking of moonlighting at the local community college."

It took a while, but she did laugh and then laughed again. When the words came out of her, they weren't the ones I was expecting: "He's not as bad as you think; he's not a simple misanthrope."

Aware of the Stockholm syndrome, I still wasn't sure what to say to that. "Excuse me?"

"I was sure you knew, when I told you I was from Wacouta and you mentioned the Red Wing factory, that there's a maximum security prison just down the road."

"No."

"That's where I met Raynaud, and I guess I was vulnerable, but he's so, well, I don't know, charming, kind of, and he loves me, really . . ." She froze for a moment, and I was worried that I'd lost her, but then her lips moved and she began speaking again. "My father had just died, and I was struggling with a thyroid cancer diagnosis and a divorce. I was working at a veterinary clinic, and maybe it was coming to terms with my own mortality when I started feeling sorry for the number of dogs that were exterminated for lack of adoptive owners. A friend of mine suggested I start a cell-dog project with the prison. You know those programs?"

I figured this was the only way to get her talking, and I was curious about how she'd gotten tangled up with Shade. "I've heard of them."

"I interviewed Raynaud for the program, and we argued at first about which method produced the best-trained dogs, discipline or positive reinforcement."

"Want me to guess which one he believed in?"

She sighed a laugh. "I asked him which one worked best with him." She tucked the blanket in a little closer. "He was magnificent with the dogs, had a real talent working with the most vicious animals—they loved him. I think he saw a reflection of himself in them." A hand crept up and stayed there at the side of her head. "One day he complimented me on my hair." She looked up at me. "I know I'm not very much to look at, Sheriff, and that's probably why it struck me the way it did—like water on a dying plant, I guess. Anyway, a few months later we made plans for him to escape so that the two of us could be together. I was going to sneak him out in my van with the dog supplies. We were going to run away to the Northwest Territories, in Canada, where he's from. I pulled forty-two thousand dollars from my bank account; it was about all I had, but he was worth it."

"What happened?"

"They had a heartbeat monitor at the gate that discovered him. I was charged with aiding and abetting, but my husband—my ex-husband—paid the bail money from what was left from the forty-two thousand. Raynaud was transferred to the prison in Utah but wrote me a letter asking me to forgive him for getting me into all the trouble." She sipped her tea. "We continued to stay in touch, and he told me there would be one last opportunity for him here, in Wyoming. We had devised a kind of code; he's brilliant, Sheriff. A genius."

I thought about how much planning this entire escapade must've taken, which reinforced my thought that Raynaud Shade was more than your usual, garden-variety sociopath. "So, he had all of this planned far in advance."

She nodded. "He said there was a body that he had buried here in the mountains and that he knew where that was and could get himself this far. All I had to do was help him get free and provide supplies, and he'd take care of the rest."

Indeed. "So you figured out the hairpin trick with the handcuffs?"

"He taught me." A quick sob escaped her, and she shook, finally speaking into her mug. "I know everybody wants me to hate him, but I don't."

I waited, thinking about all the things that affected us, things we were aware of and things we weren't. I recited the rest, hoping I could remember it all: "We must always love something. In those matters seemingly removed from love, the feeling is secretly to be found, and man cannot possibly live for a moment without it."

She turned, and I could see the tears shining on her cheeks. "More Pascal?"

"More Pascal." It was time to change the subject, and I only hoped she'd stay with me. "I'm going to be honest with you; there are some serious consequences for what you've done, but that really doesn't concern me right now. Right now, I've got only one question—do you have any idea where they might be going?"

"No." Behind the glasses, her eyes were still full of tears— maybe she was attempting to dampen the flames. "I really don't know."

I waited a little before asking again. "Anything you might've overheard?"

"No."

"You're sure?"

"Yes."

I leaned back in the sofa, and it was so soft I thought I might die there. I was tired and not sure how to proceed. The choice was to either leave her and Omar here or send them out and back to Meadowlark Lodge, and for me to continue up.

"There was something about money."

I shifted my position on the sofa. "Excuse me?"

"Raynaud said something about money."

"What'd he say?"

"There was some money that had been taken or something and that they would get the money if they helped him—that's what he told all of them."

"Who?"

She glanced toward the door where I'd duct-taped a piece of cardboard over the broken glass after I had dragged Popp onto the porch—if I had to leave the two of them in the cabin, I wasn't going to leave them here with a corpse in full view.

"The other convicts?"

"Yes, and . . ."

"What?"

"He has a package with him, a rubber duffel, and water-proof like you carry in a kayak."

This was news. "And you think it's full of money?"

"I don't know. I could have sworn he didn't have it with him, and then it was just there suddenly."

"You didn't bring him the bag?"

"No."

Perhaps the story of the money was true after all. "You are sure you don't know where they're going?"

She honestly seemed confused. "I don't . . . Away—that's all I know."

"Beatrice, there's no way out where they're headed." She continued to look at me blankly. "There are no roads."

"Raynaud said there was a road . . . Battle Park."

"You're already past that—it's about three miles back." I tried to get her to understand. "There are only a few branch roads off of West Tensleep and you're already past all of them. The main road goes on for another mile and a half but then it throttles off into trails that are going to be so choked with snow that he won't even be able to walk out of there, even with snowshoes."

"Raynaud said . . ."

"Beatrice, there are no roads."

She was confused by this information. "Maybe they turned back."

I shook my head. "No, the tracks went on."

I left it at that. There were a few other questions I had and couldn't risk her shutting down again. "You brought them supplies?"

She swallowed. "I did."

"What've they got?"

"I don't . . ."

"Insulated clothing, packs, sleeping bags, food, snowshoes? The things they'd need if they were going to try and hike out of here?"

"I guess. Yesss . . ." It was a strangled reply, like a tire slowly deflating.

"What about weapons? I know they took the marshal's rifle from our van and some sidearms from the federal agents and the two Ameri-Trans guards. Was there anything else?"

"No."

I nodded. "I've got to know: are the others, Pfaff and the Ameri-Trans driver, still alive?"

"Yes, they are." She nodded with the words—glad to have good news, I suppose. "They were fine—no one had done anything to them the last time I saw them."

"Good."

She started to say something and then paused for a moment. "There was someone they were going to meet."

I didn't move but then finally pulled in enough air to ask, "What?"

"Someone. Raynaud said something about meeting some-body who knew the way."

"The way out of the mountains?"

She nodded. "Yes."

"Who?"

The frustration rose in her voice. "I don't know." She sat there fingering the edge of the blanket like a child would, and I thought she was through talking, but she wasn't. "Raynaud, he's rather . . . Charismatic is the only way I can describe it. He has a power over people . . . not just me." Her eyes came up to mine. "I'm not crazy, Sheriff. If it wasn't impressed on me that Raynaud was a killer before, it is now. He left me here to die, and I thought I was the most important person in his life." She looked at the ceiling, and when she looked at me, there were still tears. "I just don't want you to underestimate him."

"I wasn't intending to."

"If you go after him, he'll kill you."

I nodded and rose. "Drink the rest of your tea."

Her face returned to the fireplace, and the reflection of the conflagration again replaced her eyes. I turned and looked at the fire, reveling in its warmth and letting my mind thaw with my face.

For the first time, I noticed that Omar's Sharps buffalo rifle was hanging above the mantel. I stepped forward and placed a hand on its elongated barrel; it was the one I'd used to explode a pumpkin in his backyard. It wasn't like the Cheyenne Rifle of the Dead that was securely ensconced in the gun safe in my closet, but it was close enough to raise the hair on the back of my hand. It was beautiful, a museum piece, really. It hadn't had the hard wear of the Indian weapon but had a dignity of its own. There were new additions since the last time I'd seen it over a year ago: a period military shoulder strap and a beaded rear stock cover with three .45-70 rounds tucked in the butter-like leather—the father, the son, and the Holy Ghost.

I fingered the rounds as I thought.

The hostages were easy to understand; if Shade were cornered he'd need insurance. But why corner yourself and why in the mountains? I was sure the money was bullshit and simply Shade's way of keeping them all going, but then what was in the duffel? Where and to whom was he attempting to get? Deer Park Campground was ahead, along with West Tensleep Lake proper, but no one in his right mind would be up that high this early in the season.

I was exhausted. I turned around and looked at Beatrice, who had lowered her head to the arm of the sofa and closed her eyes.

I left the rifle and carried my mug back to Omar and the butcher-block island. He seemed to be sobering up. "I've got to get going."

He stood. "What's a misanthrope?"

"Somebody who hates all of humanity."

He shrugged with his good shoulder and stood. "Workin' on that myself." He studied me for a moment. "You should get some sleep; even a little bit would help."

"I can't, I've got to . . ."

"Got to what?" He started to fold his arms but then thought better of it. "They're not going anywhere. Go back over to the other sofa and stretch out. I'll wake you up in a couple of hours and you can start. It'll still be before daybreak."

He was right, of course.

"And I'll go with you."

The absurdity of that statement played across my face. "No, you're not."

"How many of them, with hostages, and only one of you?"

"You're in no shape." I gestured with my chin toward Beatrice. "And I can't leave her here alone. I've got people back at Meadowlark, and you can wait and see what the weather does before you make up your mind to stay here or go there." I glanced around at the comforts of the cabin I would soon be leaving. "Personally, I'd have groceries delivered and just hole up till the cavalry shows."

He took a breath and cultivated it into a sigh. "I'll make you a deal; you sleep for a couple of hours and I'll let you go on your own." He glanced back at the sofa and shook his head. "What we do when we think we're in love." He looked at me. "Deal?"

I settled into the Indian blanket chair opposite the sofa where Beatrice was sleeping, pulled my hat over my face, and listened to the logs spitting in the fireplace. Omar brought my sheepskin coat and threw it over me.

"I'm still not going to help you with the horny thing."

"Shut up and go to sleep." There was a pause, and then he added, "How are you going to follow them?"

I could already feel myself drifting away. "I've got snowshoes."

Somewhere in the distance I could hear his voice: "Oh, I think we can do better than that."

There is a familiar odor to old trucks; it is a comforting smell and it is what he smells now. The knobs on the dash are large and chrome metal and he pushes one in where it stays for a moment and then pops back at him. He blinks

*and then pulls the knob the rest of the way out, turning it
and looking into the red-hot coils inside.*

*He doesn't know why they have to fish; he doesn't like
fish, doesn't like picking bones out of his mouth.*

*He points a finger into the lip of the cigarette lighter
where the burning coil is cooling, but he can still feel the
heat.*

"Stay here while I go get more worms and some beer."

So he stays, and he waits.

*He puts the lighter back in the dashboard and listens
to the breeze shimmering the yellow and stiff leaves of
the cottonwoods alongside the Big Horn River. It's warm
and he becomes drowsy, having a dream of his own. A
dream within a dream, but this one was real—where his
father, eyes wide with whiskey, broke up the furniture
and burned it one night.*

*He has that ability, they say, to blend dreams with
life. In the murmuring voices in the next room he over-
hears the old woman saying it will lead to tragedy.*

*He unwraps the candy bar the big man left for him,
a Mallo Cup in the bright yellow wrapper that feels slick
in his hands, wondering who the Boyer Brothers are or
where Altoona, Pennsylvania, is.*

*He starts at the knock on the window of the truck
and looks up to see a smiling face with lots of teeth but no
warmth. "Unlock the door."*

Snow machines scare me, and this one scared me more than
any I'd ever seen before. It was red, blood red, and huge, with

some sort of track system all its own. I guess it started out as a four-wheeler, but with all the modifications I really couldn't tell.

There were lots of other sleds there in Omar's garage, but it was easy to see why he'd chosen this one for me. A regular snowmobile would have skis on the front and those would take me only so far; with treads on the front and rear, this monster would be able to follow the narrow trails and, more important, be able to climb the rocks that were buried in the snow as well.

It was early morning, about six thirty, and the big-game hunter had returned three times with supplies stuffed under his one arm, including my backpack, my snowshoes, and a leather rifle scabbard. He gestured toward one of the snowmobiles. "This one over here is the fastest, but without experience on these things, especially this one, you'll end up piled into a tree or off a cliff." He looked down at the machine where he'd stacked my supplies. "Not that this one's for the faint of heart—more than a thousand cc's. I had it special-made in Minnesota. The suspension is custom-reinforced, and the Trax-System will not fail."

"How fast will it go?"

He studied the machine in the battery-lit garage like it might leave on its own. "Faster than you want."

"Of that, I have no doubt." I sat Saizarbitoria's pack on the utility rack of the ATV. "What if I wreck it?"

"I'll buy another one, or three." He rested a much larger pack on the rack with mine and propped the rifle on one of the rubber and metal tracks. "I took the liberty of packing you some supplies. There's food, drink, a sixty-degree-below-zero bag, and a pair of Zeiss 20×60 image-stabilization binoculars."

"I don't want to know how much those cost."

"About six grand."

"I told you I didn't want to know that."

He reached back with his good arm and pulled something from a shelf. "Here."

I unfolded a massive amount of newfangled mountaineering gear. "What's this all about?"

"A few years back one of my hunters was a Denver Bronco; he had a bunch of stuff shipped up here and then left it. It's too big for me."

I unbuckled my gun belt, took off my hat, jacket, jeans, and boots, and slipped on expedition-weight long underwear. "Which Denver Bronco?"

"Hell, I don't remember. I don't watch that shit—he was a big son of a bitch, though, like you."

Omar took my sheepskin coat and helped me sort through the pile, handing me a pair of 300-weight fleece pants and a jacket to match, a black Gore-Tex North Face Mountain Jacket and overpants, a balaclava, and a pair of insulated gloves. I transferred my pocketknife into the overpants and found that I could still get my gun belt over the entire ensemble.

"Thanks."

I pulled on my boots, thought about the cell phone, and then carefully placed it in an inside pocket of the jacket. I picked up the two-way radio and handed it to Omar. "Here, it's useless to me and I don't want the weight." I then picked up Sancho's pack, unzipped the top, and dumped the contents into Omar's. Everything but the copy of the *Inferno* made it in.

I grabbed the thumb-worn paperback and glanced at

him. "Saizarbitoria's idea of a joke, I suppose, or maybe he thought I was going to get bored and have some reading time."

He lifted the weapon onto the saddle of the machine. "You said they had a rifle?"

I zipped the tactical jacket and put on my hat. "Armalite .223 with an infragreen scope, but it's the short barrel, maybe sixteen inches."

"Dangerous up close, but not so good at distance with that carbine model." He admired the rifle in the leather sheath. "We call this 'evening the playing field.'"

I turned my head and looked at him.

"I've got all kinds of handguns and carbines, but nothing that'll reach out and touch with the impact of this one— besides, I thought it might be a sentimental favorite."

I looked at the weapon and felt the rush of heat at the remembrance of how things had turned out with a weapon very much like this one almost two years ago. "Favorite, but certainly not sentimental." I carefully lifted the .45-70 from the case, sliding the leather cover away. "The three in the stock holder?"

He sighed. "I don't even have extra ammo—just brought it up here on a lark as decoration. I never thought I'd be shooting it. You've only got the three."

I nodded, feeling the accustomed weight close to eight pounds. I liked the accuracy of the drop-block weapons, the simplicity and smooth action of fewer moving parts. "Well, this gives me an edge over that short-barreled .223."

"If you hit him, he'll know he's been hit." He leaned over and slipped open the butt of a plastic rifle scabbard mounted on the other side of the vehicle. "This is padded and should

absorb a lot of the vibration and shock should you hit something."

"Omar, it's a museum piece, worth a lot of . . ."

"Take it."

I didn't move, giving him the opportunity to change his
mind, and then reached across and carefully placed the Sharps
in the boot, and his eyes stayed on the encased weapon. I
watched him for a long moment and could pretty much guess
what was running through his mind, over and over and over
again. "Your first?"

"Yeah." His eyes came up to mine but then returned to the
scabbard. "Does it get easier?"

"Not really." I cleared my throat and stood there trying to
think of the words that would make it in some way better. "He
was a bad guy with a lot of notches; he would've killed you,
raped and killed her, and then who knows how many more he
would've killed." He nodded, dealing with the sickness that
overtakes your soul when you take a life—the sick/scared
before, and the sick/sad afterward. "It's amazing, isn't it, what
human beings can become."

When I came back from my own sicknesses he was looking
at me. "You gave me some advice, now let me give you some."
His eyes went back to the scabbard. "You better become a misanthrope, too . . . Kill 'em, kill 'em all. Kill 'em fast." His hand
went to the rifle scabbard. "And from far away."

The handle grips were heated, and the motor warmth of the
big Arctic Cat that Omar had loaned me floated up against

the trunk of my body before being whipped away at speeds approaching forty miles an hour. The ATV was capable of going a lot faster, but I wasn't. Fortunately, Omar had remembered to loan me a pair of antifogging goggles or my eyes would've been frozen to my eyelids.

Even with the blowing snow and the four hours that had passed, the tracks of the Thiokol were evident, at least until I arrived at West Tensleep Lake. It was only when I got to the fork in the road that I slowed the Cat to see which direction in the parking loop they'd taken. The wide tracks continued on the high road, which was what I'd expected, figuring the cover story that Raynaud had planted was indeed false. The snow had reached levels where no regular wheeled vehicle could go, and even trying on horseback would've been nothing but a slog.

Then the tracks simply disappeared.

I pulled up to the two bathroom structures buried in the snow and overlooking the pull-through parking area. Nothing there.

There were no vehicles in the place, and no tracks whatsoever.

Where could the damn thing have gone? It wasn't as if it a were svelte mode of transportation.

Listening to the idling motor of the ATV, and watching the trees sway with the wind, I sat there thinking about the last time that I'd been this high; about how things had not gone well, and I'd had to haul two men from Lost Twin Lakes in a blizzard. That had been difficult, but it wasn't the memory that held me still at the moment.

I'd seen and heard things all those months ago—things I'd never seen or heard before yet which continued to haunt me.

I cut the motor and listened more carefully.

There was the noise of the wind, like something colossal moving past me, something important—so imperative in fact that it could not pause for me. It was the cleaning sound that the wind made in the high mountain country, scrubbing the landscape in an attempt to make it fresh.

I thought about the dream of the boy in the truck, the trees moving—and how the dream didn't seem to be mine. Maybe our greatest fears were made clear this high, so close to the cold emptiness of the unprotected skies. Perhaps the voices were of the mountains themselves, whispering in our ears just how inconsequential and transient we really are.

The snow continually fell, and the canvas unrelentingly washed itself clean.

I saw some movement to my right, a different kind of movement surging against the insistence of the wind. I stared at the copse of trees by the sign that marked the entrance to the Lost Twin trailhead. My eyes through the goggles stayed steady, but I couldn't see anything more, just the movement of the limbs and branches.

Something else moved to my left, and I whirled in time to see a shape dart back into the trees where the ridge dropped off into the open, white expanse of the lake.

I quietly dismounted the Cat and stepped onto the surface of the snow, which crunched like cornflakes under the Vibram soles of my Sorels. I thought of the Sharps fastened to the side of the Arctic Cat, but instead slipped the glove from my right hand and unsnapped the safety strap from my .45, drawing it from the holster and moving toward the small ridge.

I was not seeing any green dots.

I kept looking at the grove of trees to the right but could catch sight of nothing more. By the time I got to the top, I could make out where the wind had struck the rise, lifted its load, and then dropped the snow, flake by flake, in a drift as sharp as the edge of a strop razor.

It was then that something made a noise very close to me. I stood there for a moment and looked around. It was muted and almost like music. I looked down at the ground, but it wasn't coming from there, it was coming from my coat. I remembered that I had put Saizarbitoria's cell phone in the inside pocket of the high-tech jacket. I unzipped and pulled out the device, took it from the plastic bag, and looked at the number on the display—Wyoming, but not one I recognized. I flipped it open and used Vic's patented greeting: "What fresh hell is this?"

There was some fumbling on the other end, and then a strange voice spoke. "What the fuck does that mean, man?"

Great—just what I needed was a wrong number eating up my battery.

"Hey, Sheriff, is that you?"

I stared at the phone and then returned it to my ear. "Hector?"

"Yeah, it's me; hey, how you doin'?"

"Hector, where are you?"

He laughed. "Where the hell do you think I am? Locked to a water pipe, right where you left me."

"How did you . . . ?"

"I got a credit card that some *tonto* left out of the cash

register and activated it for some long-distance charges. I'm bad, I'm nationwide. I called my family back in Houston, and then I called my buds down in . . ."

"How did you get this number?"

"I got it when you gave it to your secretary."

"Dispatcher."

"Whatever, man. Hey, aren't you glad to hear from me?"

"You're eating up my battery, Hector." He paused, and I thought for a moment that he'd hung up.

"Hey Sheriff, I wanna get something straight here from the beginning—I'm no snitch, you got me? I mean, where I come from, ratting somebody out is the lowest of the low." There was another pause, and then he continued. "But you been pretty good to me with the tiger and all, so I figure I owe you something."

"Okay."

"Where you're goin' and what you're tryin' to do—don't trust nobody. I mean even the people you think you know? Don't trust 'em. I'm just sayin'. Adios."

The phone went dead. I hit the disconnect button and shook my head. Just when I didn't need reception, I got it.

I stared at the hillside that led down to the lakeshore and shifted the goggles further onto my forehead. There was no one there, and no one had been—no prints, no tracks, nothing. What early morning light there was reflected across the lake, making it look like tundra. I shifted to the left to peer through the trees and saw where it was the Thiokol had gone.

I carefully placed the cell phone back in my inside pocket and thought about who I knew up here, and who I trusted.

West Tensleep Lake is almost a mile long, large for the high country of the Bighorn Mountains. I was now traveling across it and soon to be in direct violation of the 1964 Wilderness Act and the 1984 designation of the Cloud Peak Wilderness Area; they could ticket me if they could find me.

The center of the lake had been whitewashed, and the surface was a reflective sheen of about sixteen inches of solid ice, easily capable of holding the weight of the Thiokol and the Arctic Cat. They'd traveled to the center of the lake and then continued north to where it tapered into its source.

I slowed the machine as I got to the place where the hillsides rose and narrowed and where the snow grew steadily deeper. The wind had refilled the tracks where the big Spryte had gone, but now there was an uneven surface underneath that would suddenly send the Cat lurching to one side or the other and almost yank the handlebars out of my hands.

Lifting the amber-tinted goggles onto my forehead, I slowed and stared at the terrain ahead—everything had a flat, gray quality. The snow had stopped somewhat; the sun was just up, although behind a thin cloud cover, and I was glad to see its opaque glow, hoping it might lift the mercury above zero and ground some of the blowing snow. Closing my eyes for just a second, I stood there on the running boards of the Cat and soaked in a little of the warmth from the sun. I took a deep breath and thought about the figures I'd seen back at the turn-around and wondered if they might've been the ones Hector had warned me about in his phone call. I didn't allow myself to dwell on the subject for too long.

I could see where Tensleep Creek stretched to the right and then rounded to the left before continuing north. The snow would get deeper, but anywhere the Thiokol could go, I could follow.

I hit the accelerator and carefully picked my way through the miniature pass, getting to another flat and following the creek bed.

I was trying to remember what the area looked like before being smothered in layer after layer of snow, but my last trip had been in the fall two years ago. I had been up the mountain since then on a fishing trip with Henry, but that had been on the Dry Fork near Burgess Junction on the Sheridan side of the mountain.

Originally the Crow called the mountains *Basawaxaawuua*, or White Mountains, but when Lewis and Clark reported on the vast herds of bighorn sheep at the mouth of the nearby Big Horn River, the range received its modern name, rivers being ever so much more important to explorers than peaks.

Recreation wasn't my game, and that was probably why I had only a vague memory of having been up here in something other than a crisis situation. I thought there was a boulder field to my right, with scree leading down to the waterline. Better to avoid that; I kept to the left and puttered around the corner.

There was another straightaway, and I could still see where the Thiokol had burst through the drift at the other end. I rose up on the handlebars and floorboards again so that I could see exactly where it had gone. It was at that moment I thought I heard something—something louder than the exhaust on the Cat and not musical. I sat back down, but something felt strange on the saddle. I rose up a little and glanced back at the black seat, where I saw that there was a large rip in the vinyl.

I twisted the bars again in an attempt to track the snow machine to the right and under the lip of the ridge so that I might be protected from whoever was shooting, but another round went through the plastic of one of the front fenders and I lost control. The big red contraption heaved up the steep incline of the hillside like an eight-hundred-pound bronco and casually rolled sideways, landing on top of me.

I scrambled to get out from beneath it before it settled but only succeeded in catching the bottom of the Cordura pant on a peg on the other side. I bent my leg so that it wouldn't break. The snow was relatively soft underneath, but the ATV's crossbar struck me in the face and sunk me.

I lay there trying to pull my leg and left arm free, but nothing would budge. I pulled my hat from my head and yanked the goggles down to my neck with my right hand, frantically searching the ridge above to see from where they were firing, but there was only the gray of the clouded, early-morning sky.

Nothing.

If they were making their way to me, I had only a few moments to prepare. The Sharps was still lodged in the case and snowpack, so my only option was the Colt in my holster. I yanked the glove from my hand with my teeth, spitting it to the side. I breathed a quick cloud of relief as I unsnapped and drew the .45 and clicked off the safety.

They would be to the left from where I'd rolled, and from the angle of deflection they must've been above. If they were smart they'd approach me from ground level at the frozen creek, but if they didn't want to wade through the drifts, they'd stay on the ridge where they'd have to reveal themselves before they could take another shot.

I aligned the barrel of the Colt through the overturned tracks of the Cat, close to the undercarriage where it might not be so noticeable, and carefully reached up to where the kill switch was and turned the thousand cc's off; evidently, Omar didn't believe in safety lanyards. I smelled gas and couldn't afford to just let the thing run. Let them wonder if it had cut out on its own.

It was quiet, except for the wind and the swaying of the trees, and I kept my attention on the ridge that was only thirty feet away, allowing my eyes to go unfocused, evolving into motion detectors. I thought I might've heard some noise; I waited, but it was quiet again, and I took my eyes away just long enough to assess my situation.

Screwed, pretty much, as Vic would say.

The big pack had borne the brunt of the impact on my back, but my head and shoulder had taken the front. I could feel something wet trailing down from my forehead and into my eye socket, something wet and warm.

My hand was beginning to shake from lack of blood, bad

positioning, and the adrenaline rush that was still blistering through my veins. I breathed as shallowly as I could, attempting not to sound like a derailed locomotive, and waited.

It was possible that there were more than one of them, and in that case I might have the barrel of another pistol aimed at the back of my head. Maybe I was wrong about the deflection, and they were farther ahead or more to the rear.

I smiled to myself, just the tiniest grin of bitter acknowledgment of the fact that I was the prey and falling victim to the voices of the second guess. These voices are the ones that rabbits and mice hear when they think they are safely underneath the sagebrush, but they hear the hoot of an owl or the screech of an eagle that sets them to wondering if this patch of cover they've got is good enough or if they should make a run for it—maybe that patch over there is better.

Then they move.

Then they die.

I could afford to stay still and ignore the voices—I had .45 teeth.

There was another sound, coming from where I'd expected it, faint and up on the ridge. I was really shaking now with the exertion of holding my arm steady. I took another short breath and slowly let it out, wondering how long I could stay like this. I figured it had been about five minutes since my pileup.

Movement.

The pistol was the first thing I saw, which was a mistake on his part, because now there would be no hesitation in my response. I had been shot at twice; they hadn't said anything and were now approaching me armed. I figured the response I had in mind was prudent and reasonable.

I waited—they might've been able to see part of the wreckage, but it was possible they still couldn't see all of me.

A few tiny pieces of snow broke from the ridge and tumbled down the hillside in a miniature avalanche. I saw a knit cap, and the face underneath had a beard. I was sure it was one of the convicts from the Ameri-Trans van—the one with the long hair.

There was a second's pause and another round blew into the ice and snow behind me.

I fired.

It's never a pretty sight; his head yanked back and then fell forward, blood leaking onto the snow and sliding down the slope along with the pistol that now lay halfway in the ten yards between us.

I dropped my arm and just lay there breathing. Still holding the Colt, I wiped my face and could see the blood on the back of my hand, but there wasn't too much. I pushed down with my elbow and was able to make a pocket where I could slide out my other arm. I stretched it, getting some feeling back in my hand, and stared at the man's head. I decided I should check. I raised the .45 and yelled, "Hey!"

He didn't move, and I fought against the sickness that always overtook me.

"Hey, are you dead?" I glanced around and assessed my predicament. "Because if you aren't you can help get this four-wheeler off me."

It would appear that I was on my own.

The way the big machine had flipped, I was pretty much buried in the snowbank but could still feel something solid against my trapped leg. If I was lucky, the hard thing I could feel was just snow frozen in the serrated layers of thaw/freeze. If I was unlucky, it was one of those boulders I'd been thinking about earlier. I shoved the .45 back into my holster and tried to rock the snow machine. I figured that even if I got it to roll over me and the rest of the way down the bank, it was better than just lying there like an indisposed turtle.

I pushed, but there wasn't any way to get solid purchase and nothing moved. I tried again, finally throwing my head back in the trough it had formed and staring at the leaden sky. "You have got to be kidding."

I slipped my glove back on and started digging under the saddle and around my leg and could smell the gas and see where it was leaking. I wasn't sure if the tank had been rup-tured or if one of the fuel lines had been cut or partially torn loose. It wasn't a lot of gas, but it was gas and the fumes were strong.

My position was awkward, and I wasn't able to get at much of the snow below my leg, but when I finally got to my knee, I could tell that although my leg hadn't broken, it was securely lodged in the crack of what felt like ice over a granite shelf.

"Damn."

I thought about my options: continuing the struggle or waiting for the summer thaw. I carefully placed a boot against the floorboard and pushed.

Nothing, not even a nudge.

I lay there for a few more minutes in an attempt to gather some strength, but the fumes leaking from the gas tank were a little nauseating. I repositioned myself in an attempt to get farther away from the smell as something struck me in the face. I wasn't sure what it was, but it burned and I swatted it away.

I looked up the thirty feet at the dead man and was rewarded with a bloody grin as he looked down at me with the knit cap pooched up at an odd angle. He flipped another match that landed farther down the embankment.

"Hey, do you mind not doing that?"

He continued to smile with one eye puckered shut and pulled another match from the small box in his hands. You would think that his motor functions would have been impaired by the shot he'd taken in the head.

The next match struck the gas tank, but I slapped it out with my glove. "Hey!"

I pulled the .45 out and held it so that he could see it. "You remember this?"

He lay there, staring at me, and it was time to put up or shut up. I lodged my foot against the floorboard and grabbed the nearest side of the handlebars with one hand, the fumes from the gas starting to take the hair from my nose.

I gave it all I had.

Nothing.

My head dropped back in frustration, and I clamped my teeth as another match struck the machine and ricocheted off into the snow with a brief, adderlike hiss.

I aimed the .45 at him. He was smiling again, blood staining his lips, and he ducked a little. "Stop it. Now."

He tipped the tiny box of matches up and shook it, then slid the cover open further and tried to look inside.

He was out of matches.

I had to laugh, but when I looked back at him, he was trying to climb over the crest of the hill toward me. Not so funny. I looked at the Sig about halfway down. If he got his legs over the edge, he could just slide to his pistol.

I carefully aimed at his extended right hand. "This is the last time I'm going to warn you. Stop."

He didn't, and I fired. I didn't hit his hand but it must've been very close, because he yanked it back and looked at me. He wasn't smiling now, and when he lunged this time, I took careful aim.

I don't know how long I lay there before thinking of Saizarbitoria's cell phone in my inside pocket. I pulled it out and looked at it, anything to keep from looking at the dead man who was staring at me, his legs still invisible over the crest of the ridge; definitely Fingers Moser.

I concentrated on getting the cell phone up and operating, pulling it from the Ziploc and turning it around and flipping it open. The phone immediately displayed a splash of green and then the photo of Marie and Antonio. I stared at the display and watched as two words marched across their smiling faces—NO SERVICE.

I slumped back in my new spot, a little away from the dripping gas leak.

Turning the mobile off, I stuffed it back in the plastic bag and sealed it, carefully sliding it into the inside pocket of my jacket. "I can't even talk to Hector."

I lay there feeling sorry for myself and then got up on one elbow to reach behind me and see how much of the spilled supplies I could find. The first thing I located was a Snickers bar. I broke it in half and stuck part of it in my mouth—it tasted like a piece of moldy firewood and was like chewing bark. I lay there allowing my saliva to soften it a little, then chewed some more and swallowed.

Figuring there might come a time when I'd want it, I poked the other half into my pocket, flailed my hand around behind me, and finally found something else—the paperback of Dante's *Inferno*.

Great, some uplifting literature to help bolster my mood.

I dropped the paperback on my chest and started thinking about my immediate future. The weather was certainly a problem. There had been a brief break in the squall, but to the northwest I could see the broiling bank of storm clouds that was coming next. Pretty soon it was going to start snowing again, and then the wind would pick up and fill my little wallow, effectively turning me into a sheriff Popsicle.

I thought about the hungry cougar back at the lodge and wondered what else there was up here that might be waiting for the opportunity of an easy meal. There are wolves in the Bighorns to go along with the mountain lions and black bears; the Game and Fish said there weren't any grizzlies in the range, but I knew a few old-timers who called bullshit on that one. I wasn't anxious to be the bait staked out to discover if it was true or not.

I was pretty sure that the warmth of the partial sun, my body heat, and the engine would thaw the ice shelf underneath me enough that I could dislodge my leg. I just had to find some way of passing the time.

I stared at the book on my chest.

I was going to have to get pretty desperate to start in on that.

* * *

Cord never shot an arrow from itself
That sped away athwart the air so swift,
As I beheld a very little boat

Come o'er the water tow'rds us at that moment
Under the guidance of a single pilot
Who shouted, "Now art thou arrived, fell soul?"

"Phlegyas, Phlegyas, thou criest out in vain
For this once," said my Lord; "thou shalt not have us
Longer than in the passing of the slough."

As he who listens to some great deceit
That has been done to him, and then resents it,
Such became Phlegyas, in his gathered wrath.

My Guide descended down into the boat,
And then he made me enter after him,
And only when I entered seemed it laden.

I thought about the first time I'd read the epic poem in the old Carnegie library that was now my office. I'd had a draconic English teacher, Betty Dobbs, who had drilled us to the point that I'd had to go to the Durant Library to discover new ways of deciphering the text.

They used to keep a fire burning in the small, marble fireplace in the winter months, and there was a long oak research table that you could sprawl your books onto. The copy they had was a beautiful old tome, the Reverend Henry Francis Cary translation with illustrations by Gustave Doré. The thing had a weight to its presentation that had you believing that you were truly glimpsing hell in a handbasket rather than the moonings of a banished, heartbroken Florentine.

Contrary to popular belief, there aren't that many descriptions of hell in the Bible, and the majority of images most people carry around in their heads are from the fourteenth-century poem, which means that our contemporary view of hell is actually from the Middle Ages.

A depressing thought, to say the least.

I had gotten to the eighth canto and was amazed at how much history and politics there was in the thing, observations that most certainly passed me by when I was sixteen.

I marked my place by dog-earring a page and placed the book back on my chest. My eyes were tired, I had a headache, and it had begun to snow again. I'd had an eye operation a few months back that had been an unqualified success, so I was pretty sure my headache was from the bump on my forehead and the gasoline fumes and not from my eye.

I pulled the cell phone from my pocket, took it out of the bag, held it up, and looked at the two words. I turned it off, dropped the thing in the Ziploc and back in my pocket, and pulled my glove back on.

The clouds were so low, it felt like I could reach out and touch them, so I tried—my black gloves looking even darker as they rose up to the steel afternoon sky. It was getting colder, and my hopes for thawing out enough space for my leg were taking a hit. I drew my other leg under the four-wheeler and tucked the book away.

I was about to pull my hat over my face and take a little nap when I saw the horn button on the handlebars of the Arctic Cat. It was a feeble hope, but a hope nonetheless.

I pushed the button with my thumb and listened to the extended and herniated beep of the horn. I waited a moment and then tried it again, this time bleating out three shorts—three longs—three shorts. I continued the SOS pattern until I noticed a difference in the tone, indicating I was killing the battery.

I pulled up the balaclava, went ahead and put my hat over my face, tucked my arms into my body, and rolled to my left in an attempt to get as much cover from the machine as possible.

Definitely a noise.

I'd been lying there half-asleep in my little snow cocoon when I thought I'd heard something, and this was the third time I'd heard it—a snuffling, huffing noise from up on the ridge.

The wind was now howling through the swaying trees, and I was loath to poke my head out, but I was damned if I was going to be eaten and not know what it was that was eating me. Brushing away the inch of snow that had fallen, I pushed my hat off and peeled back my goggles. It was brighter, but other than that everything looked the same.

The dead convict had been partly covered over by the falling, blowing snow, but up on the ridge the wind was stronger, so it was an uneven mantle. I glanced up and down the hillside, but there was nothing else there.

I was just about to put my hat back over my eyes when I heard the snuffling and what might've been a grunt or growl. I reached down for the Colt and kept a weather eye on the ridge.

It was then that the dead man disappeared.

I blinked to make sure I'd seen what I'd seen, and I had. One moment the man's corpse had been there hanging over the hillside with only the bottoms of his legs hidden, and the next, something had yanked him by them, and he was gone.

Moser had to be at least two hundred pounds. No wolf could've done that, and I doubt a mountain lion could've either.

Bear.

Had to be a bear; no other animal up here had the power to grab a full-grown man by the legs and simply snatch him away into the air.

I did some pretty damn fast calculations about hibernation and the feeding habits of bears, both black and grizzly. It was May, and the bruisers had had ample time to get up and look for something to eat. They were known to eat their fill and then bury the rest in a shallow grave for later—another comforting thought. I figured the convict meal, the prevalent fumes of gas, and the proximity of the machine might save me an eventual confrontation, but I could also be wrong.

I pulled the .45 from my holster and brought it up aimed in the direction of the shuffling, huffing, and breathing. I half expected to hear the sounds of flesh rendering and bone crushing, but it grew silent again.

I kept the pistol pointed toward the ridge, my eyes drawn to the left by the whistling flakes. Something moved to the right, precisely where the convict had vanished. It was only a shadow, but it was a very large one, much larger than any man and much larger than any black bear.

The massive head was incredibly wide, and I could just make out the pointed ears on top and the huge hump at its back. It turned in my direction, and it was then that I saw the muzzle of the gigantic beast sniffing. I listened to its lungs tasting the air for me.

With his skull three-quarters of an inch thick, it was doubtful that I'd do any real damage to the monster, but at least it might dissuade him.

Slowly the big, ursine head swiveled until it was looking directly at me, and it was then that I fired. I saw a chunk blow off the side of its head and take part of an ear with it, and the big beast disappeared almost instantaneously.

There was no howling, no growling, nothing.

I lay there with my aim still on the ridge and hoped that the monster had decided to go with the buffet and was dragging the dead man off to a comfortable dining spot. I still couldn't hear anything but the wind, so I waited.

I was unsure how long I lasted with my arm like that, but then it kind of dropped of its own accord. I listened to myself breathe, but over the wind I couldn't hear anything other than my still-pounding heart.

I figured the bear was gone, and whether he'd taken the dead convict with him was his business. Keeping the .45 on my chest, I lodged my hat up to block the wind and reintroduced my neck into the collar of the North Face. My eyes were trying to close, but my mind kept prodding them with a stick. It was in just one of those instances that I thought I might've heard something again, and my eyelids shot open.

There was nothing on the ridge, but my heart practically leapt from my chest when something moved right above me.

I fumbled with the .45 trying to get it from my chest, but in one savage swipe a massive paw struck my hand like a baseball bat; the Colt fired harmlessly into the air as it flew away and cracked against the ice-covered stream a good forty feet below.

I scrambled to get the hat from my face and then lurched upward trying to strike at the beast, but the weight and size of the thing was too much. I was yelling as loudly as my raw lungs could support in hopes that I might scare the monster away, but it just stayed there.

I howled for a while and continued my doomed struggle until I noticed the creature was attempting to do something other than tear me apart. I froze as its massive paws dug underneath the machine and, in an incredible show of strength, actually lifted the gigantic four-wheeler off of me. The roar that came from the bear was enough to rattle my own lungs, and it flipped the Arctic Cat down the hill where it rolled once and then landed upright on the ice below.

I didn't move, and the furry head with one ear hanging comically from its side looked at me. All I could think of was Lucian Connally's adage, "They can kill us, hell, they can eat us—but we don't have to taste good."

I stared up at the shaggy head that seemed as wide as the trunk of my body. Astonishingly, it spoke. "What'chu doin' this high, Lawman?"

Virgil.

9

"The first thing I ever killed was a couple of rattlesnakes." The gigantic man shifted his weight and turned his two heads toward the opening. "When I was ten, I came upon two prairie rattlers mating. They saw me and tried to get apart, but they couldn't. I cleaned them; snakes are easy, and I remember them with their heads cut off still striking at my hand on the handle of the frying pan." He tilted the pot in front of him and inspected the beef stroganoff that he was cooking.

There may have been stranger places in which I've woken up than Virgil White Buffalo's cave in the Bighorns, but I can't remember where they might've been. As caves go, it was a comfortable one, with rugs, pillows, and even a jury-rigged exhaust flume wedged into and continuing through one of the large cracks in the rock ceiling. Assorted hides were piled against the front, and I had to admit that the whole system made the place pretty cozy.

"I don't know how many lives I've taken since then, hundreds, I suppose. None of them really in the right."

I studied my host, crouched over the fire and illuminated by the flames, and could've sworn a bear was cooking my supper. "I thought there weren't any grizzlies in the Bighorns."

"There aren't." He picked up a wooden spoon and dipped it in the concoction, moving the crustier parts at the side back into the center of the pot. "Anymore."

Virgil White Buffalo was a legend, and last summer I'd had him in my jail when I'd mistakenly arrested him for the murder of a young Asian woman. He'd assisted me in apprehending the actual culprit but then had melted into the Bighorn Mountains. I hadn't had any contact with him since then but had suspicions that the Cheyenne Nation might have.

"Where did you get the head and cape, Virgil?"

He stopped stirring the formerly freeze-dried concoction and nodded, mostly to himself. "He was a neighbor, but we ended up not getting along."

I filed away the thought that it might behoove me to do everything within my power to get along with the very large Crow Indian. I rubbed my head where the handlebars had struck it; the goose-egg lump made me feel like I was growing a horn. "You heard my SOS?"

"No."

I sat up a little, careful to keep the sleeping bag around my legs, especially the bruised one. "The gunfire."

"Yes."

Virgil's rocky abode wasn't very far from where I'd overturned the vehicle, and with a little verbal assistance he'd retrieved my .45, had gotten the Cat running, and had parked it underneath a tree. The cave was a ledge that Virgil had closed off with a multitude of rocks, almost a Bighorn cliff dwelling. Thirty feet in the air and sheltered by the towering fir trees, there was no way you'd ever notice it if you hadn't known it was there.

The elk hide that was draped across the only opening blew inward, the powdered snow skimming across the granite floor. "Still crappy out there?"

"Yes." He gazed toward the opening and then crouched over to rest a few rocks at the bottom of the hide to keep it from blowing. "It will likely continue through the night and maybe for a few days after." He went back to the fire but glanced at me. "Why, you're in a hurry?"

I shrugged. "On the job."

"Always with you people." He nodded again, occupying himself with the stirring. "The shoebox."

"Yep."

"Have they done something bad?"

"Escaped convicts."

"Oh." For the first time, he smiled, and it was a sly one. "Like me."

"Well—" I glanced at the surrounding rock and noticed that Virgil had gone so far as to decorate his walls with some ledger drawings, the one nearest me showing the epic battle between Virgil and the grizzly. "Not exactly." Strangely enough, the figure of Virgil seemed to be turned with his back toward the bear so that he was driving the spear behind him.

He carefully spooned the rehydrated dehydrated-de-jour into two metal bowls and brought me some. Virgil's entire cooking kit was in an olive drab army surplus box, probably from WWII, complete with pots, pans, plates, utensils, and cups carefully held in place by narrow leather straps and small brass rivets that reflected the fire. He reached behind him, brought over an old percolator, and poured us both cups of coffee. "I have some powdered cream, but I think it might be left over from the Ardennes Offensive."

"I'll pass." I wondered how many other people in the Bighorns knew the German term for the Battle of the Bulge. When I'd first met Virgil, I'd attempted to crush his larynx, and our relationship had been verbally one-sided. To my shame, I hadn't thought he was all that intelligent—a judgment I'd soon amended upon discovering beneath the heavy brow the fine mind capable of playing chess on a grand-master level. I spooned a few mouthfuls and sipped my coffee. "The beef stroganoff is always a good freeze-dried bet."

"Yes, it is. Thank you for including it." He sipped his own coffee and studied the expedition pack and beaded leather gun sheath lying next to me. "You have a lot of supplies and are well-armed."

"They're bad guys."

He finished the stroganoff in his usual record time and sat the tin bowl back by the fire; then he gestured toward the opening with his lips the way Indians have a peculiar tendency to do. "They have a woman with them."

We studied each other, and I had to concentrate so that I would not keep making eye contact with the grizzly's features that hovered over his own. The bear's jaws were separated into two pieces on the headdress and hung alongside the open maw along with beads, eagle feathers, abalone shell discs, and strands of rawhide with tiny, cone-shaped bells made from snuff container lids that made a faint tinkling sound when he moved his head.

"You've seen them outside the vehicle?"

"Yes."

Virgil didn't exactly offer a lot of information, so I primed the pump. "Where?"

"Near the falls, about a quarter-mile from here."

I blew a breath. "Why'd they stop?"

He gestured toward my bowl with a forefinger as thick as a broom handle. "Are you going to eat that?"

I handed it to him, waited until he was through, and then asked again.

He placed my bowl on top of his own and reached across to pull a bottle from my pack. "Can I have some of your whiskey?"

"It's not mine, but I think Omar loaned it to me for the long term; he's the one that loaded the pack."

"The hunter." He pulled the cap from the bottle of the Pappy Van Winkle's Family Reserve and leveraged a dollop into his coffee. "You have good friends, Lawman. We'll drink Omar's whiskey then."

"Bourbon." He held the neck of the bottle out to me, but I shook my head. "Working."

He shrugged and twisted the top back on. "The trail narrows at the falls, and with the timberline, the shoebox can't go any farther."

"When did you see them last?"

He thought about it. "An hour before I found the dead man and you."

"Then they heard the shots, too?"

"Oh, yes." He sipped his high-octane coffee and smiled. "Don't worry. They are bedded down, and it will be an uneasy night for them. They'll wait till the morning if they move, but the weather will break sooner and we can catch them unawares before that if you would like."

I sipped my own leaded coffee. "I would like."

He stretched his back, and it was as if the grizzly was rearing behind him. "So, you wanna play some chess, Lawman?"

Virgil had cleaned up from dinner, and we were into our third match and waiting for the weather to settle to make our move. The big Indian had placed a fat candle on one of the rocks and was using the light from it and the fire to examine the fourteenth-century giant blue devil on the cover of the *Inferno*.

His eyes came up to mine. "Looks scary."

I studied the makeshift chessboard and tried to remember if the larger stone with the smaller one sinewed together was the king or queen.

"It's got a Virgil in it; he was a Roman poet."

He flipped through a few pages. "Dead, huh?"

"More than two thousand years ago. Maybe you were named after him."

"No—I was named after my great uncle; he was an irrigation ditch digger." He opened the book about halfway. "What's it about?"

I moved what I thought was my queen diagonally on the checkerboard that was made from the remains of a Purina feed bag. "It's a poem, an allegory."

"Ah, something that's about something else. Does it rhyme?"

"Only in Italian, not in English."

His large fingers moved a small, singular rock that I assumed was a pawn, as he continued to study the paperback. "So, that is Italian on one page with English on the other?" He didn't wait for an answer. "What's the first thing it's about?"

"A guided tour through hell."

He considered the cover again and then tossed the book onto my legs. "I was in Vietnam and federal prison." He shifted his haunches and looked at me. "I don't need to go through that again." Something made a noise outside, a long, piercing cry that mixed with the wind and then died. He glanced toward the opening. "Cougar, female."

"Might be the one I saw down at Deer Haven Lodge yesterday. Maybe she's tracking me."

He took a deep breath and studied the board. "No. That noise, that call—she's looking for her mate. Not the heat call, but the one of loss." He noticed me studying him. "I didn't kill him."

"Good to know."

"She might eat some of that dead guy down there; how much of him do you have to bring back?" I didn't respond, and his eyes came back to mine. "These convicts—are you going to kill more of them?"

"Not if I don't have to." I thought about the man we'd put underneath the tree boughs by the four-wheeler. "So far I'm one and one."

"You let one live? That's good." He moved another large stone with sinew and no twig, and I thought I remembered it being a bishop. "Maintains a balance."

He looked at the opening again, the flickering light reflecting the scar that ran across his face like chain lightning. "Three men, one woman."

"Two convicts, two hostages." I studied the board, the ambiguity of the pieces reminding me of my life.

"You're sure?"

I took my eyes from the collection of stones between us. "Of what?"

"Who is who."

I pulled my hat down and shouldered the rolled collar of my jacket further up onto my back as a draft struck my neck. "What makes you ask that?"

"These escaped convicts, they had help?"

"A woman. Beatrice. She's back down the road at Omar's cabin."

He nodded. One of his large fingers rested on another stone, the turquoise and coral wolves on his ring chasing each others' tails. He nudged the piece forward. "This woman, are you sure she is the only one who is helping them?" He finished the move and then looked at me.

I ignored the board and looked back. "There was talk that they were going to meet somebody up here, somebody who was going to lead them out of the mountains."

He sat there like that, unmoving, his eyes reminiscent of the dead ones that I'd stared into at the base of the cliff. He suddenly reared back with a thunderous laugh that echoed off the rock walls. After a few moments he stopped, and the slits of his eyes would've knapped flint. "Seems like every time I see you, you're accusing me of something, Lawman."

I moved another impromptu game piece. "You brought it up."

He chuckled. "Not about me." He moved another stone that might have been a knight, and not for the first time I began wondering if the game was crook. His face stayed on the board as the grizzly one watched me, and it was almost as if the bear head was the one that finally spoke. "Checkmate. Go to sleep, Lawman."

"Unlock the door."

The boy doesn't move, just stares at the dashboard of the truck. He knows this almost-man—knows the meanness in him. Saw him once at the Greyhound bus station in Hardin placing ash at people's feet with the lost dreams of his eyes. They had seen each other for what it was worth, and they had both known that the hanging road was the line between them—even then.

The tap again. "Unlock the door."

Not of our people, says the large man about the almost-man. Stay in the truck and do not unlock the door.

"Unlock the door."

Do not unlock the door.

"Unlock the door."

He turns his face to look at the almost-man, who raises a fist as if to break the glass and it is suspended in the air there like a falling tree, trapped by its branches. He thinks how angry the big man will be if he returns and finds the glass in his truck broken.

"Unlock the door."

He unlocks the door.

★   ★   ★

These dreams were so real they left me shaken and unsure of which world I was in. I shrugged the buffalo hide farther up onto my shoulders and listened to Virgil snore—I was sure in no less a decibel level than that of a real grizzly—and then rolled over and returned to my restless, vision-haunted sleep.

"Bad dreams?" Virgil woke me with a hand on my arm, and I have to admit the rawhide-laced lance in his other hand was a little disconcerting. The weapon was about eight feet long with a painted coyote skull near the hilt, and it was wrapped in red flannel and studded with brass tacks, elk teeth, horsehair, and deer hooves that rattled when he moved. "It's time—they're asleep."

I stretched my eyes and tried to clear my head. "How do you know?"

He stood and pulled the grizzly head back from his own, the snow falling like dandruff. "I have been watching them."

It was a little more than a quarter-mile walk following Tensleep Creek. I had the advantage of the recovered snowshoes, but Virgil had the advantage of knowing the terrain, and we followed his footprints and walked in the rut where we'd dragged the dead convict.

He'd been right about the weather, and the full moon shone above us, broken by the passing clouds like camouflage. We made our way across the same ridge, the cold grinding the snow beneath us as the deer toes on Virgil's spear clack-a-tated like wind chimes.

"Hunter's Moon."

I glanced up again thinking about the Native designations that even NASA had agreed upon for each monthly moon; Hunter was October. "Little early for that."

His voice resounded in his chest. "Never too early for that; besides, it's a moon and we're hunting." He stopped just below the ridge, careful not to concede a target even when no one was looking. "In the Snow Moon, I about froze my ass off."

I had to think—February.

"What month is it now?"

"May."

"Hmm . . ." He grunted. "Day of the week?"

"I believe it's Sunday, early Sunday morning."

It was clear and colder than before, and the moonlight made it feel as if, even in the wallow, we were walking across a spotlit stage. I was rested and feeling a lot better, the bruise on my leg not giving me any trouble. Virgil continued to carry my pack; I'd asked him why, but he'd only shrugged and walked on. I had the Sharps over my shoulder, just in case we didn't have the element of surprise that the big Crow Indian had guaranteed.

We followed the frozen creek through another ridge and stayed to the left before crossing into the open again, still following Virgil's earlier tracks. The timberline was on a hillside to our right, and he motioned for me to follow him to an area that overlooked a four-way split in the stream that made a wide meadow before the falls. In the cerulean light of the moon, I could make out only one rectangular outline nestled in the aspens below.

You could see where the driver had circled to the right, but then, when faced with the steep incline and more trees, had returned to the field to the west and parked.

We were going to have to take the long way to the east and circle the meadow or backtrack in plain view across the creek. We chose the long way, and it took the better part of a half hour, but I felt assured as we looked down on the vehicle that we hadn't been seen. I adjusted the binoculars that Omar had thoughtfully given me, and my eyes drifted in and out of the shadows playing across the snow.

The area around the Thiokol had been trampled flat; there were no lights, and no one was outside—at least as far as I could see with the aid of the powerful optics.

"There has been no movement for two hours. They are city people and don't know that the bad things happen at night?"

I shrugged the binoculars from my eyes. "They know about bad things, day or night. I'll bet they're asleep. It's where I'd be if you hadn't woken me up." I was just starting to figure out a plan on how to approach the vehicle when in my peripheral vision I noticed Virgil holding the expedition pack out to me. I stood, took it, and rested it against the tree beside me. "You headed back?"

"Unless you would like me to stay?"

"No."

It wasn't fair to dragoon Virgil into official business that wasn't his own. I slung the strap of the binoculars around my neck, pulled a glove off, and extended a hand. "Thanks."

"For what?"

I continued to look up at the giant. "Well, for getting an eight-hundred pound four-wheeler off me, for one—I'd still be down there near the creek bed if it weren't for you."

He nodded and then glanced at the Thiokol. "Maybe that would've been better." His double head turned back to me, the bear one sitting a full foot taller than mine—short, really, for a grizzly. "Anyway, I got beef stroganoff out of the deal."

"And a bottle of Omar's Pappy Van Winkle's."

He shuffled his enormous feet. "You saw that, huh?"

I rubbed the lump on my head—the cold must've reduced the swelling. "I did."

His eyes came back to mine, and he finally took my hand, enveloping it in his. "You don't miss much, do you, Lawman?"

"Nope." I liked him, as much as you can like a giant sociopath who had killed so often he couldn't even remember all the lives he'd taken, human and otherwise. "You better get out of here before the shooting starts."

He stood there looking down at me, and I was sure that even if I could've made out more of his face, I still wouldn't have been able to read his expression. It was hard not to try, though. His mammoth chest rose and fell, but he said nothing more, then stooped through the lower limbs and walked away without comment.

I listened as the deer hooves chattered into the distance, then turned and, bringing the binoculars back up to my eyes, studied the vehicle below just in time to catch someone standing in front of one of the frost-covered side windows strike a match and light what looked to be a cigarette. I lowered the binoculars and remembered one of my late wife's slogans about smoking: "Cigarettes are killers that travel in packs."

Following the tree line around the meadow, I found a pretty good spot where I could approach the Thiokol Spryte from the rear where it had no windows. One side mirror hung crookedly and the other was completely encased in ice, so if they were going to see me they were going to have to stick their heads out or open the rear doors.

The closer I got to the thing, the more it reminded me of one of the old APCs we'd used in Vietnam, the one with the clamshell doors. Still a good fifty yards away, I could see the handles and figured the direct approach was the one I would use—simply yank the doors open and lead with the Colt. I certainly didn't see any reason in yelling out who I was and, more important, where I was until I had the drop on them. I was walking slowly, but the snow was so dry and cold it crunched even under the snowshoes; hopefully, they couldn't hear it.

I'd left the backpack at the edge of the clearing but had the Sharps cradled under one arm, the binoculars still hanging from my neck. A gust of wind carried over the western ridge, causing the pines to sway and giving me a little white noise with which to work as I traversed the last fifty feet and stopped only a few yards from the Thiokol. I stood there, not moving and listening for any sounds that might escape from the Spryte, but could hear nothing. If my calculations were correct, it'd been about fifteen minutes since I'd watched someone inside light their cigarette—plenty of time to smoke it and go back to the sleeping bag, if not to sleep.

I slowly let out my breath and watched as the vapor trailed to my right, dissipating and fading into the half-moonlit meadow as I took the last few steps.

The handle on the vehicle was a large lever-action one, like those you saw on walk-in freezers in grocery stores. There was a small trip mechanism at the end of it with matching holes where a padlock could be used to secure the two doors. If I'd had enough padlocks and the other doors were so equipped, I could just lock them in and let them drive around until they ran out of gas.

I carefully played the small trip mechanism out of the way of the bar, placed a hand on the foot-long lever, and remembered to breathe, hoping that the moonlight would illuminate the interior enough so that I could see who it was I might have to shoot.

I yanked the handle up and swung the door wide, jamming the .45 into the opening. There was no one inside near the doors, but something glowed to my right, so I aimed the Colt at the small amount of light and movement.

The other Ameri-Trans guard sat covered in a blanket against the bulkhead. He was puffing on a cigar, his right hand cuffed to the grating that divided the cab from the cargo space. He pumped the stogie like a bellows and rocked back and forth; I could barely make out his eyes, he'd pulled his knit company logo cap so low on his forehead. "Thank God, I thought I was going to have to be here like all night."

I kept the .45 on him but allowed my eyes to scan the interior—empty—and then looked back at him. "You're alone?"

"Yeah."

"Where are the others?"

He nudged the cap back with the butt of his free hand. "Gone, man. They've been like gone for hours."

"Where?"

He shrugged. "Hell, I don't know. I don't know where I am." He shoved himself a little farther into the corner but continued rocking. "You mind coming in and closing that door? I'm like freezing my ass off."

"What's your name?"

"Brian Heathman. We've met."

"We have?"

"Yeah, back at that lodge where the Bureau guys set up camp; it was like just a handshake."

I readjusted the Sharps and lowered the Colt. "Sorry, Brian, that seems like a million years ago. I'm going to get my pack. Stay here."

He nodded his head and squinted his eyes through the irony and cigar smoke as he rattled the handcuffs. "Very funny."

I holstered the Colt, made the round-trip to the tree line, and returned with the pack. I removed my gun-hand glove, tucked it in my inside pocket, and then pulled the Colt out again and stuffed the semiautomatic into the side of my coat.

I opened the door and tossed the pack onto the floor of the Thiokol. Heathman had pulled the blanket up around his neck. I climbed in and shut the door behind me, careful to leave it unlatched, as he reached overhead and turned on the dome light.

"You're going to run down the battery on this thing."

Still rocking, he removed the cigar from his mouth and shook his head. "The transmission is like shot; it's a lawn ornament. Hey, you don't have anything to eat, do you?"

I pulled the pack up, unzipping and rooting through the detachable top. I found the aged bag of Funyuns and held it up.

He tucked the cigar into the corner of his mouth and took the bag. "Oh man, these have the cutout. Frito-Lay hasn't used those since like '05."

"Cutout?"

He held it up for my inspection. "The little window where you can see the product; they've all got solid bags with a photograph now." He turned the bag to look at it. "Who knows how old these things are."

I glanced into the pack, aware that I had a few sandwiches further down, but I wasn't giving those up just yet. "I've got some very old Mallo Cups, and some beef jerky that appears to have hardened into iron ore."

He transferred the cigar into his attached hand and ripped open the vintage chips with his teeth. "Anything to drink?"

Pulling one of the water bottles from the side of the pack, I placed it on the bench at his covered feet and took another for myself. I unscrewed the top, resting it on the seat beside me, and took a swig. No need for ice. "Didn't they leave you anything?"

I took a little time to study him—he looked rather incongruous with the cigar in his cuffed hand. He was a little heavy, which might've explained why Raynaud Shade had left him behind. Maybe.

"No."

"What did they expect you to do?"

Reaching in and pulling a few of the ringlets from the bag and examining them for bugs, he seemed satisfied and popped two in his mouth. "He said you'd be along."

I took another swig from my water bottle. "He did, did he?"

"Yeah."

"He didn't think that Fingers Moser would finish me off?"

"Hell no. That guy was a nutcase, and Shade like wanted to be rid of him in the worst way."

I leaned back against the interior side of the Thiokol and

could feel the cold emanating from outside. "How's the other hostage?"

"The FBI agent? She's fine; a little roughed up, but she was okay when they left."

"And you have no idea where they went?"

"Nope." He rested the bag in his lap, plucked the cigar from his opposite hand, and stuffed it back in his mouth. Then he wiped his fingers on the blanket, bunching it so that his hand was underneath the fabric.

"Hey, Junk-food Junkie."

The tone of my voice and the use of his nickname gave him pause.

"Let's say for conversation's sake that you've got a Sig 9mm under that blanket, and that I've got a Colt .45 in my right pocket aimed at your guts, and my finger on the trigger; we would continue to have this nice conversation without any rude interruptions, now wouldn't we?"

Freddie "Junk-food Junkie" Borland blinked, but that was all he did.

"Now, I don't know if your hand is already on that Sig, or that it's aimed, or the safety is off—but I am ready to pull the trigger on you right now." In the dim light, I could see his eyes widen just a bit and the glow at the end of the cigar flare a little brighter with his intake of breath. "Something else for you to think about is what's going to happen afterward. You might shoot me and kill me, but I most certainly will get you—center shot, right in the guts."

I tapped my boot against the door, and his eyes shifted to the noise. "The other thing I'll make sure I do is kick this door open so that just in case the cold doesn't get you, whatever carnivores might be out there roaming around looking for a little Bighorn buffet will smell the blood. I've had a cougar following me for the last few miles, and I'm pretty sure there's a good-sized grizzly out there, too—and brother, when those professionals come in here they are not going to concern themselves with which meat is alive and which meat is dead."

The last part was mostly horseshit, but I didn't figure his Phoenix-born ass would know the difference any more than Hector's Texas one did—besides, the abstraction of a bullet was one thing, but being eaten alive was something else.

"I figure that putting you in the Ameri-Trans driver's uniform was Shade's idea, but after seeing how the other flanking efforts had fared, especially with your buddy Calvin back there, you took exception. That's when he cuffed you to the grating and left you here with a pistol that's only got one bullet." I shifted my weight forward. "What were you going to do after you shot me, hope that you could fish the cuff keys out of my belt?"

He still didn't move, but the end of the cigar flared again.

"Well, I'll make sure I fall out the back. Then you can sit here eating Funyuns and fattening up for what happens next."

He finally swallowed and shifted; the semiautomatic pistol clattered onto the metal floor between us.

10

"Only a professional criminal would neglect to ask an officer to uncuff him, but the dead giveaway was the Funyuns. Who but the Junk-food Junkie would know that the cutout window in a bag of chips was replaced in 2005?"

He nodded and rubbed his wrist, trying to work the blood back into the white and stiffened hand now cuffed to the other in his lap with those cuffs attached with my own to the bench seat.

"Fuck."

"Yep, it never pays to have a *nom du criminal.*"

Along with the 9mm, he'd had one of the next-generation satellite phones, which I activated. The battery was fully charged and should be plenty good enough for my purposes; within thirty-six hours I intended to be sipping an Irish coffee somewhere warm. "Were you supposed to call him when you were done with me?"

"Yeah."

I stared at the phone and then tossed it onto his lap. "Call him."

His eyes widened. "What?"

"Call him; tell him I'm dead and that you've uncuffed yourself and need to know what to do next."

He looked at the phone but made no move to try to dial. "We're supposed to like meet somebody."

I plucked a Funyun from the bag beside him and ate it; it wasn't the usual and tasted like onion-flavored insulation, but it would have to do. "I'm aware of that, but I want to know who and where."

He sat there. "I can't lie to him."

"What, you've suddenly developed scruples?"

He picked up the phone and held it out. "He'll like kill me; after he kills you he'll come back here and kill me."

"So, they are coming back this way?"

"No, but he'll make an extra effort after I lie to him and he kills you. Hey look, I don't know who we're meeting or where. Shit, man . . . I don't know where the hell I am right now."

Still holding the 9mm, I sat on the opposite bench and looked at him. "Call him, or when I go I'll leave the door back here open and let nature take its course." He still didn't move. "Survival of the fittest."

He looked like he might cry but thumbed the CALL button and bent down so that he could hold it to his ear. After a moment, he spoke into the receiver. "He's dead."

There was a pause.

"No, like really. I shot him and got the keys off of him. He's like lying here and I think there are animals outside . . ." He stopped talking for a moment and swallowed, the fear wafting off of him like a bad smell. "What? No, like he's dead and . . ." He paused again, froze like that, and held the phone out to me, the tears openly flowing. "He says he wants to talk to you."

I sighed and took the phone. "Yes."

The singsong rhythm of his voice sounded close. "You should be getting kind of tired about now, Sheriff."

"Actually, no. I'm used to the altitude, and I've been cooped up most of the winter and been looking forward to getting out of doors."

"It's beautiful up here isn't it—sacred land."

"Yep, it is." I waited, but he didn't say anything. "I'm sure we've got more to discuss than the scenery. Look, Shade, I don't know where you think you're going, or who you think you're going to meet . . ."

There was a long pause, and then his voice bounced off the satellite in the cold dead of space and landed in what was left of my ear. "You should stop now, Sheriff. I gave you those four in hopes that that would be enough. Remember, there are only the two hostages and me. I've given you all I'm willing to give; if you continue to pursue me any further—I will begin taking."

I measured my next words carefully, knowing we were playing a balancing act, attempting to get into each other's head. "I want you to listen to me very carefully, Shade. Those two people are the only reason you're still alive. I know you've got that .223, but if you keep going up on this trail you're going to hit some long meadows and then open areas above the tree line, and when you do you're going to feel an itch between your shoulder blades, a .45-70 itch. That'll be me—and it'll be the last thing you ever feel."

I listened to him breathing on the other end of the line; then he spoke in a voice that was monotonous and unemotional. "Tell Freddie that I'll be back for him."

The line went dead.

"What'd he say?"

I thumbed off the phone. "He says he's having a wonderful time and wishes you were there." I drew the pack onto my shoulder along with the Sharps and grabbed the snowshoes beside the door.

"Hey look, you're not going to like just leave me here, right?"

"I am but don't worry, I'm going to use the phone to bring the cavalry to you."

"What about the bears and the mountain lions?"

"When I leave I'll close and latch the door. Both of them are amazingly adaptable hunters, but one thing they don't have is opposable thumbs, which means the next thing that opens the cargo hold will be human. It'll probably be Henry Standing Bear, a big Indian fellow, or a mean little brunette deputy of mine by the name of Victoria Moretti—if I were you, I'd hope for the Cheyenne."

I stood there for a moment, thinking about what I was going to do and how I was going to do it. I had limited resources and a limited amount of time. I pulled Saizarbitoria's cell phone from the inside pocket of my jacket, rescued it from the waterproof Ziploc, and flipped it open; it was still out of service. I closed it and put it back—insurance, just in case I was to get to an altitude where it might get a signal.

I looked at the satellite phone in my other hand and thought about which of two calls I wanted to make. I punched in the office number.

"Absaroka County Sheriff's Department."

"It's me."

"Where are you!"

I held the receiver a little away from my ear. "Ruby, I need you to listen. I've got one of the Fed satellite phones now, so this is the number where you can reach me, and I was right, the numbers are sequential. I'm at the waterfall meadows on Tensleep Creek where I've got a vehicle broken down. Is there any backup nearby?"

"Wait . . . meadows at the base of the falls at Tensleep Creek, right? Yes, they broke through on the east and west slopes. Saizarbitoria is arranging transport for that agent."

"McGroder. He's alive?"

"Yes, and Henry's with search and rescue. They're getting ready to head out from there. Did you really leave a man hand-cuffed to a water pipe at Deer Haven Lodge?"

"I did, and I'm about to leave another one handcuffed at this location."

"Another one?"

"Yep, and there's a body at Omar Rhoades's cabin at Bear Lake."

"Oh, Walter." There was a rustling of some papers. "Tommy Wayman, Joe Iron Cloud, and a detachment of High-way Patrol are at the last turn at Tensleep Canyon and should be joining Henry before too long. Do you know about the weather?"

"It's cold but dry up here for now."

"It's going to get much worse. The NOAA says that was only the front of the storm and that this blizzard is carrying fifty-mile-an-hour winds with severe mountain temperatures that will likely reach forty below zero. It's going to be a com-plete whiteout by midmorning." There was only a short pause. "Walter, you have to stop."

I placed my thumb over the OFF button.

"Walter, please? They are on their way; at least wait until Henry and the others get there."

"Don't worry, they'll find me." My thumb hovered over the button. "I've got to go."

"Walter . . ."

I punched it and looked at the indicator, which still read fully charged. I turned the satellite phone off and hoped for the best.

The Junk-food Junkie was looking at me when I raised my face. "Popp's dead?"

"Yep."

"Good, he was a prick. How about the Mexican kid?"

"Hector. Alive and well."

"What about Fingers?"

I didn't answer.

He seemed to take a certain amount of satisfaction in that at least one of his companions was alive, but the troubled expression returned to his face as he began rocking again. "You cannot like leave me here."

"I don't see as how I have much of a choice, Freddie. Unless you want to leave the comfortable environs of the Thiokol and accompany me farther up the range, but the weather report isn't good." I studied the Fed phone and wondered if any of the other ones had been left. I held the device out. "I don't suppose they left any more of these, dead or otherwise?"

"No." He wiped his hands, rattling the restraints that held them close to the bench, and looked at the water bottle beside him. "How am I supposed to drink that, cuffed like I am?"

"Pour it into the lid a bunch of times, but I'd not wait too long or it'll freeze. The other option is keeping it close to your body." I pushed my own water bottle inside the pack to help it stay insulated and then placed the satellite phone in one of the outside pockets of my jacket in hopes that the cold would do the battery some good.

"Hey, have you got any more food?"

I dug into the expedition pack, dragged out Omar's sandwiches, and handed one of them to him. "Here."

He took it, crouched down to reach his hands, and began eating. He studied me from under the knit cap, his eyes shifting like bad cargo. "You should just let me have the other one, too."

"How do you figure?"

He swallowed and took another bite. "You're gonna be like dead here in a few hours anyway."

I stood there looking at him for an elongated moment. "Dead, or *like* dead?" He didn't say anything more, so I repacked, starting with placing the other sandwich back in my pack. "Beatrice said that Shade had a waterproof duffel with him. Do you have any idea what's in it?"

"He's got a lot of stuff with him, some of it that she brought and some that he took from those FBI guys." He took another bite and chewed, suddenly sullen. "You don't get it, do you, Sheriff?" He licked the mayonnaise from the corner of his mouth with his tongue and shook his head. "It doesn't mean shit that you've stopped us; he's not like us. I mean, we're the kinds of guys that give people nightmares." He shifted his weight and leaned back against the bulkhead with one shoulder. "He's the kind of guy that gives *us* nightmares."

I lifted the pack up onto the seat by the door to make it

easier to hoist onto my shoulder, stretched my eyes, and rubbed my face. "Then I guess you'd better stay awake."

It was starting to snow again, but through the tides of the storm I could see small leaks of moonlight seeping to the ground. I was able to follow their tracks, but before heading into the timber, I checked the early morning western sky for stars—there weren't any. This was not a good thing. I was feeling tired again and that wasn't good, either. I took a deep breath and exhaled through my nostrils, the vapor blowing across the expanse of my jacket like the twin trails of two locomotives. Maybe what I needed to do was work up some steam.

Even as cold as it was, there was still a discernible amount of water dropping from the rocks above; of course it was smothered under a two-foot casing of ice, but the dull thudding of the falling water pounded a rhythm and I settled into a comfortable pace. It'd been a long while since I'd had this kind of physical activity at altitude, and I figured the burgeoning headache that seemed to be mushrooming in the front of my head was just that. Of course, the knot on my forehead probably didn't help.

I wondered once again where Raynaud Shade thought he was going.

The path straightened at the ridge along Mistymoon Trail, bypassing some smaller ponds I remembered. I knew this area better than Virgil's since we were now approaching the main trail. Of course, I'd been here mostly in the summer and that was a different landscape. I'd fished Gunboat Lake with Cady and before that with my late wife, what seemed like a few lifetimes ago. Before my daughter was born, Martha and I made summer pilgrimages in an attempt to break up the heat and to supplement my civil service wages with a freezer full of brookies and a few rainbows—some as large as ten inches, big for being that high.

I remember my wife on those trips, mostly with her hair tied back with a bandana, as she dutifully breaded the fillets and carefully browned them over an open campfire. I remembered the closeness in our double sleeping bag and the smooth soles of her feet as she attempted to keep them warm by pressing them against my legs.

A surge of wind pulsed against the trees on the far ridge as if trying to push them aside and then swirled into a snow devil in the frozen meadow below, the tiny tornado jumping the hard surface of the water and moving across the small valley toward me. Just as suddenly as it had appeared, another gust caught it, and it was gone.

I wasn't even aware that I'd stopped walking.

Standing there on the ridge trail, I realized I'd come to a fork and my subconscious mind had been unable to make the choice. The main path led north, the one to the right went east toward Mirror and Lost Twin lakes.

I felt a shudder run through me that had nothing to do with the temperature. I could feel a slight twinge in my fingers and in that little portion of my ear that was missing, and felt kind of like those amputees that reach to scratch limbs that have long been removed.

I adjusted my collar, pulled the balaclava over my nose, stuffed my gloved hands in my pockets in an attempt to further insulate my long-healed wounds, and stared at the path east. There were no tracks, but I could swear that someone was watching me. It was the same feeling that I'd had at the West Tensleep parking loop at the start of this trail. My mind made the logical connection and moved back to the time when I'd been even more sure that I'd been watched, prodded, cajoled, and enticed.

I thought about the questions I'd asked Henry after I brought George and him out of the wilderness, and the inadequacy of his answers. Maybe there were no answers to what had happened on my multiple trips to and from Lost Twin Lakes that time on the mountain—maybe there were no answers because there was nothing there at all.

Perhaps, but it still felt as if something had been there and that something was here now.

I glanced up the main trail where there were three sets of snowshoe prints. Looking for movement, I let my eyes unfocus, but there was nothing there. I took a few steps and felt a sudden sense of loss, snow devils being better than the real ones.

I lifted the binoculars just to check the trail more closely and saw what I must have sensed—there was another set of footprints along the creek bed. I tromped my way down the slope, kneeled—careful not to let the top-heavy pack topple me over—and gently blew in the nearest print. It was a huge track, moccasins, smooth with just a trace of the stitching on the side—crude stitching that could only have been homemade.

Virgil.

I glanced back up and half expected him to be standing there with the paws of the giant grizzly swaying in the breeze beside his massive girth, but there was still nothing, only the tracks that continued to follow the other three. It took the better part of a mile to get to Lake Helen, and Virgil continued to follow the others. As I trudged along, I thought about the Crow Indian. Had he known that they had left Freddie in the Thiokol and continued on? Why was he following them? Was he the guide whom Hector had alluded to, that Beatrice had mentioned? If he was, then why had he taken the time to fool with me?

He said he'd been watching them last night before waking me, and if that was the case, wouldn't he have seen them leave? If he was the so-called guide, then why wouldn't he have simply joined them there?

The moonlight had given way to dawn, and I could see some movement on the trail far ahead. I pulled the binoculars up again and looked.

The blue patches of the early morning sky were succumbing to a wall of gray, but it was light enough that I could see the Cloud Peak massif rising above the valley. The granite-ribbed peaks gave way to the subalpine forests trickling down to scattered groves of conifers that strung all the way to Mistymoon, one of the last lakes before the true high country.

I used the ridge as a guide and followed the trail from there to the area below where I could see three people struggling to make their way up to the next hanging plateau. The one in the back was stumbling under the weight of a large pack and was unarmed—must be the real Ameri-Trans driver; the one in the middle with the blonde hair had to be Agent Pfaff; and the one in front carrying a large pack, an automatic rifle, and what looked to be a black duffel had to be Raynaud Shade—confident son of a bitch.

I lowered the binoculars and thought about what Omar had said in his cabin before I'd left: "Kill 'em, kill 'em as fast as you can and from far away."

I unclipped the center strap of my pack and carefully slipped the rifle off my shoulder. I figured just a hair over six hundred yards—at the edge of my limit. All my instincts were telling me to take the shot, to do it now and end it. I would never have a better opportunity or conditions.

It would take about a half second to reach out to Raynaud Shade, but there was something about shooting a man, even a guilty man, unawares from great distance that didn't sit well with my job description.

They'd made the ridge but weren't moving too rapidly, mostly because of the Ameri-Trans driver, who seemed to be having trouble keeping up. I looked at him for a moment, then moved the rifle back to Pfaff, and then to Shade. He had dropped his bags and was standing on the ridge, the .223 aimed with his eye pressed to the scope.

Watching me.

I had that same eerie feeling I'd had every time I looked at him and had found him looking at me. It was possible that there was no surprising Raynaud Shade.

He knew that the Armalite wouldn't reach this far. He was aware, also, that what I was carrying would, but he still didn't move. We stood like that, the two of us, for a long second.

Waves of unease overtook me, and I remembered the last long-distance shot that I'd taken with a Sharps buffalo rifle and how it had ended in tragedy. In some ways they all ended in tragedy, no matter which end of the slug you were on.

He lowered the tactical carbine but continued looking at me. After a moment his left arm came up and he waved, but it was a strange wave. Then he closed his fingers as if grasping something.

The satellite phone in my pocket rang.

I lowered the rifle, pulled the device out, and hit the button.

"Hello, Sheriff. We are somewhat at an impasse."

I measured my words. "You need to stop this."

He breathed into the phone. "That is what I'm trying to do."

"Let the two hostages go, and maybe we can figure all of this out."

"They tell me you don't believe in them."

Of all the conversations I wanted to have with Shade, this was the one I wanted to have least. "Shade, look . . . We need to get you some help."

He laughed, but there was nothing but depravity in it. "I have all the help I need." He was silent for a moment. "More than I can stand."

I waited.

"You should acknowledge them; so few of us can. They discovered me when I was very young, but from the reading I've done and what the psychiatrists and therapists tell me, that isn't abnormal."

"No."

"They took part of me with them then. I've been trying to get that part of me back ever since—that's why they speak to me so much; that's why I listen." He stopped talking but didn't disconnect, and I pulled the binoculars up to watch him remove something from the bag he carried and place it on an uncovered boulder alongside the trail. "I'm leaving this for you because they tell me it is what I must do."

The phone went dead, and I watched him for a few more seconds as he loaded up and continued on over the ridge with the other two following.

Adjusting the optical ring at the back of the binoculars, widening the aperture, I scanned the slope behind them, half expecting to find a giant Indian wearing a bearskin. I trailed the optics along the path all the way back to the southern edge of the lake but still couldn't see any sign of Virgil.

I needed a drink and settled for water. I sat my pack on the trail. The bottle was on top and, as I pulled it out, the satellite phone began ringing again from my inside pocket. "Shade, listen . . ."

"Hey Sheriff, there are fucking Indians up here."

"Hector, how did you get this number?"

"You were right, they're sequestered or something like that . . ."

"Sequential."

There was a jostling. "I'm not kidding. These two Indians were just here, and they're looking for you."

"I know. They're on our . . . they're on my side."

"Well, I just thought that with you bein' a cowboy and all I better call you up and let you know. These were some really tough-looking hombres. The one guy, the really big one? I mean, they had guns all over 'em, but the one guy, the big one? He had this axe thing between his shoulders." There was a pause. "He took the gun away from me. I told him it wasn't loaded, but he took it anyway."

"It's okay. He's a friend of mine."

"I'm jus' sayin'." There was some noise in the background, and I could hear someone else talking. "I'm tellin' him about the Indians."

I held out the phone to look at the display. "Hector, you're eating up my battery."

"Sorry, Sheriff, but I've got this Wop cop here who wants to talk to you." More fumbling, and I heard Hector say ouch. "Hold on, here she is."

"What the fuck do you think you're doing?"

"I'm providing a phone messaging service for the entire Bighorn mountain range." I waited and was glad she wasn't nearby. "It's really good to hear your voice."

"Where the hell are you?"

I glanced around at the eye of the storm. "I am currently enjoying an exquisite alpine idyll." I'd loaded up, discovering that I could multitask—both talking and tracking—and, keeping an eye north, made my way down the cutback of the boulder field. I figured I could stop if the signal started breaking up. "Lake Helen, then Lake Marion and probably Mistymoon here in about an hour—I figure that's where I'm going to catch up with them."

"The weather is going to turn to frozen shit in a matter of hours—stop."

"I don't think so."

There was an audible sigh of exasperation, which was my undersheriff's usual response to me. "Why not?"

"He's more likely to play nice if he knows I'm here."

There was a pause. "He knows you're there?"

"Yep. We just had a nice conversation."

"You what?"

I slid a little on the ice at the base of the trail and steadied myself. "I took the satellite phone I'm talking on from the convict in the Thiokol, which, by the way, is when I had him call Shade—then he called me."

"Get the fuck outta here."

"Yep, we had a wide-ranging confab about conversing with dead people." She didn't laugh. "He's the only one left, and he's got two hostages, Pfaff and the Ameri-Trans driver."

She readjusted the phone in her ear. "Walt, he's going to kill them."

"Not if he thinks they're the only thing that's keeping him alive."

"He's got the marshal's .223 for that."

Indeed. "Speaking of, where the heck is my backup?"

"Bear was with Joe Iron Cloud and Tommy Wayman's just above. Hey, were there any trees across the road when you went up West Tensleep?"

"No."

"Well, lucky for you Wayman's an old-school Wyoming sheriff and keeps a Husqvarna 42-inch chain saw in his truck. He said the last time he saw Henry and Joe they were leaping over the fallen trees in the finest James Fenimore Cooper tradition and were headed out at a high rate of speed." I thought about how the odds were evening. "Tommy said there was no way the Bear and the Cloud were going to keep up that pace." She laughed. "I asked him if he wanted to bet."

"What'd he say?"

"Not now, not ever." It was my turn to laugh as she continued attempting to bolster my mood. "Why don't you wait; you've got some pretty intense Indian backup coming—both the Arapaho and Cheyenne nations."

"Yep, the mountains are full of them."

There was another pause. "What's that supposed to mean?"

"Virgil's up here, too."

"The jolly red giant?"

"Ho, ho, ho."

"That's not good. Does he know that evil scumbag is the one who murdered his grandson?"

I stared at the trail as if approaching a cliff, and maybe I was. "That's how it stands?"

"Yeah." I stood still and could hear her lodging the phone against her neck, which, as I recall, was a very nice place to be. "It would appear that Virgil's son, Eli, had a child out of wedlock—the boy, Owen White Buffalo. There are no reports of a missing child, because there are no records of him, period. We're attempting to find the mother, but so far—nothing."

"Okay."

She could read the tone of my voice. "Are you getting ready to hang up on me?"

"I'd better—I've got to catch up."

She gave me Joe Iron Cloud's satellite number. "Give them a call to see where they are and what the weather is doing before you do anything stupid, all right?"

"Roger that, nothing stupid." I would dial it into the phone after we hung up. "Gotta go."

"And call me before you do anything stupid."

"Anything stupid, my SOP. 10-4."

She hung up. I turned the device off and tucked it back inside my coat. Annoying Vic was always the simplest way to get her off the phone and, all in all, it was usually pretty easy.

I started out again, looking up the valley at the west ridge of Bomber Mountain, so named because in 1943 an unfortunate B-17 had abruptly come to rest there with all crewmen on board.

I know how they must've felt.

So it was quasiofficial that it was Virgil's grandson. Could he know, and how could all of these horrible coincidences have fallen in place the way that they had?

I suddenly remembered Joe Iron Cloud's cell number, so I

pulled out the phone and dialed. Even if he didn't answer, the number would be recorded. As expected, it connected me to an answering service—the Arapaho had even taken the time to record a message. His halting voice made me smile, and I could just see those two very tough men racing their way up West Tensleep Trail; God help anything that got in their way.

"Hey, hey, this is Sheriff Joe Iron Cloud. I'm unable to answer your call right now, but if you'll leave a message I'll get right back to you. Ye-ta-hey."

I waited for the beep and then spoke. "Joe, this is Walt Longmire, president of the Give America Back to Americans movement, and I was wondering if you'd help the three-hundred million of us pack? Give me a call."

I closed the phone and tucked it away.

"That should get their attention."

Keeping an eye on the cloud mass that seemed to be leaning on me, I worked my way around the west side of the lake. If I was lucky, I'd get them pinned in the open meadow adjacent to the big peaks, and I would have cover at the ridge of Mistymoon Lake. Raynaud Shade would have the choice of either giving it all up or taking a chance on the delivery of a high-powered, high-mortality package at long distance.

I began to climb to the next level that would lead to Lake Marion and started feeling the burn in my legs, mostly the tops of my thighs. I was doing pretty well with my lungs, but my legs were another matter, and after twenty minutes more I was starting to resent the supplies in Omar's pack—the very supplies that, if everything went bad, were going to be responsible for keeping me alive. I trudged on, every once in a while lifting my face to scan the ridge where they'd disappeared.

When it happened, it hit like a wall. The second front of the storm came in. I knew it was just the barometric pressure, but it still felt like I was being inhaled by that giant blue devil on the cover of Saizarbitoria's book. The exhaling riptide came quickly, and I watched it bend the trees like a sweeping claw as it topped the extended northern backbone of Bald Ridge.

It was like the winter had shattered, and the shards were now blowing in my face, small bits of the last season, blasted and blown.

My eyelids were starting to freeze, and I remembered the amber-tinted goggles that were hanging around my throat. I fumbled to pull them up as I climbed and concentrated on just putting one foot in front of the other as I pushed up the last part of the hillside trail where I'd last seen the three. Every time I looked away from my boots I'd stumble and veer from the path, so I tried to focus on their tracks. It was only when I got to the point where Shade had called me that I almost stumbled over the huge man in the grizzly bear hide. He was sitting on a boulder with the lance balanced between his knees, his back to the storm, his moccasined feet stretched out onto the path.

His booming voice carried above the keening wind that bucked me sideways as I stood above him.

"He left this for you."

In the surrealistic amber hue of the blowing snow, the giant sat holding a small human femur in his gigantic hands.

11

"You know, when the Iichihkbaahile formed people, we used to have ears at the back of our heads so that we could hear if anything was sneaking up from behind."

I'd been listening to Virgil's galloping monologue for about ten minutes now. "Does that include white people?"

"I suppose. Even with all your faults, you're people too, right?"

"Right." I watched through the bizarre view afforded by my goggles as the massive grizzly skin swayed along the trail, the hind claws dragging across the snow as if the White Buffalo was packing a bear in a fireman's carry.

"The reason they got moved to the sides was because while he was working, us people kept moving our heads back and forth to see what the Iichihkbaahile was doing." He paused on the trail for a second, and I almost ran into him. "Doesn't that sound like something white people would do?"

"Uh huh."

"Anyway, now we only know what goes on when it's right beside us." He'd hung back a moment, just long enough for me to hear the statement, but I said nothing in return, so he went ahead and we shambled our way across the hill adjacent to the frozen surface of Lake Marion. The giant was providing a partial wind block as the ferocity of the storm blew down the ridge at our left and followed the contours of the valley into our faces.

Personally, I was glad for the insulation.

Virgil had handed the bone to me as if it had little significance, asked me what I thought it meant, and then started off as if this had been his plan all along.

I found it hard to believe that he was their guide; more than likely that portion of Raynaud Shade's story was, like the money, simply leverage to get the others to follow wherever he led—but where was that? If Virgil really didn't have any connection with these people, then why had he reappeared and taken up my cause in pursuing them? It was impossible that he knew about his grandson, which meant there was no personal stake in all of this for him. He'd helped me enormously a few months back and had even gotten himself seriously injured in the process. Why was he chancing that again?

I stumbled on the slick surface of one of the rounded stones along the shore. It was hard to keep up with Virgil's extended stride. One of the promises I made myself was that I wouldn't be the one to tell the man about the fate of his grandson; it would've been like pulling the trigger on an avalanche.

At least I now knew what was in the duffel, but why would Shade have taken the remains of the boy with him? Why had Shade left the bone for me on the boulder? What could he possibly have hoped to gain from antagonizing me any further? Did he know of the connection between Virgil and the boy he'd killed? Had he left the bone for Virgil and not so much for me? Did he even know Virgil existed?

There was a thicket of trees just off the path on a peninsula that divided the two main parts of the lake that provided a remarkable amount of cover. Virgil pulled up short under the snow-covered overhang and sat on a fallen log, turned, and looked at me. "I thought you might need some more help."

I nodded and stamped my feet, allowing some of the snow I'd collected on my snowshoes to fall off, and was just thankful to be out of the wind. "I figured." I could feel the weight of the leg bone in the inside pocket of my jacket, along with the weight of the words I was trying not to speak. I settled on some others as I looked out at the lake from the relative shelter of the trees. "We must be getting up close to ten thousand feet."

"They will rest before they reach the final ridge, so we will also rest." His two heads turned, and he looked through a narrow opening at the table-flat distance between the ridges that were as tall as skyscrapers. "What is it the whites call this lake?"

Slipping the rifle off my shoulder and lowering the goggles, I came over and sat on the log with him. "Marion."

"Hmm . . . I call it Dead Horse." He paused for a moment, and it was a pause I was used to, the pause that a lot of people have before they tell someone with a badge something. "There was a party of elk hunters up here doing a little fishing last fall, and they had their horses tied off to a group of dead pines down by the rocks." He flipped a massive paw from the cloak. "A bear came down from the ridge over there and started circling toward the horses while those elk hunters were fishing over this way. The horses went crazy and most of them pulled free, but there was one that was tied up pretty good. He kept yanking on that lead until finally it broke off the base of the trunk with a bunch of the rocks still attached to the roots. The horse bolted, trying to get away from the bear, but the dead tree fell in the lake and dragged the horse in after it. You could see him fighting to get loose from the halter, but he just disappeared into that water, kicking the whole way down."

I stamped my feet again, seriously trying to keep them from freezing. "What'd the hunters do?"

"Oh, after the bear was killed they fooled around and built a kind of half-assed raft and tried to get the horse because it had some expensive tack on it."

"How'd that work out?"

"One of them drowned."

I looked at him. "You're kidding."

"Nope; watched it happen—big like you. He went down but never came back up." He gestured with his lips toward one of the ridges to our east. "Saw it all from right over there."

"What'd the hunters do then?"

"They got the hell out of here."

"They left him?"

The giant looked down at me as if to discern which particular village was missing its idiot. "They already lost one horse, one bear, and one man; nobody else wanted to go." He actually yawned. "Can't say that I blamed them."

I glanced out at the lake. "The man and the horse are still down there?"

"Yeah; the bear, too."

"Did anybody report it?"

"You'd be in a better position to know that than I would." He took a deep breath and tried looking toward the ridge above us to the north. "Different rules up here. Good for the water spirits, though. Not much water in the high country, and they need the company. That or the Water Monsters took them in revenge for their defeat at the hands of the Thunderbirds." He glanced at me. "They had the help of a human hunter, you know."

"You don't say. I must've missed that in Bible school." It was Sunday morning, after all.

"Yeah, people don't remember that part. See, the reason the Thunderbird had to go get help was because the Water Monsters kept eating his young."

I pushed my hat back for a closer look at Virgil's face. "Really?"

He studied me for a few seconds and then returned his eyes to the ridge, giving me the full view of the indented part of his forehead where a drug dealer had pounded it with a claw hammer. "The Water Monsters or Long Otters would come whenever there was a fog and eat the young Thunderbirds before their feathers were mature. So the Thunderbirds got the help of one of my people to do battle against the Long Otters. The warrior shot them with arrows and poured red-hot rocks down the Water Monsters' throats to kill them."

"That'd do it, in most cases."

Virgil smiled, suffering my trace of sarcasm. "Yes, then the warrior was given many powers by the Thunderbirds so that he could change his shape, becoming many different animals and birds. He lived by the big water for many years but came down with a case of lice and longed to go home."

The big Indian could see me smiling at the details of Crow mythology.

"Lice? You'd think if you had all those powers, you could get rid of lice."

A little indignation crept into his voice. "Hey, this stuff is handed down."

"Right."

He ignored me and continued. "Anyway, the warrior remembered that he wanted to return to his native land, the Yellowstone Country. He turned himself into a crow and flew home. Once his travels were over, he saw an elk by the river and thought he would kill it."

"A crow could kill an elk?"

"It was a big crow. Anyway, it grabbed him and drew him into the water where the Long Otters were waiting. The Thunderbird thundered and shook the earth, but the Water Monsters paid no attention and tortured the warrior, finally asking him if he knew what he was. He said he was a crow. They told him, no, you are an Indian and you have killed many things here in the water, but we do not wish to kill you. We will release you back to your people—and that is how the Crow got their name." He sniffed a little in indignation. "It is also how the Elk River or Yellowstone got its name, but that is not so important."

I nodded my head. "And the moral of the story is?"

He raised an eyebrow, and it was as if the dent in his forehead was looking to dig deeper. "What is it with you white people and morals? Maybe it's just a story about what happened." He paused for a moment. "If an Indian points at a tree, you white people are always thinking, What does that mean? What does the tree stand for? What's the lesson in this for me? Maybe it's just a tree."

"Okay." I wanted to get going but was still curious. "What happened to the young Thunderbirds?"

"How the hell should I know?" He glanced up to where the sky would've been if we could've seen it. "My great uncle, the ditchdigger, he said they grew up and populated the earth as eagles."

I waited for more, but there didn't appear to be any so I asked the next question that had been on my mind. "Virgil, back down the trail at the meadow, did you know there was only one of them in the Thiokol?"

He continued to study the lake, possibly looking for either a hoof or a monster that might be sticking out of the ice. "Yes."

"How come you didn't tell me?"

The double head dipped, and it was the first time I'd ever seen a grizzly shrug. "You had to arrest that one before you could come after these. I thought I could keep an eye on them while you were busy." He studied me. "You don't tell me everything down below, Lawman, and I don't tell you everything up here. Like I said, the rules are different this high—we do not have the final say."

"How so?"

He breathed deeply and thought about it. "Down there—it is so loud and so busy we can block them out, but up here is different."

I wasn't sure I knew what he was talking about, which was nothing new with Virgil White Buffalo, Kicked-in-the-Belly band, Crazy Dogs warrior society. Nonetheless, I thought I'd give it a shot. "Virgil, that wasn't you down at the West Tensleep parking lot that drew me over and showed me where the Thiokol had gone, was it?"

He looked around, his gaze stopping here and there as if he were seeing something or someone I wasn't. He didn't move for a moment, then the wind struck his wide back as if urging him onward, and the dark hollows above his cheekbones turned toward me. "There is the singing water and the drumming rock and this is the way of it. Listen."

Foolishly, I thought he was going to say something more. "What?"

"I am serious now. Listen."

I finally got his meaning and stood there trying to hear the report of Shade's .223, cries for help, or even Water Monsters and Thunderbirds, but all I could hear was the wind and snow scrubbing the high country like an unforgiving brush. "I can't . . ."

"Listen."

I tipped my hat back in exasperation. "What the hell am I listening for, Virgil?"

"They follow you still."

My skin prickled, and my mouth grew dry. All I could think of was what had occurred since my experience on these mountains more than a year ago. I thought about almost drowning in Clear Creek Reservoir, racing a borrowed horse across Forbidden Drive in Philadelphia, hunting a killer in a ghost town, and being drugged on a mesa in the Powder River country. Strange things had happened to me in all those places, including the parking lot at West Tensleep only yesterday, but I'd filed all those instances away as explainable phenomena. What stood before me now was much larger and more powerful than the giant cloaked in a bear hide. As strange and mystifying as it might be, I needed to know. "What are you saying, Virgil?"

"The Old Ones, they have spoken to me for the first

time—or maybe it is the first time I have been able to listen."
He smiled a little and turned his head to catch the corners of
the wind as it redirected itself around him, and it was like the
snout above his head tested the air. "They tell me to watch
over you and to keep you safe—which is all very strange."

I stood, now especially anxious to stop talking and get
moving.

"They don't watch over white men."

Slipping the rifle strap onto my shoulder, I took a few steps
toward the opening that led toward the trail. "Well, I don't
know what to say to that, Virgil."

He let the smile play on his lips like a warped board. "You
saved an Indian the last time you were up here, yes?"

I froze, and not because of the temperature, and thought
about how Henry had taken a bullet that could've easily been
mine. "Sort of."

"So . . ." The giant nodded his great, hooded face, the slight
glimmer from the reflection in his pupils remaining steady as
he lowered his head to look me in the eye. "What Indian are
you saving this time?"

It was a command performance asking for a response, but
now was not the time to discuss things that would derail the
entire venture. It was hard, but I remained silent.

The wind gusted against him again, but he stood in front
of it, unmoved. "Still keeping secrets from me, Lawman?"

A few flakes blew into our protected area and lit on my
face, burning like ash. "Maybe it's like you said; up here we
don't have final say." He was still, like a hunter is before the
defining act, and all I could feel was the sympathy I'd had for
the giant when I'd heard the boy's name.

"No, we don't." He shrugged the cloak higher with a roll of his shoulders; maybe the inactivity of not moving was beginning to have an effect even on him. "You have great sorrows burning in your heart, and you'll have more sorrows with someone very close to you in the not so distant future. The Old Ones have told me this, and that's probably the most important thing I have to say to you."

I readjusted my goggles and watched the world suddenly glow as if in a warm fire. "Are you telling futures now, Virgil?"

He smiled as he stood and approached me. "I am. How do you like yours?"

"Couldn't you have just told me I was going to be rich someday?"

He considered it. "No. Now, do you have something you wish to tell me?"

I chewed on the inside of my lip. "Not just yet." I readjusted my hat. "And now, if you're through gazing into your crystal ball, how about we get going?"

He stared at me a few moments more with the smile still in place and then raised his arm, inviting me to take the lead. "I'll assist you for as long as the Old Ones tell me to." With the next statement, the smile faded a little but was still there. "Pax?"

I smiled back till I was sure my teeth were going to crack. "Pax."

Rather than follow the trail and face the drifts, Virgil decided that we would make better time crossing the frozen, wind-scrubbed flat of Lake Marion or Dead Horse, depending on your Maker.

After climbing over a few boulders, I removed my snowshoes and attached them to the pack. We stood at the precipice of the expanse, and I studied the ridge at Mistymoon that appeared and disappeared with the changing cloud currents. "We're also going to make some pretty majestic targets out there on the ice if somebody, and I mean Raynaud Shade, is aiming a laser sight at us from up on that ridge."

Virgil had draped the remnants of a wool trade blanket across his face for protection against the wind, and pulled it down with a forefinger to address me as he scanned the deadstand, beetle-killed trees. "No one there."

I stepped off onto the slick surface under the skim layer of snow that the wind had left as change. "Fine with me; you're a bigger target than I am."

He muffled a laugh as he re-covered his face with the red cloth and then wrapped one of the grizzly arms across it and over his shoulder with the panache of a high-fashion model. "Like a tin bear in a shooting gallery?"

Boy howdy.

After a couple of hundred yards I came to the conclusion that the surface was slicker than I'd thought, and the light layer of driven snow made ball bearings under my boots, causing me to slip and catch myself with each step. It was getting to be like a tightrope act, and I was about to turn and tell Virgil to forget about this route when I took a long split and rolled to my right, the weight of the pack and rifle forcing the side of my head to strike the ice with full force.

"Where are we going?"

"If I tell you, it won't be a surprise."

He watches as the almost-man drives the truck, newer than his grandfather's. The truck is loud and he watches the strange territory pass by the window, growing higher and more rocky—mountains unfamiliar to him.

There was a time when his grandfather took him to a place like this, telling him stories of the mighty warrior that had helped the Thunderbirds in their battle against the Water Monsters. He said the man had gone so far that he had forgotten who he was and from where he came. This will never happen to you because you will find the hard edges of the earth rounded by those who love you, he had said.

After many miles the boy begins to cry, softly at first and then stronger.

"Shut up or I'll really give you something to cry about,"
the almost-man said.

I lay there for a few seconds and fought against the concussion, but my eyes refused to focus. I closed them for a moment and thought I could hear something in the ice as though the plates of frozen water were colliding underneath me, grinding like glaciers. I opened my eyes and watched the snow skim across the surface toward me and could feel the warmth of my face adhering its skin to the lake.

I peeled my face away and looked at the sky, half expecting Virgil to yank me back up to a standing position, but nothing happened.

I stared at the lower part of the clouds that raced overhead and could hear a thumping noise, loud and insistent. The noise was steady, but it wasn't coming from above—rather, from below. I could feel it in my back, through the expedition pack, as it set up a rhythm. It was a song in counterpoint, one that I'd heard before but was unable to identify.

The noise settled into my heartbeat and the pounding in my head. My legs moved okay, but when I pulled my hand away from my temple, there was blood. The pain was tremendous and once again reminded me of the headaches I'd had only a few months ago, before my eye operation. I stretched my jaw and probed the wound under my hat—more blood. "Well, hell . . ."

My hat fell off as I rolled onto the pack on my back and sat there looking for Virgil.

There was no one.

As far as I could see, there was no one on the ice of Lake Marion but me.

I immediately felt panic, disconnected the breast strap, and shrugged the pack and rifle from my shoulders. I wrestled myself to my feet, assuming that with Virgil's weight he had hit a soft spot in the ice and had broken through.

I kneeled, sweeping my arms across in an attempt to find the hole that must've been covered by the snow, but there wasn't anything. I scrambled my way back along my tracks but could see only the dull, opaque sheen of the flat surface with not so much as a crack.

My head was still killing me, but I couldn't stop jerking it from left to right in an attempt to find him. I took a deep breath and stood, turning three hundred and sixty degrees, but there was nothing except undisturbed lake. I walked in a spiraling circle emanating from where I'd fallen, fully expecting the giant Crow to be somewhere in my field of vision, either approaching or disappearing into the blowing snow, but he wasn't there and there were no prints.

I stretched my jaw again and blinked my eyes. "Virgil!"

"Virgil. Virgil . . ."

My voice ricocheted off the cliffs, and I swallowed and stood there for a moment more before noticing that my hat was skimming away on the surface of the lake. Carefully, I trudged across the smooth, hard surface and had just begun to lean over to grab it when a ripping gust carried it out toward the center until it lodged in a small drift a good twenty yards away toward the ridge. I sighed and thought about how I'd lost my last hat and how I damn well wasn't going to lose this one.

Figuring I'd not have to backtrack if I took the entire load with me, I gripped the strap of the pack and hoisted it, picked up the Sharps and examined it to see if I'd done any damage, but it appeared intact. I put the rifle on my shoulder and looked through the binoculars.

All I could see were the acres of beetle-kill pine that spilled over the ridge and down the valley toward me. I followed the trail to make sure Virgil hadn't gone ahead and then followed it behind to see if he'd retreated.

I lowered the binoculars and looked around just one more time, forcing his name from my lungs like a bullhorn. "Virgil!?"

Nothing.

I approached my hat and watched as it started to flip up again. I scrambled over and got ahold of the crown and tried to pull it up, but it stuck to the ice, probably from the warmth of my head.

I yanked at it this time, scattering the snow and revealing a freeze-dried, mummified hand.

I blinked hard to clear my head, thinking that it must've been a frozen branch, but it was still there when I opened my eyes. I knelt down and used my hat as a fan to scatter the snow that had built up around the thing.

There was a lot of skin left, with a few tendons, and the nails were purpled and black. The wrist was bent, the thumb contracted toward the palm, the forefinger extended and the other three digits slightly curved, almost as if that one finger were pointing up the trail.

I was sure this had to be the hunter that Virgil had mentioned in his story about the dead horse, though it seemed odd that the body of the man had drifted north, away from where the accident had occurred.

There was a ring on the one finger, so I thought I should retrieve it for identification purposes and reached down to carefully remove it, but when I did, the entire hand broke off in mine. Kneeling there holding it, the whole situation felt rather surreal, not to mention macabre, and I was beginning to think that I'd hit my head harder than I thought.

"Jesus . . ."

To make matters worse, my disturbing the hand had loosened the ring so that it was now sliding back and forth on the bony finger. More carefully this time, I placed the ring between my own thumb and forefinger and slid it off the end. It was silver with coral and turquoise wolves chasing each other around the band, and I couldn't help but feel that I'd seen it before. There was an inscription on the inside, but the print was far too fine and worn away for me to see what was engraved.

I dropped it in the breast pocket of my jacket and then looked at the hand in my hand.

It seemed somewhat disrespectful to just throw it into a snowbank and walk away; then there was the DNA that might give us the name of the poor, missing hunter in case the ring didn't narrow the field.

I stuffed the gruesome remains into a different outside pocket and figured since it was my lot in life to be the Bighorn Bone Collector, I might as well gather up all of them.

I tightened my hat onto my head and kicked off north toward the gully of trees that led up the creek that fed Lake Marion, which connected with the ridge. Maybe it was Virgil's sudden disappearance or maybe it was my growing collection, but I felt very alone and hoped I wasn't going to eventually add to the assembly.

12

It was a ragged forest decimated by the bark beetles—a standing forest of the dead. They say that if you're quiet and you listen, you can hear them chewing.

They're only about an eighth of an inch long, like a grain of rice, which is appropriate since they're indigenous to China, Mongolia, and Korea. Word is they hitched a ride over on truck pallets, crates, or some such—and so far they've eaten more than 1.5 million prime acres of our woodlands. The forest service figures that in a few years the bark beetles will have killed every mature lodgepole pine in Wyoming; by then the epidemic will be under control, because there won't be anything for the little monsters to eat.

The other thing that will kill them is an extended cold snap of subzero temperatures that lasts more than ten days. Now, I figured that this winter alone we'd already accomplished that many times over, but evidently some of the little buggers were frostproof.

The effects of beetle-kill on water flows, watersheds, timber production, wildlife habitat, recreation sites, transmission lines, and scenic views is already horrific, but the thing that's got everybody really nervous is that, if given half a chance, there will be a forest fire unlike anything ever seen—Smokey Bear's worst nightmare, a wildfire that would run from New Mexico to Colorado, through Wyoming, all the way into Montana.

When I saw those standing lifeless brown streaks of dead trees running through my forests, I always thought that I could hear the chewing, too.

But maybe that was just in my mind.

The northern tip of Lake Marion was fed by a healthy amount of water that also filled a couple of kidney-shaped ponds that had no names. The snow was deep in the gullies, but the wind had polished the banks, making the footing pretty good; with recent developments, footing was foremost of my priorities, so I took the shortcut that would help me gain ground on the party ahead. I could still see the ridge trail they followed—it wasn't as if I was going to cut them off, but I'd be gaining ground.

When I got a little higher, I turned and looked for Virgil in the valley below, but there was still no one there. What I could see was where we'd diverged from the path and started across the northern part of the lake from the peninsula. The odd thing was that there appeared to be only one set of tracks in the portions I could make out.

It was possible that the giant had been careful to walk in my prints, just to make sure the ice would hold him, but it seemed odd.

I shook my head, immediately regretted it, and slipped a hand up under my hat. The blood was congealing in my hair, and it was hard to make out the damage by fingers alone. The lump on the front of my head still hurt, but it was nothing in comparison to my newest wound. The pack straps were biting into my shoulders, and the muscles in my thighs were really starting to ache. Running for exercise is one thing, but carrying a pack at altitude on broken ground through snowdrifts on snowshoes is something altogether different.

I looked back up the rise. I could cut left and find the trail, but that would be where Shade would be expecting me, so I decided to take the more direct, if exhausting, route. I knew once I got to the glacial moraine at Mistymoon Lake there would be alpine meadows that trailed to either side, one leading toward Florence Lake, Solitude Trail, and the Hunter Corrals, which would be the only way out, and the other leading toward the dizzying heights of Cloud Peak and no exit.

The weight of the snow had felled a number of the trees leading up the slope; where the bark had sloughed away, I could see the crazy-quilt patterns that the beetle larvae had made in pursuit of the soft cambium underneath.

I was studying just such a log when I got to the second of the two pools and stepped onto the ice. When I put my full weight on the surface, there was a discernible crack, and the water rushed underneath complete with multicolored bubbles crowding against the underside; I eased back on my rear boot.

The larger of the ponds had been rock solid, but this, being the shallower of the two, didn't have the capacity to maintain a thickness. I decided to follow the right bank in an attempt to stay with the creek and give myself a little relief from climbing over logs.

The storm had let up, but the wisps of fog and intermittent snow were still driven by the wind, and visibility was still negligible. It felt like I was pushing up from under the clouds through half-shadows and hazy-looking stands of eaten-alive trees. I was starting to think that Mistymoon Lake had come by its name honestly when I got that sensation that I was being watched again.

I froze and felt it full force when I thought I saw something beside a stand of the dead trees up and to my left. Someone was there—a small, slim someone.

I scrambled to get my .45 out of my holster since it was the easiest weapon to get to, snapped off the safety, and held it ready as the vapor between us grew stiffer. I could've sworn that directly where I was pointing, someone laughed like a child.

The front sight of the .45 wavered a little with the exertion of holding my arm steady. I took a deep breath but kept the pistol pointed at the spot ahead. When the elongated streams of mist cleared a little, I glanced to my left and then my right, but there was nothing. The rows of monochromatic lifeless trees stretched away like bars on a universal and reminded me of something from my past, something important—the Old Cheyenne.

I lowered the Colt and reassessed. If I was getting to the point where people were appearing and disappearing in front of me, then perhaps I needed to holster my weapon and wait for some backup.

I thought there was some movement to my right, and I snapped the sights of the .45 on it and waited, but once again there was nothing. My heartbeat reminded me of the bubbles struggling against the underside of the ice, and I just stood there, finally lowering the semiautomatic pistol and laughing.

A second later, I heard a giggle to my right.

This time I didn't even raise the Colt—but I did laugh again.

He mimicked me in triplicate, and I leaned my head against a tree. You fool—you're aiming at your own shadow and attempting to shoot your echo.

I punched the safety, holstered my sidearm quickly, and tried to remember if I'd laughed first before hearing the echo— but I must have.

Must have.

I took a deep breath and looked around at the bursts of fog surging past the trees like the flow of a river. The effect pulled me forward, and I left a hand on the tree to steady myself. Maybe it was the altitude, maybe it was the exhaustion, or maybe it was cracking my head open on the ice, but I had to get a quick grip on things.

I met up with the creek feeding the small pond and started climbing the hill again. There was a large log lying over the area where the water spilled in under the ice, and I could gain some more yardage by stepping up and crossing over. I placed a hand on it and could feel its structural integrity.

It was massive, still sturdy, and unlikely to move. Scrambling onto the rooted end, using some of the larger limbs as a handrail, I stepped onto the log and started across. I kicked the snow off as I went, clearing a path so that I could see the wood and make sure I didn't slip.

It was a balancing act, and I felt like Errol Flynn in *The Adventures of Robin Hood*, but where was my Little John, let alone the rest of the Merry Men? I turned and looked at the drifting currents of fog erasing Lake Marion; no Virgil, nobody.

As I stood there, I noticed that the mist had turned from white to gray to black, which only reinforced the two-color landscape, and it took a while for me to realize that something was not specifically right about this.

Black fog.

Then there was the smell.

I tasted the tang of smoke in those glands at the front of my throat, and when I took another breath, I choked and my eyes underneath the goggles began to tear.

I swung around and almost lost my balance, especially when a cabinet-size sheath of bark fell off onto the ice. I caught myself, careful not to let the weight of the pack and the rifle pull me over the side, but what I saw on the ridge above me almost dumped me anyway.

It was a wall of fire with an inverted layer of smoke below and flames at a height of over two hundred feet above, arching down the hill with the forty-mile-an-hour gale-force winds.

The tops of the dead-standing trees were on fire, and I could see the ones along the ridge and the ones that surrounded it on both sides lean forward and start to collapse down the hill toward me.

It was a ground fire that had crowned, every firefighter's worst-case scenario, the one that the old hands used to say you'd fight by finding an ash pile, curling into a fetal position, and praying for hard rain.

I'd worked as a smoke jumper in Greybull in my youth with the advantage of being big for my age—ten feet tall and bulletproof. The largest fires I'd fought were a few class Ds in the sixties and then helping with the evacuation during the Yellowstone fires in the late eighties, but none of them had looked anything like this, and I'd never been anywhere near this close to any of them.

It was as if the immediate world was like some giant coliseum suddenly on fire.

I looked to my left. It was a good hundred yards to clearance—a death trap, with fallen trees and dry brush between here and there. I yanked my head to the right, but the forest was denser in that direction and I couldn't even see how far it was before I would be able to get into a clearing. Straight ahead was sure burning death, so the only avenue of escape was back down the hillside.

Some wildfires have been clocked at over six miles an hour, able to bridge gaps and jump rivers and fire blocks; this one, with the advantage of fuel in the dead treetops and plenty of oxygen from the ferocious wind, seemed alive and was leapfrogging, transforming from a crown fire to a whirl. The vortex of flame, preceded by the poisonous gases, superheated air, and reflected heat, would be on me in less than two minutes— well before that, it would cook my lungs.

I looked down the hill.

Never make it.

I looked back up the hill. The black fog had changed direction, pulling the oxygen from the arching wind that continued to blast its way down the valley, the fire using the ridge as a jumping-off point, not even backing up for a run at it. Lodgepole pines were exploding with the heat, and a crisscross of timber fell down the incline. The darkness lifted long enough to reveal massive logs exploding as the resin inside them reached boiling levels, branches, pine cones, and needles swirling in armies of winged fire devils.

The tower of flames reached out from the top of the forest

with a sound like a freight train, and the vacuum pulled at my chest, trying to topple me from the log where I stood as live ash struck at me from the dead trees. I stood in a spot where flammable material, oxygen, and a temperature above the point of ignition would spontaneously combust and essentially detonate.

I twisted my hat down tight on my head; in the next few seconds, I could die, still erect in a state of astonishment, or I could tuck in my arms and legs and . . . I clutched the binoculars to my chest and stepped off the log.

The expedition pack on my back absorbed the majority of the shock just as I'd hoped it would. I'd thought of leaving the rifle on the bank, but it would've been nothing but a smoking husk of charred wood and burnt metal if I ever got back to it, so it went into the drink with me as well.

I'd felt water this frigid just over a year ago when I fell through the ice in Clear Creek Reservoir, but I didn't remember the chest-seizing cold that struck me like a ball bat and forced the air from my lungs; all I could think was that I was going to need that air in a matter of moments.

I felt the pack hit bottom and estimated that the pond must've been only about four feet deep, hopefully enough to insulate me from the coming hell above. I stood and fully inhaled.

The steam vapor rising from the expanse of ice made the entire pond look as if it were being whipped away up the hill and lifted into the pitch-colored sky. The noise was deafening, and as I looked back at the log that I had been crossing, I could see the smoke beginning to pour off the thing.

I unsnapped the pack, shifted it around and over me, and

heaved myself backward into a cleft of rocks where the water spilled into the pond, any sort of shelter being an advantage.

Generally, except for the very heart of the inferno, there would be a stratum of oxygen up to about fifteen inches from the ground. I didn't know how the water would affect this pocket, but my hopes were that the vapor would provide added insulation without parboiling my lungs.

I forced a massive amount of air into my chest, hoped there was enough there to suffice, and plunged into the water again.

The fire's heart struck it like a cannonball, and I could feel my ears deaden with the brunt of the blow. Tiny explosions of blue, white, orange, and finally red covered the surface, and it was only when I noticed the temperature of the water rising that I realized it was attempting to boil.

I was sure I was in the belly of the beast now. Those fire devils were circling above, hunting for me, hoping to turn me into a hairless, bloated, purpled, and slick-skinned corpse—a collection of blackened bones wearing nothing but a charred leather service belt with all my extra ammunition exploded.

As I buried my face into the pack and slunk deeper into the crevasse, I thought about the phones in my pockets and all the calls I should have made to all the women in my life. I thought about Cady, about her wedding and what she was going to look like standing in the golden grasses of the Little Big Horn country in July. I thought about my wife, how long she'd been gone, and how she wouldn't forgive me for not being there to represent us at our daughter's wedding. I thought about Ruby, who would want to know exactly where I'd died. I thought about Vic, who would likely pound her fists on the chest of my corpse for being such a dumb ass.

I couldn't die—I had too many women who would kill me.

The log I had been standing on exploded like a pipe bomb, the resin inside finally reaching the temperature of napalm, the dead husk no longer able to contain its fury. The force of the eruption hit the pond like a depth charge, the pressure making it feel as if my mouth, nose, ears, and eyes were being pressed back in my head, I stifled the scream that would kill me; instead, I crammed my face against the backpack and just lay there, crushing it against me.

The panic from lack of oxygen was yanking at my chest, trying to get me to the surface, but I held on with my face pressed against the Cordura fabric for what felt like another eight hours but was likely twenty seconds. I felt the involuntary heave of my diaphragm and knew that I had to get to the surface before the next one.

I disengaged from the pack and turned my head; the roar of the freight train was distant now, but I wasn't sure if it was because my eardrums were partially, if not totally, shot, or if the fire was receding. My eyes were still working, however, and I could see that red had subsided to amber.

I figured I had about five seconds before I pulled in two solid lungs of pond water. I carefully listed to the side and raised my face slowly to the surface, barely allowing my nose and lips to break the tension where air and water met.

As horrifying as it was, it was magnificent. About a foot and a half above me, the air was burning like some gargantuan convection oven, jets of undulating flame coating the air and water vapor steaming from the surface of the pond. I was actually fortunate in that the water's temperature had started at just above freezing, which was keeping me from being boiled alive.

I coughed uncontrollably and inhaled. The air was super-heated, just as I'd expected, but it was air and breathable. I could feel my face beginning to burn, especially my eyes, so I closed them, hurriedly filled my lungs, and sank back into the warm and insulating water.

I lay there, thinking that if I could just hold on for another couple of minutes, the majority of the fire's front would've passed and I could reemerge relatively unscathed—well, as long as a flaming tree didn't fall on me.

I wasn't taking anything for granted.

The reflections on the water continued to change from red to orange, finally fading to yellow. My air was running out again, and I was pretty sure that that last gulp had held a lot less oxygen. It seemed by the color refracted that the fire had receded to the banks. I really didn't have much choice and carefully raised my head again.

The ceiling of flame was gone. There was a thick layer of ash on the surface of the pond, which I wiped away with the back of one of my gloves, and sleeper fires were still burning along the banks of the pond.

I rose up to my full height, the ash water rolling off me as I stood, leaving me cloaked with a grayish-black soot.

It was like hell on earth.

There was not a tree standing in the gulch leading toward the ridge, only blackened husks in the forest where I had stood only five minutes ago. The flat plains of scree and boulders steamed from the heat, and the pond had dropped about a foot since I'd entered it, the exploded tree trunk sunk into the black water from both ends.

I could hear nothing, not because there was no sound, but

because I was stone deaf from the compression of the exploding log. I stretched my jaw again and felt a popping in my ears and a ringing, muted like an alarm clock under a pillow, with a dull thrum as accompaniment. I could feel the air going in and out of my lungs, but I could swear that there was no sound.

I turned my head and looked down the mountain where the fire had burned itself into the draw at the shore of Lake Marion. The valley was protected from the wind, and there was a larger snow load on the trees there that had smothered the flames so only a red and orange edge showed fire.

With my hand still holding the strap of both the pack and the rifle, I pivoted to my left and looked up the hill. There was some movement to my right, and I watched as a charred elk stumbled forward down the incline toward the edge of the pond, his blind eyes dead in the sockets but his nose drawing him to water.

I stood silently as the elk came closer, hobbling on hooves that had burned away. He bumped into a scorched tree, momentarily catching one of the points of his antlers, then yanked free and continued more carefully.

His body was telling him that he needed to drink; his body was telling him that if he could only go a little further it was possible that he might make it. His body, of course, was lying.

I wondered how many lies my body was telling me—maybe my hearing was gone for a reason. Perhaps my body didn't wish to be the one to break the news to itself about things I shouldn't hear.

Hairless and black, he lowered his blistered nose to the soot-covered surface. The great rack on his head bobbed as his lips pulled in the water with a shudder from his midriff. I was amazed that he could stand, let alone drink.

I stood there with him until his legs collapsed and, with a shiver and one brief exhale, he died. I waded out to him and placed a hand on his magnificent antlers as I paused and returned my eyes to the ridge, the dead silence crowding in on me and hardening like my clothes.

The animal's horn still looked alive with the glow of the many fights the majestic old beast had won. Every rutting season he would've taken on all comers: younger elk, bears, cougars, wolves, and the human hunters that would've followed him to the very heights of the Bighorn range.

He had survived them all, only to end like this.

I could feel the air around me cooling, and the water that had protected me was solidifying underneath, in, and on top of my clothes; it was like I was wearing one of Dante's lead cloaks. The ridge was naked, with just a stubble field of nubbin trees and scalded earth. The only thing I'd ever seen that approached it was a war zone, but somehow, in so many ways, this was worse.

I thought about all the recently lost lives, of all the current destruction, and could feel a stirring deep in a place where my ears wouldn't have heard it harden even if they'd still worked. The ringing continued, bells of warning along with the continuing tattoo of distant drums, but the one sound that rustled over the others was the sound of the blackened, leathery wings of wrathful vengeance folding themselves around me.

13

Icicles fell off me with each step, but I could only imagine the delicate sounds they might have made when they struck the stones near my feet. After only a few minutes, it was getting impossible to move, so I stopped by one of the flaming logs, at least partially sure that the resin in it wouldn't explode.

I set the pack against the outcropping of rocks just a little away from the flames. The sodden thing felt like a boulder with shoulder straps, and I was glad to be rid of it. I pulled off my gloves, turned the cuffs inside out, and placed them along with my goggles on one of the already-burnt sections of the log.

I held the rifle up and looked at the drop-block mechanism, which appeared fine until I jacked the lever, slid down the action and, after catching the round that feebly fell from the breech, could see the traces of ice inside the chamber.

I slipped the bullet into my pocket and breathed into the Sharps as if I were giving it mouth-to-rifle resuscitation. I turned it around and did the same thing to the end of the barrel—amazingly enough, it appeared unharmed. I checked for any signs of mud, but there was nothing. I set it by the pack and hoped the heat of the fire would override the ambient

temperature. Then I glanced through the binoculars still hanging from my neck and found that they too were unharmed,
but I hung them from a blackened branch just to make sure.

I took off my hat, hung it on another convenient branch,
and reached into my jacket to retrieve the mummified hand.
The pocket was empty. I turned it inside out, but there was
nothing there, not even the ring that I'd taken. I must've lost
both in the nameless pond below. Remembering the femur
that Shade had left behind, I quickly checked my other pocket
and was relieved to find that bone still there.

I felt my teeth rattling and turned, moving a little closer
to the flames. I could feel an ulcerous sore at the top of my ear
where it had gotten frostbitten before—chilblains, I believe
they were called—and gently fingered it, just the thing you're
not supposed to do.

The convulsions continued, and I was pretty sure that if
I didn't get my clothes and myself warmed up I was going to
become hypothermic, delusional, and useless.

I shed my stiff-armed jacket and placed it beside the log
flambé, where it literally stood on its own in a three-point
stance, and then slid off my boots, the overpants, and the
fleece that Omar had loaned me, hanging them on another
blackened branch.

Dressed only in my Capilene underwear, I backed up near
the log to dry off and keep warm, squinted through the blowing ash, took a deep breath, and coughed the soot from my
mouth and nose; the faintest touches of what felt like rain-
drops struck my upturned face—the falling snow was melting
in the heat.

I rubbed my eyes with my fists and looked around. The

cold and snow were already creeping back in, and it wouldn't be long before all the charred black would be covered with white—and me too.

I dragged the backpack over, flipped off the top, and started pulling items from the cavernous main compartment. There were an extra pair of socks that I strung on a limb and some food   the energy and candy bars looked pretty good in their foil wrappers—and the bottle of Pappy Van Winkle's Family Reserve that Virgil hadn't taken after all was unbroken.

That, among so many things, was odd.

You're not supposed to drink under these types of conditions because the only thing the liquor does is dehydrate you and widen your blood vessels, allowing greater blood flow to your extremities, which may feel better in the short run but which eventually robs you of core heat. I knew a lot of old fellows who had survived these kinds of circumstances and wasn't sure if I'd ever seen them *not* drink. Anyway, I was more concerned with my mental well-being.

I unscrewed the top and took a swig of the bourbon and waited as I always did for the aftertaste that never came because the first taste was so good. I took another and carefully set the bottle on the rocks before digging into the pack and yanking out the soaked sleeping bag that had already hardened into a clump. I pulled the bag from the stuff sack—it hung there in my hand like a reluctant snake, refusing to uncoil. I shook it, and surprisingly, the man-made, water-resistant fiber released and the length of the thing flopped to my feet.

I carefully unzipped it and noticed that the majority of the water hadn't soaked the fiber inside the bag, so I wrapped it around me and felt better immediately. I wrested my way into the outside pocket of the pack and came upon Saizarbitoria's copy of the *Inferno*. I resisted the urge to throw it in the fire and just dropped the soggy pulp onto the ground.

Seeing the Basquo's reading material reminded me of the cell phone that Sancho had carefully put in the waterproof Ziploc. I fetched it from my jacket and hoped that the bag was truly what it advertised. Then I pulled out the satellite phone and looked at it. I could see that the rubberized coating seemed to have no seams; was it possible that the thing was water-proof as well?

I hit the button, and it lit up. Thank goodness for the high-tech FBI.

I stood there for a moment or two, finally deciding to give my Indian backup a call; I was one of the only white men I knew who felt better when he was surrounded by Indians.

"Hey, hey—you're alive!"

Joe's voice cheered me even though I could hardly hear it.

"Just barely."

"We got another one of your leftovers."

"You're going to have to speak louder; my hearing is kind of shot." I smiled in spite of myself. "You guys are at the Thio-kol?"

He was shouting into the phone now. "You betcha, just collecting the trash. Hold on, the big guy wants to talk to you . . ."

I waited as a familiar voice came on the line; he was shout-ing, too. "Where are you?"

I sighed. "I've been asked that a lot lately." I felt the jacket and turned it—it was drying nicely. "Near the ridge at Misty-moon Lake."

"You . . ." There was a flare of static. ". . . traveling fast."

"I had help up until Shade set the whole forest on fire."

The concern in his voice increased after another static burst. "We could smell that. What did he do?"

I looked up the hillside but couldn't see anything except the rushing clouds above and the soft rain of the melting snow. "He must've set the beetle kill on fire; the wind took it and burned all the way down to Lake Marion." I fought to not let him hear my teeth chattering. "I had to go for a little swim to get out of it."

There was more static, probably from atmospheric conditions. "You are kidding."

"Nope; I'm drying my clothes right now."

"You mentioned help?"

I smiled. "Yep, one of our old buddies is up here—Virgil White Buffalo." I waited for a response, but there was none. "Are you there?"

Static. "Virgil."

"Yep, he keeps popping up."

More static, stronger than the signal this time. ". . . more to the story than you know . . ."

I thought about it. "That wouldn't take much, considering how little I do know."

The static was so strong now that I could barely hear him. ". . . need to stay where you are. We are only two and a half miles . . ."

I held the phone out where I could speak directly into it. "If you can hear me, I'm going to keep the pressure on Shade." I could barely make out his voice in response. "I'll call you back when I make the ridge at Solitude Trail."

★　★　★

I didn't move for a while, just stared at the flame on the log and watched the infinite swoops and swirls of its dance. I found myself half hypnotized by the life-giving warmth, and it seemed like I'd forgotten how long I'd been standing there. Another wave of shivers came over me, though, and I reached for the bourbon.

It was gone.

I looked to see that I hadn't knocked it over in a shivering fit and then looked down at my feet, sure it must've been lying on the ground, but there was nothing there. I was just about to utter a curse about disappearing rings, bourbon, and Indians when two out of the three reappeared.

He didn't look any worse for wear, neither burnt nor marked by the fire, as he rested his lance against the rocks.

"Where the hell have you been?"

The giant smiled in the shadow of the grizzly headdress. "What do you mean?"

"I mean where did you disappear to? One minute I was standing down there on the lake with you, and the next minute I was alone." I shook my head and couldn't help but smile. "Hey . . . I can hear you really well."

He looked at me with questions playing across his face along with the reflections of the fire. He took a swig of the bourbon and studied me. "I went up to the west ridge following the trail after you fell. I told you what I was doing. You don't remember?"

"No." I picked up my hat to feel if it was dry, and when half of it wasn't, I hung it back on the branch the other way. "Virgil, what are you talking about?"

His eyes narrowed, and he looked at me uncertainly. "After you fell, you were a little disoriented, so I told you to stay put and I would come back for you."

I felt my head; it wasn't as tender and also wasn't bleeding anymore—the pond water must have washed the cut. "You did?"

He studied me, even going so far as to tilt his head to get a good look at the side of mine, the bear jawbones, beads, and elk teeth gently clacking together in counterpoint to the tinkling bell cones. "I was very clear. You should have stayed on the ice where you would've been safe." He lifted the bottle to his lips and took another tremendous draught, then lowered it but didn't offer to give it back. "Maybe you hit your head harder than we thought."

"Maybe so." I shivered again. "Gimme the bottle."

"Not until you have really warmed up."

"I have really warmed up." We stood there, staring at each other, and I clutched the sleeping bag a little closer.

"Turn around and cook your front; that's the part that needs it."

I did as he said and moved in a little closer to the flames at the branch end of the log. He glanced around at the wreckage. "Hell of a fire he set."

I nodded at the giant. "You saw him light it?"

"I did. He made a bomb out of one of those backpack stoves."

I studied him and noticed that not even the moccasins he wore carried any black on them. "How did you avoid it?"

"I told you. I took the trail to our far left. You sat down on the ice of the lake and wouldn't move." I turned my head a little in the folds of the sleeping bag, and he extended a hand that blossomed fingers like a gigantic sunflower. "You don't remember."

"No."

"That isn't good." He made the statement flatly and without judgment, which made it sting that much more.

I reached up and felt my ear again, then held the palm of my hand against it in an attempt to warm it back to normal. "No." I sniffed the air, and the smell of wood fire came off his moosehide war shirt, a scent stronger than the fire in front of us.

Virgil White Buffalo looked down at me and placed an all-encompassing hand on my shoulder; I was sure it was more for my benefit than his. "Maybe you've gone as far as you can go, Lawman. Maybe you should wait here for the others, and I'll go ahead."

I looked back at the fire. "No."

"There's no dishonor in this. You've done everything that you could; everything that could reasonably be expected—of any living man."

"No."

He took a deep breath, and the flames wavered in his direction. "Then perhaps you should tell me why going after this man is so important to you."

I paused. "It's my job."

He watched me. "No, I think it's something more than that."

He removed his hand from my shoulder and waited, and it was that continental-drift pace, Indian wait, an otherworldly motionlessness that only the best hunters have. I turned my head all the way and looked at him, and even in the wind it was as if the feathers and the bear fur that surrounded him didn't stir a single hair. I was afraid that my faculties had gone again.

"Virgil?" I was relieved to hear my own voice.

"Yes."

When he spoke, the spell was broken and everything about him came to life again. I stretched my hands out to the flames and tried to concentrate on what had to be done. "Nothing."

He nodded as if he knew what I was going to ask, and his head dropped. With happy surprise, he stared at the paperback lying beside my boots. "You're not reading anymore?"

I nudged the book with my toe and was a little concerned that I couldn't feel much of my foot. "It's kind of ruined."

He stooped and picked it up by the binding—it opened to a random page. He flipped the bloated book over and read from the English side of one of the curled pages.

> "They all wore robes with hoods hung low, that hid
> their eyes, tailored—in cut—to match those worn
> by monks who thrive in Benedictine Cluny.
>   So gilded outwardly, they dazed the eye.
> Within, these robes were all of lead—so heavy . . ."

He lowered the pulpy mass and looked at it from the cavernous depths of the grizzly cape. "Leaden cloaks; he is on to something there."

I reached over and plucked my steaming pants from the limb.

"Life is like that." He flipped through a few more limp pages. "You collect things as you go—the things you think are important—and soon they weigh you down until you realize that these things you cared so much about mean nothing at all. Our natures are our natures." He grunted. "And they are all we are left with."

I dropped the sleeping bag—my underwear was reasonably dry—and struggled to get the damn pants on. Without the gloves, my hands were stiff and cold. "You think?"

The bass rumbled in his chest, but his eyes stayed on the paperback. "I think." He raised his head, but this time his black eyes stayed with the fire. "All the horrors in this book are the horrors of the mind, and they are the only ones that can truly harm us." He reached behind him and culled the bottle of bourbon from the rocks, then turned and poured the remainder of the liquor onto the log near the flames where the fire, now blue in tint, leapt forward and strung its way down the charred bark. "I think that's enough old damnation for now." He gestured with the book in his other hand. "Do you mind if I keep it?"

I hastily retrieved my gloves as he tossed the bottle onto the other side of the log. "You're not supposed to litter; don't you remember the commercials with the crying Indian?" He ignored me till I gestured toward the *Inferno*. "I thought this kind of literature didn't suit your tastes?"

He shrugged. "One can be too picky—books are hard to come by this high." He stuffed the blown-out, spine-split paperback inside his shirt. "Almost as hard as shelves."

I tried not to laugh. "I bet." I took the fleece from its drying rack and put it on, picked up my jacket and stuffed my arms into the sleeves, and deposited my assortment of phones. The jacket had thawed and was even warm, but I flapped my arms around in an attempt to gain a little mobility anyway, then reached down and fumbled with the zipper.

When I looked up again, Virgil was still watching me. Patiently, he stepped forward and zipped the jacket, and I felt like I was being dressed for school.

His voice echoed as it resounded through me, and once again his words were the last thing I could hear. "Leaden cloaks."

The forest is never silent, no matter the season; there are always sounds, and the trick is simply slowing yourself to the point where you can hear them. My situation was different, though. I can't explain it, but it was almost as if I was laboring under a selective deafness; I couldn't hear the wind or the sound of my own footfalls, but I could hear voices—at least I had been able to hear Joe's, Henry's, and now Virgil's.

"My grandfather told me the story of how, before I was born, his mother, my great-grandmother, died. Our village was on the Little Big Horn. He said that one day when he was very young the sun was very hot and the lodge skins were propped open so that any breeze might pass through, but even these winds were hot."

I tried to concentrate on his words and glean the warmth from them as I stumbled forward through the deepening snow.

"A large party of my people was moving camp into the mountains, and my great-grandfather told my great-grandmother to water his horse while they were gone. My great-grandmother forgot this until the afternoon when she went to the horse that had been staked out near the lodge, but when she approached, he was startled and pulled the stake from the ground and ran away toward the pony-band."

I stumbled but caught my footing and continued on after the giant.

"My great-grandmother ran after the horse, but she tripped and fell. When she got up, there was a man there with the horse's lead, and he handed it to her. She took the rope, but when she did, she saw that it was not one man, but two. She thanked them and then watered my great-grandfather's horse and returned to the lodge."

His strides were longer than mine and, even with him carrying the pack, I was having trouble keeping up. My mind was wandering, but I kept being brought back to the trail by his voice.

"When they returned, my grandfather said she told them that she would be going to the Beyond-Country, that two of her sons, my grandfather's two brothers who had died in the wars, had come to take her there."

Virgil stopped at the top of the ridge, and I ran into him, knocking my hat over my face. When I pulled it away, he had turned and was looking down at the half-filled tracks that led west around Mistymoon, across the meadow and into the freezing fog.

"They wrapped my great-grandmother in a buffalo robe, and she went away in her sleep. I tell you these things even though we Crows are forbidden to speak of the dead—you know this?"

I was breathing hard, trying to catch what was left of my breath. "I've heard it said."

He nodded and knelt down to give closer inspection to the tracks, even going so far as to blow in them to clear away the drifting snow, his breath like a bellows. "The experiences you had before, the one on the mountain that you have chosen not to share with me—have you told anyone else about them?"

I knelt down with him, curling my arms around my knees. "No, not really. I discussed it briefly with Henry, but that's all."

His eyes rose after the grizzly's as he looked north and west into the strands of mist. "The ones you call the Old Chey-enne."

I shivered and not just because of the cold. "Yep."

"They are not only Cheyenne."

I looked through the binoculars, tracing the edge of the cornice with the power of the Zeiss lenses; the tracks contin-ued across a sloping meadow and around the overhang to our left. "Where does he think he's going?"

His shoulders rose. "Up."

The satellite phone had no clock feature that I could find, and I was afraid to see what the water might've done to my pocket watch, so I glanced west to try to figure out the time; there was a vague glow within the clouds. "Late in the after-noon—they're going to have to settle down for the night somewhere."

"Yes." He stood and stared down at me. "What did the Cheyenne say?"

I glanced up at him. "What?"

"The Cheyenne, Henry, what did he say about the Old Ones?"

I tried to realign my thoughts, but my mind remained off topic. "The Cheyenne, Henry, said . . ." I forced myself to con-centrate. "He said that he wasn't singing."

"Singing?"

I stood and was a little uneasy, feeling confused and angry. "When I carried Henry and this kid off the mountain, I was dehydrated, hypothermic, concussed . . ."

"Like now?"

I bit my lip but could hardly feel it, remembered the balaclava and pulled it up over my nose. "Worse; a lot worse."

He laughed. "Well, the evening is young."

I was fully annoyed now. "I thought I heard singing, and when I finally . . . when I got him back to the trailhead and the emergency people, the EMTs . . . I asked him if he thought—if singing with the kinds of injuries that he'd sustained was a good idea."

The giant grunted and repositioned the base of his lance. "What did he say?"

I forced the next part out with my breath. "He said *what singing?*"

"Hmm."

I stepped around him and looked up at his chin. "Hey, Virgil?"

It took a while, but he finally looked down at me and it seemed like I'd gotten the attention of Mount Rushmore. "Yes?"

"To be honest, I don't care about any of that stuff right now. I've got two innocent people who are being led off to God-only-knows-where by a schizophrenic sociopath and no backup besides a seven-foot Indian who wants to stand here and discuss paranormal phenomena." I breathed deeply after my little tirade, watching the clouds of vapor fly from my face and thinking about what exactly I was going to do if Virgil, my only volunteer, dropped my pack in front of me and went back to the comforts of his cozy cave.

He didn't say anything for a moment but then smiled. "Just curious." The indentation in his forehead deepened as he turned a little toward me. "Would you be upset if we continued the conversation while we walked?"

Now I was feeling stupid, and my head was starting to pound again. "Of course not; I just want to focus on what's important."

He smiled some more, then turned and continued over the top of the tracks on a course of north by northwest, his words tossed over his shoulder. "Me too."

I was feeling bad about my little outburst. "I'm sorry, Virgil."

The snout of the bear cloak swung around, but I still couldn't see his face. "It's all right; I suppose I have become talkative in my isolation."

"Self-imposed isolation. You know there are no charges against you. You're a free man and can go wherever you'd like."

I suppose it was the sheer bulk of the man and the deepness of his voice, but even though he was a good two paces ahead on the trail, his voice sounded as close as if he were talking into my ear, the sore one. "Where would I go, back to the VA hospital?"

I wanted to be sure that Virgil understood that there were no official reasons prohibiting his return to civilization. "Back to the Rez? I don't know . . . You've got a son who lives over in Hot Springs."

"He wouldn't want me there, and I have none of my people left on the reservation."

"Last of your kind?"

"Yes, in a way. Something like you."

I shook my head. "I've got a daughter in Philadelphia."

"A daughter, yes. When she has her daughter, she will not carry your name."

I laughed at the ridiculousness of our conversation as we were slogging our way toward the crown of the Bighorn Mountains.

"She is to be married this summer and when she has the daughter she now carries, that daughter, your granddaughter, will carry another man's name."

I stopped, but he kept walking.

His voice drifted back as the fog slithered over the meadow and surrounded us. "C'mon, Lawman, we don't have time for all this talk—we have innocent people to save, remember?"

"Virgil, have you been talking to Henry? I mean, did he . . ."

"I have not spoken with the Cheyenne—they are a handsome people, but they are difficult." We reached the cornice, and he floated into the mist, only his voice remaining. "I don't know how I know these things; perhaps they're told to me by the Old Ones, but I know in my heart of hearts that your daughter will bear a daughter."

He reappeared next to a rock shelf and placed the pack on the ground between us. "Do you want a candy bar?" He unsnapped the top and sorted through a few items, finally bringing out two of the aged Mallo Cups. "I want a candy bar, and these are my favorites."

He handed me one, took one for himself, closed up the pack, and threw it back on one shoulder as if the burden were a windbreaker. "I had a grandson once and a daughter. I had a beautiful wife. Family is important, don't you think? I mean, they can make you crazy, but they're very important."

He knew he had a grandson? How did he know about Owen? Was it something that his son had told him while he was in my jail? I brushed a hand up to the pocket of my coat and could feel the bone there.

He was watching me, and I knew he had noticed my hand, but then he turned and started off. "C'mon." He chortled. "Innocent people."

I climbed over the top of the cornice and followed the hulking mass of him swaying with the effort of battling the headwind. "You know that story I told you about my great-grandmother, the one about her meeting her two sons, the brothers of my grandfather?" He mumbled, and I assumed he was eating his Mallo Cup. "I saw her the other day."

I paused before responding this time. "Your great-grand-mother?"

I could see him gesturing. "Yes, she was a strong woman, built like my father."

"Your dead great-grandmother?"

"Yes, but do not refer to her in that way—it's disrespect-ful." I started to stuff the Mallo Cup into my coat, but he spoke without turning. "You should eat that."

I looked up at him and then back at the candy bar. It was easier to eat than to argue, so I unwrapped it and fumbled part of it into my mouth—it broke off like balsa wood in the cold.

He continued along the winding rock outcroppings as I concentrated on his words and his footsteps. I wondered how he was able to keep his feet warm with only the moccasins to protect them—he didn't seem to mind the cold at all.

"I was near water, or in water, I can't remember. I was small, young. I turned and she was there, holding her hands out to me. I never met her, but I knew it was her. You know how you know these things?"

"Yes. I do."

He finished his candy bar and stuffed the wrapper in his pocket. "I told her that I couldn't go with her; that I had things I still had to do. She said that she knew of these things so she left me there." He stopped and knelt down again, the fog and falling snow so thick that I felt like I was watching him on my old television at home, the one that didn't get any reception. "Do you think that means I'm meant to follow the Hanging Road to the Beyond-Country with the Old Ones?"

I drew up beside him with the thought that the Hanging Road was the Crow path to the other side and referred to the horizon-to-horizon bow of the Milky Way in the nighttime sky. "I sure hope not."

His wide hand lifted and a finger pointed down the hill into the whiteness. "They have left the trail and are now going across Paint Rock Creek."

"Then what?"

His breath condensed, and it was as if Virgil was exhaling clouds. The twin heads rose, and I knew he was looking at the top of the Bighorn Mountains.

"Up."

14

Whiteout.

Not only did it sound as if I were hearing through cotton, now it looked like it, too.

The falling snow had increased to the point where we were now in a true whiteout—not the two to three inches an hour sometimes mistaken for a whiteout, but the honest-to-goodness, mountain-effect, windless blizzard where you couldn't differentiate between the air and the ground. Visibility was cut to less than twenty feet, and the only thing that kept us going was Virgil throwing his war lance ahead and then the two of us following.

He'd made me stop and put on my snowshoes again, but he still seemed to be punching through the drifts faster than I could walk over them.

I knew it was a quarter of a mile from Solitude Trail across the creek and through the meadows to the falls and the ascent inclines that led up the west ridge of Cloud Peak. As near as I could tell, even though it felt as if I were still falling forward, we were on the flat and approaching the first climb.

Virgil tossed the lance ahead of us, and I watched as the feathers and deer toes spiraled with its trajectory. We walked after it, and he trailed a hand down and picked up the lance again.

"We used to use snowballs when I was growing up out on the Powder River. Everyone in this country has lost someone to these kinds of conditions."

He stood and inclined his head upward toward the cliffs and ridgeline I couldn't see. "Why do you suppose my great-grandmother was the one they sent to fetch me from this life?"

I should've guessed; it seemed that all he wanted to talk about was his theoretical impending death, but I was amazed at his ability to distract himself from the exhaustion that was continually causing my chin to stab my chest. I sighed. "I don't know, Virgil."

"You would think that they would've sent someone I knew—someone I'd met."

He turned and looked straight at me. "Which leads me to believe that she was not really the one sent to take me to the Beyond-Country." He shook his two heads. "What is it the Cheyenne calls it?"

"Calls what?"

"The afterworld."

"Henry and a friend of his, Lonnie Little Bird . . . they call it the Camp of the Dead."

"Yes, that's it." He gestured with the lance. "We can climb beside the falls—there."

I looked up but could see only vague shadows through the amber lenses of my goggles. I began thinking that perhaps they were more of a hindrance than an asset, so I lowered them and was immediately blinded. I yanked them back in place. "Whatever you say, Virgil. I learned a long time ago that you don't argue with the Indian scout."

He nodded. "It gives me hope."

I blinked, aware that I was becoming more and more confused. "What?"

"That it was my great-grandmother who came for me. When they're serious, I imagine that they'll send someone I know." His head was very close to mine as he hunkered down to stare into my face, and it was as if he was blocking out the rest of the world. "I've thought about this, and I think they should send my wife. Don't you think that's a good choice?" I could smell the Mallo Cup on his breath and maybe even a little of the bourbon he'd poured onto the flaming log. "You don't look so good, Lawman. White—whiter than usual."

I laughed and converted the next series of teeth-chattering shivers into a nod. "I'm cold and kind of tired, but I'm all right."

He bent down and unstrapped my snowshoes. "You won't need these for this part, but you'll need them farther up." I stepped off them like a dutiful child, and Virgil drove the butt ends into the snow next to the trail; it looked as if someone had been buried there head first. "This will help the Cheyenne and the Arapaho find you."

"I thought you said I was going to need them."

He turned his great bulk toward the rocks. "We will get you another pair."

"How?"

He ignored me, and I gestured toward the granite escarpment with my chin. "Up?"

He brushed away some of the snow to reveal a good foot- and handhold at his shoulder level—it must have been where the others had gone. "Up."

Even with the expedition pack on his back, he had no

trouble and disappeared into what the old-timers called a buttermilk sky. I made the mental note to remember where he placed his hands and moccasins, aware that in my depleted condition, his judgment was better than my own. After the first shelf there was a gully, which made for easier climbing, and I just used the giant's prints as footholds.

A few times I could see the cairns jutting from the snow that pointed out the classic route to Cloud Peak, and we followed them when they were visible, taking the lesser drainage along the base of the southwest ridge. The climb became real and more strenuous as we got to the northeast ridge and continued east and up, ever up.

I stopped by one of the rock pillars to take a breather. Virgil continued on, first blending into the falling snow and then disappearing. "Virgil."

There was no response.

"Virgil!"

I was just beginning to think that my hearing was going again when his voice drifted back from above. "Who would you want to see? If someone were to show up to guide you to the Beyond-Country, who would you choose?"

I shifted my weight; luckily the dry-stacked stones stayed solid, probably frozen together. "I don't know. I'm not sure."

"You should be, Lawman."

We fell into a steady, silent rhythm and arrived at the first scree field where there was a large overhang looking like the capsized hull of a ship.

There was a bit of light that just penetrated the veil of

low-flying clouds and I thought that maybe those last horizon-tal rays of the sun were defining the highest portions of Cloud Peak and Blacktooth and Bomber mountains even though we couldn't see them. I thought about the rays' warmth, how it felt when they left the sky and you forced yourself fur-ther into your sleeping bag. I was thinking about all of these things as we traversed the ridge and followed the trail that led toward the vast boulder field that rose above us like the fallen city of Dis.

As near as I could tell from the voice that echoed back to me from the cirque, Virgil was reading from the *Inferno*, the words sometimes drifting back to me through the storm.

> *"In that still baby-boyish time of the year,*
> *when sunlight chills its curls beneath Aquarius,*
> *when nights grow shorter equalling the day,*
> *   and hoar frost writes fair copies on the ground*
> *to mimic in design its snowy sister . . ."*

Virgil's voice lulled me into a stupor, and I found myself trudging along allowing the cold and snow to envelop me like cotton ticking. I was asleep on my feet, and the boy's dreams once again became my own.

The almost-man stops the truck near an old wagon with a rounded top alongside a creek bed, high in the mountains. He flings the door open and yanks the boy out by his arm.

Skidding in the gravel as he falls, the boy looks around but there is no one else there. He stays without moving, judging the distance between them and thinking of what he should do, but his mind is like an empty sack—the only thing he can think of is a joke another boy told him on the playground. What is it when an Indian kills another Indian? Natural selection.

He had made up his mind to not give him the satisfaction of his tears; instead, he will be a warrior—what is the worst this almost-man can do to him?

I ran into Virgil's back again.

I straightened my hat and, coming back from walking sleep, fumbled for my words. "Why'd you stop?"

We were in the shelter of a large crevasse, the blowing snow having arched a bridge over us, providing sanctuary in a false cave. "Someone is up ahead."

In both a physical and metaphorical sense, I froze in my tracks. I tried to look around the White Buffalo, but visibility was limited and I couldn't see anything, not even shadows. "How far?"

His voice was quieter than it had been. "Not far."

I slipped the binoculars up and scanned the area ahead as he leaned against one of the rock walls. After a moment, I tracked something a couple of hundred yards ahead, something darker within the white. It disappeared, so I kept the binoculars on the area and waited. After a moment the fog and snow thinned a bit, and the outline reappeared; I quickly readjusted the power on the Zeisses.

"It's a cairn."

"A what?"

"One of these piles of rocks we've been following that mark the trail."

He looked back at the scree field that tilted upward to the right. "No, there's something else."

I squinted across the incline with its thousands of pebbles, stones, and boulders. I was looking for a shape, a shape different from the ones I was seeing. I continued to pan my way up the sides of the cliff and across the horizon, dipped down along the valley that led toward the east face and the Wilderness Basin, and lowered the binoculars again. "I don't see anything human."

"Huh."

"Virgil, there's nowhere else for him to go. He's boxed himself in on all sides." I slung the rifle farther onto my shoulder and jammed my hands into my pockets for extra insulation. "Any other direction is a drop-off of a couple of thousand feet." I could feel the bone in my pocket, and the burden of it was as great as the conditions. Here I was risking Virgil's life, and he didn't know that there was any connection with my chase and his family.

I'd just about committed myself to telling him the truth when he spoke. "My grandson."

I didn't look at him. "What?"

From the direction of his voice, I knew he was staring down at the side of my face. "I had a grandson, the son of my boy."

The women in my life have told me that I am the singularly worst liar ever. They also say that this is one of the reasons that they love me. I suppose it was that and the fact that I owed the man that I decided to do what I normally did in situations when I had cataclysmically bad news for somebody I cared about—I dissembled. "What happened to him?"

"I don't know."

The crusted snow had built up to where I was feeling like a living, breathing snowman. I coughed and could feel something liquid in my chest. In need of some type of movement, and because I wasn't willing to take my word over his, I brought the binoculars up to my eyes again, even going so far as to lift my goggles onto my forehead and to pull the balaclava down around my throat. "What was his name?"

The muffled quiet surrounded us. "Owen, his name was Owen White Buffalo."

I concentrated on the aperture and stayed as still as I ever have in my life. "Did you ever meet him?"

I could feel the steady vapor of his breath on the side of my face. "Yes."

"When . . ." I tucked my chapped lips into my mouth. "When was that?"

"I was taking care of him many years ago. I had periods when I wasn't in prison or in the hospitals." He chuckled. "Sometimes even when I escaped."

"Uh huh." The scree field was more visible now, and rather than face him, I continued to look through the binoculars; it was safer there.

He shifted his weight, and I could feel the bear fur brush against my shoulder; it was almost like having a grizzly for a spotter. "I was caring for him on a Sunday afternoon. His mother and father went to Billings, and I took him fishing; we had a deal, and I made him play chess with me the night before. It was one of those warm days at the end of the Hunter's Moon when the leaves have turned but before the first snowfall—a day that seems to make the promise that winter will never come."

"Indian Summer."

"Yes." He paused for a moment and then continued speaking into my ear. "He was tenderhearted—didn't like putting the hook through the worms. We'd used up all the bait because he had set the worms free, and he didn't want to go back to the bar at the landing to get more. I made him go with me in the truck, but he wouldn't go in."

I swallowed and lowered the binoculars.

"When I came back to the truck, he was gone. I remember the seat cover; it was one of those saddle blanket ones that you can buy anywhere."

He wasn't looking at me any longer but had his eyes focused on the snow.

"I remember the weave of the fabric—what it looked like with him not there, the depression in the seat." The great bear head lifted. "It was the last time I ever saw him."

It seemed like time was holding its breath; I could feel the pressure on my lungs and against my eyes, and it was almost as if I was back underwater.

"I don't know why they didn't send him. I know that he's dead. Maybe it's because he's not with my people; perhaps his spirit is uneasy and they can't find him—maybe he can't find me." I couldn't see his eyes under the maw of the grizzly mantle, and the only part of his head that was truly visible was his jaw and the scar that dissected the side of his face like an erosion in an emotionless desert. "If that's the case, then his body will have to be returned to my people, so that someday I might see him again."

It was at that moment that the Crow turned and stepped outside the safety of the crevasse, and I heard the only other steady sounds I'd been able to hear besides the voices since I'd crawled out of the pond—two three-thousand-feet-per-second rounds passing through Virgil's body.

Thwup.

Thwup.

It took a second for my dulled wits to understand what was happening, but when I did, I threw myself into him in a behind and to the side body block, forcing him onto the snowbank to our left. "Damn it to hell!" I yanked the rifle up as I lay over Virgil and, closing my finger around the trigger, trained the sights on the overhang and the ridge.

I played the Sharps along the horizon and could make out just the slightest aberration on top of the outcropping—the outline of something that just didn't look right. I waited and hoped he would shoot again and miss so that I could be sure that he was where I thought he was. I saw the muted muzzle flash along with the spectacular illumination of the snowflakes between us as another round buried itself into the snow alongside Virgil.

I aimed at the exact spot where I'd seen the four-point flare, squeezed the trigger, and the big-bore kicked. I was certain that if I didn't kill him, I hit part of him. I jacked the lever action, replaced the round from the butt stock, and slammed it home, placing another round at the ready.

I held the sights on the exact spot where I'd fired. If he was still alive, he might try for another, but if he was smart and ambulatory, he'd move. There hadn't been much of him revealed, but even a fragment shot off the edge of the rocks would've done the trick.

I lifted my head a little and became aware of the beer-barrel chest of the giant Crow rising and lowering. "Virgil?"

He coughed, grunted, and then strangled out a laugh. "I told you I saw something."

"How bad are you hit?" I adjusted my weight so that I wasn't lying on him, then reacquired my target as much as the whiteout would allow.

His voice was strange. "Bad enough—don't let him shoot me again."

"I promise." I kept my eyes on the rimrock.

I noticed that my shivering had stopped and that my mind was now relatively clear, evidently the side effect of every bit of adrenaline in my body being dumped into my nervous system. I wondered abjectly how long the high octane would last.

His words were slurred. "Did you get him?"

"I'm not sure."

There was a pause. "I would like to think that you got him."

"Me, too." There was no more movement on the granite shelf, and if I hadn't gotten him, he'd moved to another spot or retreated. I thought again about the old maxim that had crossed my mind when Raynaud Shade had fired on me back at Deer Haven Lodge: "The first one to move is the first one to die." Shade held the advantage in that I wanted to check Virgil's wounds and possibly move him to the overhang ahead, but I had to be sure that we weren't drawing fire while I did it.

So, I waited.

"How do you feel, buddy?"

He grunted again. "Not so bad; I think only one got me good. The other one deflected and climbed up my chest and face."

The original 55-grain lead-core round had a propensity to fragment at the cannelure at certain ranges, but that was crazy. "A tumble round? I haven't seen that since Vietnam—they haven't made those since '67. You must be imagining things."

"It climbed over my face, so I think I would know."

I suppressed a smile. "Sit tight, and I'll take a look at you."

He was breathing regularly, talking, and even joking, so I figured our situation must not be too bad. Trying to carry the monster to the overhang was going to be the hard part; as near as I could estimate, Virgil White Buffalo probably tipped the scale at almost four hundred pounds.

I hoped his legs worked.

I growled in my throat, knowing every passing minute wasn't doing the big Indian any good. "Virgil, I'm going to check you and then try and move us to that overhang."

"I would like to sit up."

"Okay, here we go." I lowered our only defense into my lap and turned, watching in amazement as the giant pushed off with one arm and rolled up to a sitting position. He turned to look at me, and the effects of the .223 round were evident. The bullet had ripped up over the surface of his jawbone, had continued across his cheek, and deflected from the ridge of his brow toward his hairline. The wound was deeper at the side of his face where the distended tissue was opened like a flap, and the majority of the blood was coming from there. The socket was already swollen but appeared operable. "Can you see out of that eye?"

"Yes. I have a matching set of scars now?"

"Like train tracks." I yanked off a stiffened glove and attempted to lay the flesh back together on his cheek, but it wouldn't stay. "Virgil, I need to see where the other round went, so I realize this is a pretty absurd situation, but can you hold your face?"

He gently nodded, and one of his enormous hands came up to press the skin back in place. I pulled the cloak open, revealing the moosehide shirt underneath, and could see two small marks where the slug must've fractured and split away into three separate pieces. I felt the spot where the round had hit and had to laugh. It was like a cliché from an old pulp western—the slug had struck the thick paperback. The book hadn't stopped the bullet, but it had deflected it enough so that it hadn't killed the behemoth—maybe it hadn't been a tumble round after all.

I started laughing. "Jesus, Virgil, Dante saved your life."

For obvious reasons, he didn't smile but grunted.

I yanked at the shirt, even going so far as to pull the book from underneath, noticing the .223 had gone as far as page 305. I tossed the book aside and gently peeled the hide shirt back— it was then that I saw where the second round had gone. Dead center, but with the angle of deflection and the big Indian's response, it must've traveled down and not into the heart or lungs. Where the hell did it go? Virgil had the unfortunate disadvantage of having the larger silhouette, thus being Shade's primary target, but he also had the advantage of having more room for bullets.

The only thing left to do was check his back for an exit wound, so I leaned him forward against my shoulder. It was like bulldogging a steer, but I could hear his breathing and it was steady. I pulled at the bear fur cloak that fortunately wasn't trapped underneath him, and then pulled the shirt and a thermal top away from his vast back. "Virgil, you may be the luckiest son of . . ."

The words caught in my throat when I saw the exit wound at his lower back.

The pack was lying next to him, so I snagged the first-aid kit that Omar had included from the bottom cavity. I put a number of pads over the wound, and then used the packaging as a seal to keep air out of the cavitated tissue. I tore open rolls of medicated gauze, which I wrapped around his chest and closed off in the front. "How are you feeling?"

He nodded.

"Breathing no problem?" He nodded, and I was pretty sure we weren't looking at a sucking chest wound or any sort of lung damage. I pulled the thermal, shirt, and cloak back down; with the loss of blood, he'd be facing hypothermic symptoms soon enough without keeping him exposed. I concentrated on his face and packed snow on the wound to try to stop the bleeding. It worked, and I was able to get a gauze pad and medical tape to stick. "Can you move?"

He swallowed, and I could see that he didn't like the idea.

"I wouldn't ask, but there's cover up ahead and I want to get you to it."

His legs shifted, indicating that his core was intact, but he didn't seem to be able to get them underneath himself.

"How about if I try and help?"

He nodded, but even between the two of us we didn't get much lift. He looked at me, and there was something I'd never seen in the giant's face before—just that little bit of panic.

"Virgil, can you move?"

He shook his head and slumped a little.

"Virgil?" Air escaped from between his lips, and more than a little panic now shot through me. "Virgil . . ." I placed a hand against his throat but couldn't feel a pulse, which wasn't unusual with the conditions. I moved my hand and felt along the side of his heavily muscled neck, still finding nothing.

"Lawman." I glanced up and could see one large eye, the other now completely closed. "You must go ahead."

"No." I tried pulling at his arm, but he didn't move; it was like trying to lift a grain mill. "C'mon, Virgil. I'm not going to leave you here."

I pulled on his arm again, but his eye just stayed there, passive—almost as if I wasn't there with him at all. Finally, he spoke in a soft but insistent voice. "You must go. The others are just ahead and you must save them—innocent people . . ."

"Shut up."

He sighed a laugh. "Go. I will follow you very soon. Just let me sit here for a few moments and catch my breath."

My voice broke as I lifted at his shoulders again. "Virgil, you're going to die out here."

He laughed again, softer this time. "Go, Lawman. I will follow, I promise."

I stood and looked down at him and at the snow that had collected on the bear head. I tore into the pack, pulled out the sleeping bag, jerked it from the stuff sack, and then wrapped it around him.

As I started to leave, his hand came up and rested in his lap. He was holding the battered copy of *Inferno*. I looked at him, and he fumbled with the book. "This book . . . You know who the lowest ring of hell is reserved for?"

I kneeled back down. "Virgil, I don't think you should be talking."

"Traitors."

I didn't say anything at first, but the words were in my mouth, looking for a place to go. "I thought you said you hadn't read this book?"

He tried to smile with a bunching of one of his cheek muscles. It must have hurt.

"Are you trying to tell me something, Virgil?"

He didn't say anything more, but the smile faded and he looked sad. I glanced up the trail and then back to him. "I'm going to go up there and finish killing that son of a bitch, and then I'm going to come back with the others and get you under that overhang. Understand?"

He didn't move, and his eye returned to the snow.

I tucked the bag around him a little closer and stood. "I'll be back, you understand?"

15

I cradled the rifle in my arms Indian-style as I walked, a fresh round in place and my underlying finger on the trigger.

We had been closer to the overhang than I thought, and it seemed to move toward me like some devilishly open mouth yawning from the snow, the frozen stalactites looking like teeth.

I continued to follow the tracks that Shade and the two hostages had made, Virgil's words echoing in my head. Traitors. Was it a confession? An indictment?

My eyes kept drifting to the rim overhead. The spot where I'd tagged Shade was disturbed, and there was no snow there. The closer I got, the less chance there was that he could hit me from above, but that didn't mean he wasn't waiting in the relative gloom of the shelter straight ahead.

There were a few dislodged boulders that had fallen in front of the overhang a long time ago; I stepped between them, and it was like a curtain parting. A few flakes floated like fireflies following me in, but other than a drift that had sealed the western side, it was bare underneath the granite precipice.

From the light of a battery-powered lantern, I could see there were two of them toward the back, and the man jumped when he saw me. The FBI agent, Pfaff, was tied with nylon zip cords and a bandana tight around her mouth. She was leaning against the back wall with a sleeping bag underneath her and was evidently unconscious.

The Ameri-Trans guard was seated a little away with another sleeping bag hanging over his shoulders; he was apparently neither bound nor gagged. He leapt to his feet with his hands behind his back, a little unsteady. "Thank God."

Some of the snow slid off of me and fell to the ground as I leveled the barrel of the Sharps. "Don't move."

He glanced at the woman and then back to me. "What?" He took a step forward, this one a little more composed. "Hey, I'm one of the good guys."

I raised the barrel slightly, centering it on his chest. "I said, don't move."

He stopped, and I studied him, especially the way the sleeping bag seemed to hang up on something at his back. He was the one from the truck, the heavyset man who had been having trouble on the ridge when I'd spotted them through the binoculars. His nose had been bloodied, and it was probably broken, the swelling overtaking his eyes that shone in the darkness like wet paint.

The stocking cap on his head was pushed up but the rest of him looked normal—except for one thing: he still wore full ammo clips on his belt.

Traitors.

He tried to distract me by talking. "Hey, we need your help."

"Why aren't you tied up?"

He started to say something, realized it wasn't something he wanted to say and certainly something he didn't want me to hear, and then settled on something else. "I am. I mean, my hands are."

"Show them to me."

He started moving, and it was a little too fast for my taste. "Slow."

I Ie hesitated, and there was that briefest of moments where I could see him trying to make up his mind. It all came down to judging—if you were a good judge of the man in front of you, you might survive; if not, then you were the honored dead. It's never about who's the fastest, strongest, toughest—it's always about who, when everyone else would pause, will commit.

"I'm really tired, and I've already done this drill with the convict you left in the Thiokol. He made the right choice and is still alive—you make the wrong one, and I'm going to dislocate a couple of your solid organs."

He remained motionless, and there was a dead silence as more flakes flickered to the ground in a semicircle behind me. "What do you want me to do?"

"Just drop it."

"It might go off."

I felt my finger maintaining a slight pressure on the trigger. "Well, then, bring it around carefully—like your life depends on it, which it most certainly does."

I guess he thought he could make it.

I guess he thought I was in worse shape than I was.

I guess he felt like this was his only chance. In a way,

I suppose he was right, but in another way, he was terribly wrong.

The Sig came around quickly in his left hand, but he could have been Billy the Kid and there was no way he could've aimed and fired in the time it took me to pull the set and final trigger. I had turned sideways for two reasons, the first to aim the long barrel of the rifle, which, unlike the short barrel on the semiautomatic, would place the bullet exactly where I wanted it. The other was to provide him with the smallest target I could—an old duelist and gunfighter trick.

Maybe I was still affected by my condition, or maybe it was that I simply didn't want to take his life, but I paused and he fired first. The round went to my left as he overcompensated and drew the Sig's barrel past me.

I pulled the trigger, and the buffalo rifle delivered its package at a much shorter range than it had been designed for in one hell of a thunderous response.

Nobody flies backward when they're shot; no matter how large the caliber and how close the shot, they just slump. You die falling down, which is a terrible way to die—it destroys the confidence before it destroys the body, and that must be a terrible thing to be left with in those last few seconds.

I stood there for what felt like a long time as the echoing sound of the .45-70 subsided in my head, finally stepping across the broken rocks and around his foot. I nudged the .40 out of his grip with the toe of my boot, bent over what was left of him, pulled off my glove, and placed my fingers at his neck. Nothing.

Must've been my day for it.

I looked at his eyes, hazel-green and staring at the granite ceiling, and then reached down with two fingers and closed them, completing the ritual.

The second jolt of adrenaline had produced no tremors, which told me that the surge was only enough to keep me going for a short time and get me back to barely operable condition.

I shrugged the pack off and turned to look at Kasey Pfaff, who, thankfully, was breathing. I could see that she had a monster of a goose egg at one side of her forehead, which might've explained why the sounds of the shots hadn't awakened her. I remembered that I had put my old bone-handled case XX knife in the zippered pocket in my pants, so I took off my gloves, retrieved it, and reached down to cut her free.

I kneeled and propped her up enough to get the bandana out of her mouth. She still didn't move but made a noise in her throat and then coughed, closed her eyes even tighter, and then opened them, looking up at me. As near as I could tell from the expression on her face, she had no idea who I was—after what I'd been through lately, I wasn't so sure myself. Covered in soot, ash, soaked with snow and frozen hard with ice, I figured I looked like some sort of golem. "You're okay, just relax."

She swallowed, blinked, and continued to stare at me. "The sheriff."

"Yep, the sheriff."

She smiled and shivered. "Nice to see you." Her glance went to the surrounding area, settling on the boot of the Ameri-Trans driver.

"He's dead."

"Good."

I laughed. "Not a nice guy?"

She coughed again. "No, he's the one who hit me. Besides, he made a deal with the devil for some money, which, by the way, turned out to be nonexistent."

"Where is Shade?"

She rubbed her wrists where the zip cords had left ligature marks. "He went ahead to the top."

"Do you know why?"

"No." She sat up a little and stretched her back. "I've been lying here forever. I'm sorry. I think my ankle's b-busted."

"You want me to look at it?"

"No, it's probably just sprained, but I don't think I'd get very far out there." She sat up a little more, coughed again, and looked at me with an odd expression. "He's carrying the bones of that boy we excavated from behind the rock."

"Owen White Buffalo. I know." I patted my chest. "He left me a souvenir."

She nodded and then glanced around some more. "Where's your backup?"

My thoughts exactly.

She looked puzzled. "What?"

"Excuse me?"

She smiled a crooked smile. "You said something, but I didn't catch it."

I thought I'd said it to myself but evidently I hadn't. I guess I was more tired than I thought. Talking with people was more confusing than being confused by yourself. "They're coming, but right now I need to go get one of them and bring him in here." I pushed off the rock. The driver was dead, and she was in no condition to help, so I was back to square one.

I reached over, picked up the .40 from beside the dead man, dropped the clip, and pulled the action, watching a round fly out, and was amazed when the federal agent snatched it from the air.

She held it in her palm and smiled at me. "My hands are all right."

"I guess so." I took the round, reinserted it into the magazine, and slammed it home. I handed her the sidearm and tossed the 9mm from the Junk-food Junkie onto the blanket at her feet. "A full mag in the .40, but only one round in the 9—I'll be back in a minute with our reinforcements, so don't shoot me, okay?"

I stood, readjusted my goggles, pulled my gloves back on, and started out.

He was gone.

Again.

The swale was still there where he'd fallen and where I'd left him, the sleeping bag was still in the semicircle where I had wrapped him, and even the paperback was still lying there in the snow.

No Virgil.

I looked around but couldn't see any tracks other than mine leading in any direction. I stooped in the trough we'd made and picked up the book and sleeping bag. What if he had become confused and followed me? It was possible that the ever-falling snow had covered his tracks, but there still should've been something, anything, showing where the giant had gone.

Surely he hadn't continued on after Shade; he couldn't even walk when I'd left him. "Virgil, damn it, this is getting ridiculous!"

My voice echoed off the granite walls. *"Ridiculous! Ridiculous!"*

You said it, brother.

The snow continued to fall, and the faint glow of the late evening sun was opaque, lean, and dying. Sunday; it was still Sunday as near as I could remember—a good day for all of this to end. If I was going to make any time before it got really dark and visibility dropped from twenty feet to two, I needed to get going. I drew the sleeping bag over my shoulder, stuffed the book under my arm, and started tramping my way back to the overhang.

I thought about some of the things that the big Indian had said about my daughter having a daughter. Could it be true? Could Cady have told Henry and Henry have told Virgil on his monthly grocery drops? Why would he tell Virgil? Why wouldn't anybody have told me? I was used to the clandestine relationship that Henry Standing Bear had with Cady, but this? I had wondered why there had been such a rush to get married, and maybe even suspected, but why hadn't she told me? Through the exhaustion and confusion, I was hurt.

And where the hell had Virgil gone?

Traitors. The last thing he had talked about was something about traitors—the final ring of hell, the ninth circle, surrounded by giants with sinners frozen at different levels in an icy lake that stretched to the horizons. Most thought that Dante's hell was a flaming, superheated place, which was true for part of the Florentine's journey, but in the *Inferno*, the real hell was an arctic, glaciated, and windblown place far from the warmth of God.

Traitors.

Was Virgil trying to tell me that he was involved or was he warning me about the Ameri-Trans driver?

I stumbled into the overhang, the sleeping bag dragging behind me, the distressed book in my hands. I looked at it again and noticed that there was something in it—a marker Virgil had left behind that looked like an owl feather from his lance. I shoved the paperback into my inside pocket with Saizarbitoria's phone. I had enough to try and think about.

"Who is Virgil?" She had moved as far from the dead man as possible.

"He's the Crow Indian who was with me. I don't suppose you've seen a seven-and-a-half-foot man wearing a grizzly-bear headdress and bear cloak roaming around here anyplace?"

She looked at me, understandably worried. "No."

I put the sleeping bag next to her along with the satellite phone and my backpack, took the ascent portion from the top, and detached the straps. "This is all I've got."

She took the sleeping bag and covered herself. "The rest of the task force, the marshals?"

I looked at her, trying to decide what to say. She had nice eyes, smart and resilient.

I spoke looking straight at her, so that there wouldn't be further questions. "McGroder survived. The last time I spoke with anybody they said that he was being transported down the mountain, but everyone else is dead."

She was looking at me strangely again.

"What?"

Her expression changed from amused to concerned. "Did you know you're talking to yourself?"

"I am?"

"Yes."

I laughed through a yawn and nodded. "I have a tendency to do that, but we'll be all right as long as I don't start answering." I yawned again. "Maybe I've been up here too long. Anyway, I've got to find sensible conversation somewhere." There was a hip harness in a Velcro panel underneath the ascent pack, and I pulled the straps loose and connected the buckle. I sorted through the supplies I had, dropping the majority onto her lap. "I'll take one of the water bottles and a little of the food." I tossed the Fed phone where she could reach it more easily. "The reception on this thing has been going in and out. Strangely enough, it's when I'm with Virgil that it doesn't seem to want to work—maybe he's tall enough that he's causing interference. The battery is at about half, but keep trying and maybe it'll work."

She took the phone, glanced at the ascent pack and then up at me. "Where are you going?"

"After Shade."

Her eyebrows collided over her bloodshot blue eyes as she leaned a little to the side. "Are you crazy?"

I turned my head and looked out into the gloom. "I'm beginning to wonder about that myself."

A couple of moments passed as she tried to decide if she was going to argue with me and which point of attack on my lack of logic she was going to take. This was not a pause I was unfamiliar with in my dealings with women. "If you don't mind me saying so, Sheriff—you look like shit."

I placed the supplies in the ascent pack and zipped it. "Thanks."

"I'm not kidding; do you know that the whole side of your head is covered in frozen blood? Did he hit you with one of those shots?"

I turned back to her, an old pro at hiding wounds. "No, I just fell."

"Lean in here and let me look at your eyes; I think you're concussed along with being hypothermic and who knows what else." I didn't do as she instructed, so she tried another line of attack. "I don't know what the ambient temperature is or the windchill."

I smiled at my boots. "Thankfully, the wind's died down."

Her voice took on a little edge. "What's the elevation up here, something like twelve thousand feet?"

"Probably closer to thirteen."

She shook her head at me. "It's nighttime."

"Yep."

"You'll die."

I threw the strap over my shoulder, pretty sure it wasn't going to fit around my coat. "*He's* made it this far."

She shook her head. "He's certifiably insane."

I stared at her. "Look, I don't know what he's thinking. I don't know if he's planning to sacrifice his life to finally stop those voices and visitations, or if he's got some sort of escape in his head." I sighed, pulled the strap of the rifle up, and settled my elbows on my knees. "You were his case psychologist."

"Yes." The .40 and the phone were still in her lap. "I wish I knew what he was doing, Sheriff. I was just recently assigned as part of the task force, so I've only been familiar with him for about a week." She reached down, and I imagined she was massaging her ankle. "I'd like to think that he was making progress in coming to terms with what he'd done and what was going to happen to him, but I don't think he's suicidal. He initiated the contact with us, no preconditions, nothing. He said he just wanted to show us where the boy, Owen, had been buried." She took a breath. "Whatever he's got planned, though, the boy's remains are key."

I stood, aware that depleting my reserves with even a short conversation wasn't wise. "The fellow who was with me, Virgil? He's got a knack for showing up at some of the most unpredictable places. He's hurt, and if he appears, keep him here. He's kind of scary looking but don't let that put you off."

She picked up the semiautomatic. "I could stop you by shooting you."

I yawned again; a big one this time. "You could, but I'm so tired I'm not sure if I'd notice."

She nodded and then translated it into shaking her head. "Don't worry about me. I'll look for your friend. What else have I got to do?" She pulled at the sleeping bag. "How am I supposed to keep him here if he shows?"

I thought about it. "Tell him stories; he likes stories." I pulled the goggles down over my eyes and watched the world turn amber-glow again. I wondered how long I could wear them outside in the darkness. I pointed at some of the candy in her lap. "Give him a Mallo Cup; he really likes those."

I took out my gloves, careful to keep the bone lodged in

my jacket. "This whole thing with Shade, it's kind of gotten personal."

"Between you and him?"

I pulled up the balaclava, fixed the rolled collar of my jacket, and pushed my hat down on my head. "Well, yes, and between Shade and Virgil; Owen White Buffalo was his grandson, and even with a slug and a half in him, Virgil is some kind of formidable."

She looked at me, incredulity playing across her face. "You're worried about Raynaud Shade?"

"At this point . . ." I reached over to get the dead man's snowshoes, unbuckling the more modern version of the ones Virgil had left upside down on the trail. "I'm worried about all of us."

I smiled at her one last time, but with my frozen features, who knew what it looked like. I turned and walked out into the steadily falling snow.

I trudged up the mountain not expecting to find much, relatively sure that Shade had continued toward his final goal, which I assumed was the top of Cloud Peak. There was a slight depression in the snow where he'd made his way, but I couldn't see any tracks where Virgil might've followed.

The spot beside the cairn where he'd lain near the edge was still evident. I knelt and brushed some of the snow away. There was blood, and I could see where the round from my rifle had hit the lip of the rock and had splintered it, effectively turning it into shrapnel. The majority of the frozen blood was near where his head and shoulders would've been.

I'd gotten him, but he was still moving.

I readjusted the goggles; it didn't seem to make much dif-ference with or without them. I knew that if I followed the cirque up the last scree field, I would finally get to the Knife's Edge, a redoubtable spine about as wide as a city sidewalk that dropped off a thousand feet on either side.

I'd probably take my goggles off for that.

Then it would be a case of simply bulling my way up the incline that led to the lightning-hammered top of Cloud Peak. At that point, there would be nowhere else for Raynaud Shade to go, or me either, for that matter.

I rose, turned my back to kingdom come, and started up, steadying my rate into the mule pace that had gotten me this far. That's how I was thinking about myself as of late, like some Marine mule that didn't have enough sense to lie down and die. It wasn't the most comforting of thoughts, but it got me up the hill.

Thankfully, the majority of the snow had been swept from the ridge, making it easier to spot solid footing. It was now fully dark, and the only good thing about that was that I couldn't see the passes that led east and west thousands of feet below.

The wind seemed to have let up, and I was glad that of all the elements I was contending with, the ever-prevalent Wyo-ming wind had been the one to decide to give me a break. That was a miracle in itself.

Maybe the Old Cheyenne in the Camp of the Dead or the Crow from the Beyond-Country were holding back the wind for me with their arms outstretched, battered by the gusts and ceding none.

Sacred lands for the Cheyenne and the Crow, we whites had been in the Bighorns for only a couple of hundred years—they had been here for thousands. There is a knowledge that comes of a place you've lived in for that long. These high mountain canyons that had served as highways for the indigenous peoples, allowing them passage from one hunting ground to another and relief from the summer heat below and the gathering of medicines, are their most hallowed grounds. At the center of all this grandeur and history was the mountain that I was climbing—Cloud Peak, 13,167 feet of geologic event.

But right now, it was just cold as hell.

I tried to distract myself by thinking of other things; I thought about the story that Virgil had told me about how he had lost his grandson that sunny October afternoon. I'd wondered about the animosity that seemed inherent in the relationship that he had with his son, a man who, after not seeing his father for so many years, had responded by spitting in his face. I could only imagine the panic that must've overtaken Virgil when he'd returned to the truck to find only the indentation in the saddle blanket seat cover. To not know what had happened to the boy—it was almost as if the gods themselves, the ones from the giant Crow's stories, had come and whisked Owen White Buffalo away.

The boy stands, and there was no fear in him; he could see the other that would welcome him and make him whole again. He dreams of the truck from which he was taken, silent now without his breathing. It is almost as if it is as it was meant to be, in that he never saw himself as a man; never saw himself as tall and broad-shouldered.

He sees the knife the almost-man carries at the side of his leg and worries for his grandfather, the one who has blamed himself for so many things. The one who will sit in the tin shack, the television the only voices to hold the silence of lost battles away—one more tragedy to take the place of all the others. The sound of breaking glass thrown against the thin walls as the boy's memory stands before him, eagle-armed, waiting to be lifted by his grandfather and the gods.

Shade's bullet had detoured at the thirty-fourth canto, which described the lowest ring of hell, the ninth circle, reserved for those who would betray. Traitors—Virgil's last remark. He had warned me about the driver, just as he'd taunted me with the words *innocent people*, over and over again.

Granddaughter.

Had Virgil developed shaman tendencies since cloistering himself in the mountains? He'd made those prophecies with so much certainty, just as he'd predicted the death of someone close to me as we'd crossed the frozen surface of Lake Marion. I don't think he'd meant his own death or mine—but then, whose?

Granddaughter.

I was glad it was a girl, if it was at all. I continued to cultivate the fantasy. She would look like my daughter; she would look like my wife. I held that thought since it comforted me above all the others.

I tripped over something, stumbled and caught my balance.

I looked to see what it was and saw that I'd angled toward the very edge of the cliffs between Cloud Peak and Bomber Mountain and almost stepped blithely into the limitless void.

The ice water that ran through my bowels wasn't figurative.

There were swirling masses of snowflakes that changed direction with the brief gusts that moved the air—and then nothing—blackness, farther than I could see, a thousand feet at least.

I breathed in and consciously told my feet to step back. I must've been getting close to the Knife's Edge; as a matter of orienteering, it should've been just to my left.

Pushing the goggles up, I glanced in that direction but everything was still invisible. It was as if the world fell away from me in all directions.

I was feeling disoriented and dizzy, so much so that I was afraid I might fall down and a hell of a lot farther than I wanted. I planted the butt of the rifle stock in the snow and kneeled in front of the raised lip at the precipice. My stomach surged, and I felt nauseous, almost as if I had fallen.

My lungs burned as I forced air in and out, and I finally laughed at myself for coming so far to almost end like this. The laugh echoed across the divide and bounced back at me again and felt so good, I did it a few more times.

It was a good thing I'd stumbled over the stones at the edge, or I'd have joined the Thunderbirds of Crow legend. I thought about how it would've felt flying for those few brief seconds before I dropped like a two-hundred-and-fifty-pound side of beef.

I reached out and patted the rocks piled at the edge that had up to this point resisted the urge to follow their brethren below. The flat of my hand thumped against their raised surface.

It didn't feel right.

The snow was stubborn where it had melted from the warmth of something underneath and then frozen again. The rifle fell to my side and clattered in an attempt to throw itself over the edge, but I slapped it still and pulled it back to me. I finally pushed the chunks of ice and snow away, revealing what appeared to be the great, silver-humped back of a grizzly bear.

"Oh, Virgil." My voice sounded strange in my mouth, and my eyes risked tearing; I could feel them freezing in the stubble on my face. "Even dead you find a way to save me."

16

I sat there for a while with my hand on his immense back and then carefully stacked a rock cairn at the edge of the cliff with the few loose stones that I could find so that if anything happened to me, someone would recover his remains.

It was the closest I'd come to just quitting, sitting down in the snow and going no farther. I would just stay here with my buddy and collect snow till the spring thaw.

But that wasn't what he wanted.

I thought about all the things that Virgil had told me and wondered what he'd been thinking about when he died. I imagined that he was probably thinking about the same thing I'd be thinking about when my journey ended: about his family, his loved ones—and even the not so loved.

Rising up slowly, I was aware of the weakness in my legs, the numbness in my feet and hands, and the fog in my head—it was as if I could feel myself, bone by muscle by tendon, slowly coming apart. The headache had returned with a dull thumping and with pain behind my eyes. I thought about the dreams I'd been having, what they meant, and maybe even who could've sent them.

I looked down at the mass of fur, once again covering with snow.

He wanted his grandson back, and I was the only one here to do the job.

Feeling the bone in my pocket, I knew it was time to go get the rest of Owen White Buffalo. I could feel the cold, creeping ruin that Raynaud Shade brought with him, an infection that trailed him like a curse. He and I were coming down to it now. There would be nowhere to go for either of us.

I picked up the rifle that I'd left lying in the snow and turned east. I looked at Virgil for just a moment more. "A-ho, baa-laax."

I stepped down onto the Knife's Edge on my numb feet, my hobbled legs, and with a headache that split my skull with the shearing force of a blue-green glacier.

A lot of people who try to climb this mountain make it this far but no farther. You can convince yourself that you're on solid ground and nothing's going to happen to you up to this point, but when you have nowhere to look but down, the game changes. I had the benefit of not being able to see very far, but it was as if the dancing flakes snapping into the distance and disappearing from view were pulling at me, reaching and trying to take me with them into the darkness.

I thought again about the spirits that I'd encountered in the mountains more than a year ago and the resonance they'd placed in my life, even though I still refused to believe that they existed. Maybe they'd left me, deserting me in the same manner in which I had deserted them.

There was a high ridge to the left that flattened and then

sloped away, unlike the one on the right side that just fell off precipitously. If I fell, I was going to concentrate on falling to my left.

The snow was deeper on the downhill side, making it that much more treacherous, so I found myself listing to the ridge. I put a gloved hand along the edge, using it like a rail, and kept my vision sturdily planted ahead of me in hopes that my meandering boots wouldn't lead me astray.

There were shadows ahead, indistinct and nebulous, writhing with the flying snow. I tried to concentrate on the shapes, but as soon as I looked, they would swirl away and dissolve in the dark air.

It was getting a little spooky so I did what I usually do when I got those feelings; I took off my one glove and slipped the .45 from my holster. The long gun was fine, but I couldn't see further than twenty feet and decided the sidearm would do for indiscriminate shooting. There wasn't anyone else up here other than Raynaud Shade, so it wasn't like I was going to hit anybody who was innocent.

There was no reason for it, but I stopped, hesitating on taking that next step almost as if I were standing in a minefield. My head was killing me, but I must've heard the faint *click* in my synapses. He was somewhere out there, and it was possible that he was seeing better than I was.

"Move."

I threw myself to the left helped by an aberrant gust that seemed to propel me, and fell against the spine of the Knife's Edge. I felt the air move along with the two rounds from the Armalite as they bored holes through the snowflakes like angry, hunting eyes. Both shots passed through the spot where I'd been standing only a second ago.

Lying there in the snow, I tried to triangulate the fire at least enough to give me an idea of where he might be—with the visibility as limited as it was, he had to be close.

The Sharps was underneath me, but the Colt was pressed against my chest and I turned my head, looking at the slight ridge that broke up into another scree field. There were a few large boulders off to the break line west where I knew from experience there was another drop-off of a couple of thousand feet. I could make out secondary fracture lines in the snow just back from the edge, one in particular about four feet in width that ran from the crest. Climbing off the Knife's Edge in that direction was a death trap of crevasse-ridden overhangs. One minute you would be walking, the next you'd have broken through and be falling close to a mile.

In the other direction, there was a steep incline that simply sloped off into nothing.

Cloud Peak was like an island in the sky with only one gangplank, the one I was on. I had him trapped, but he also had me; in fact, this was the perfect spot to pin somebody down, and here I was, pinned like a cushion.

He could move farther down the scree field, but that meant revealing himself. I could hope that he'd do that, but I had a suspicion he was too smart.

Time, in a sense, was on neither of our sides; reinforcements were eventually coming, but unless they showed quickly, it was just a question of when they'd find the two of us dead—not if. I wasn't sure of his condition, but I was starting to ebb. My extremities were numb, and I was shivering violently again. My body was trying to tell me that enough was enough, and was focusing its last resources in trying to keep my vital organs warm.

I raised my hat from my head and moved it around a little, but my feeble attempts didn't draw his fire. The steadily falling snow made it impossible to see, so I slumped back, careful to slip the strap of the Sharps from my shoulder along with the ascent pack. I rubbed my head with a hand that was rapidly feeling like a club. I swiped some of the snow onto my face to try to revive myself but still felt lethargic and a little confused.

I put my hat back on my head, rested the .45 on my chest, and shoved my hand into my armpit, my middle finger feeling like a stick. In any other situation it would've been funny; generally, the middle fingers, being the longest, are the first to become immobile from frostbite—Vic would've been mute.

That was when the wind resurged, climbing and slapping me to blast over the black rock of the west face.

I've heard it said that the Eskimos have hundreds of names for snow; Wyomingites have just as many for wind—few of them complimentary. I rolled to my side, giving the blasts of heat-robbing cold my back, but it wasn't going to do a lot of good.

Cold always wins—it's the natural state of things. I was going to have to get moving soon. If I didn't move, in less than two hours I would be dead.

The snow was already creating ridges around me, the high points of my profile forming sculpted edges, but it seemed different, as if the snow was not only changing color but texture, too. Sand; it was like sand, and as I watched, the wind began to winnow the dunes—and then me along with them. First the shoulder that I'd damaged in Vietnam folded into itself and blew away, my ear, then a leg, a hand, quickly followed by a wrist, a foot. It was all very strange, as if I were watching myself disintegrate into the wind.

Eroded.

I closed my eyes to try and stop the pounding in my head and drifted away with the dense fog—just for a few seconds.

Just for a few seconds.

The boy can see the knife even as the almost-man holds it beside his leg, knows what it means. He raises his fists at him and remembers the story his grandfather told him about the mating rattlers, and how their chopped-off heads struck at his hands. There was another story that he had told the boy, one in which the big man killed his first snake, a bull that his grandfather's father said you should let live so that the field mice don't eat you out. His grandfather's father had tied his grandfather to a bucket and lowered him into a well because of killing it. Down in that darkness he said that he had seen stars in full day. It is like that now for the boy, as if he is looking out of a well. He looks for stars, but there is only the almost-man. He waits, and at the last moment throws himself, all fists and feet flailing. He feels a fist connect with the almost-man's nose and sees the spasm of anger that leaps in the cold eyes. He is satisfied with this; he will not die without passion.

Spindrift powder was flung around me so quickly that I was sure I was still blowing away with it, and I pulled my legs and arms into a parachutist's tuck.

The hurting was gone, and it was good not to have to feel the pain any longer. The creeping cold was working its way through me as if it were something alive, but at the core of my body I still felt warm and almost calm. It made no sense, but that's how it felt and it was almost as if it had a voice as it inexorably continued to immobilize me. Humming, that's what it was like humming.

I listened to the noise that flew away with the pirouetting flakes, distorted and inhuman. I was sure I must have been the one singing, but I couldn't seem to stop. Besides, it felt good, and I kind of forgot about my tired legs, my bursting lungs, and my throbbing head. I lay there hunched against the jumbled rocks, convulsively humming and shivering. I could feel the two parts of myself, the one unemotional and objective, the other, manic.

I felt disembodied and limbless. All my thoughts of death were matter-of-fact. Maybe I was too tired to be scared. Maybe if I were more afraid, I would be able to fight harder.

It wouldn't be long.

Long.

A couple of hours.

Hours.

I was facing east after all. The sun would rise, but would I see it?

"Longer than a couple."

My eyes almost disjointed themselves flying open. "What?"

"Sunrise will be at five forty-three—seven hours from now. You will have died long before then."

The voice was coming from behind me, and I partially raised my frozen body onto one shoulder as I fumbled with the .45, turned my head, and looked into the wind, sure that Raynaud Shade had snuck up on me somehow.

I studied the outline of something huge right there beside me in the darkness. Its head was immense and had two small ears on top—the damaged one turned toward me in attention.

"You're dead."

The bear head shifted down to look at me, and I swear the ears again articulated. "Hmm?"

"I saw you; I saw your body."

The great opening below the bear's snout hung wide, and it was as if he was speaking from its maw, already swallowed. "I do not remember dying."

I sat up a little more. "You weren't breathing, and you were frozen."

"Was I?"

"Yes, right down there before you get to the Knife's Edge."

"Hmm . . . I must have been resting."

"Virgil, you were dead." I thought about it. "You are dead."

He placed his huge hand on my shoulder where I could feel the weight of it, heavy like the granite on which we were crouched. "I guess I'm not; I'm here." He scooted his girth in closer to me, and now I could see at least part of his face in the shadows. "What are we doing?"

He looked normal—well, with the exception of the ears on the bear-head cloak that continued twitching. Distracted by this, it took a moment for me to remember my situation, and I grabbed his arm. "He's up there with that Armalite."

He ignored my urging and looked past me, retreating once again into the shadows of the grizzly. "He is? He must be getting low on ammunition."

"Virgil, get down or you're going to get killed again."

He seemed surprised. "I was shot?"

"Twice."

He considered my remark and made a gratuitous move-ment, but not exactly one that moved him to safety. He shifted his arm around, and I could see he still had the war lance with the painted coyote skull and the rattling deer hooves, elk teeth, and wisps of horse tail. The hooves shifted as if they were running, the teeth moved as if they were gnashing, the tails swished, and the paint on the coyote skull seemed to undulate and move. "I don't think he's there anymore."

"Was I asleep when you got here? How long has it been?"

"I don't know." He took a deep breath and exhaled, and I watched the wind hold it in front of his face like a caul before snatching it away. "You were talking to yourself."

Maybe it was Virgil's reappearance, maybe it was the rest I'd had, but I was feeling better. "I've been doing that a lot lately." It was almost as if I was feeling too well and suddenly felt like I was on fire. I dropped the collar down to my chin. "Is it getting warmer?"

Virgil reared back, and again it was as if the two heads were doing the work of one. "I don't think so, colder maybe." He looked past, his eyes returning to the sullen darkness of the mountain, the broken terrain of the summit, ghostly and vague in the fast-traveling fog. "Very cold at the top."

I rolled over and looked up at the boulder-covered hillside. "I guess I'm getting my second wind."

"Maybe so." Abruptly, with the help of the war lance that stamped the snow like a horse's hoof, he stood. "We should get moving."

I half expected to hear the .223 again, but there was no sound except the returning wind. When I stood, something heavy slid from my chest and hit the rocks. I thought there would be more resistance, but my legs pushed out and steadied me as I rose.

"Perhaps you are the dead one."

I glanced up at him. "What?"

He studied the face leading to the summit. "Maybe you're the one who was killed."

I started off past him. "I'm not the one that got shot, Virgil."

He fell in behind me, unperturbed. "How do you know? You said I got shot, but I feel fine."

"How do you explain the fact that half your face is laid open?"

I felt the hand on my shoulder, stopped, and turned to look at him as he crouched down to place his features close to mine. "I have always had this scar."

I didn't move at first but then dropped the goggles so that I could see better.

There was no fresh scar there; only the original one.

I reached up and touched the unmarred side of his face with my glove. "Virgil, I remember that you had two wounds, a center shot and a tumbling round that hit the paperback and climbed up your face—I had to patch it myself while you held it."

He looked at me strangely and sniffed a laugh. "I don't remember any of that, Lawman. Are you sure you didn't dream it or make it up in your head?"

"It was no more than a couple of hours ago." I pulled his cloak apart so that I could see the blood-soaked mooseskin shirt, but when I did, it was whole and unstained. I stood there staring at him. But then I remembered the paperback in my coat and drove a hand in to pull it out. "Wait a minute, there was this book; the one you were reading when you got shot." I yanked the *Inferno* from my coat and held it out to him. "There."

He took it and examined it before handing it back, turning and sheltering us from the wind. "Is there supposed to be something special about this book?"

In exasperation, I took it and flipped through the pages to show him the damage it had sustained—but there was nothing there. The pages were swollen and sullied from the dunking I'd taken in the nameless pond, but there was no bullet hole stopping at page 305. I looked up, my mouth and eyes wide.

He sighed a deep yet uncomplicated sigh. "You know what I think?"

"No." I looked around, trying to get my bearings; I felt more and more lost and not just in a geographic sense. "And I'm not sure I want to."

"I think that one of us was sent to guide the other one to the Beyond-Country."

His words had a ring of truth that stung like hopeful loneliness verging on desperation. "Well . . . that would mean that one of us is dead."

"Yes."

The words hung in my throat, thick and lugubrious. "And that the other one is soon to be dead."

"Possibly."

I reached up and placed the goggles back over my eyes, chortling a sad laugh at the ludicrousness of the conversation we were having and where it was taking place. "Well, I remember you dying, so I think you're the dead one."

The grizzly reared a little in indignation, and Virgil's words were gruff and clipped. "I remember you dying, more than once. You died under the four-wheeler, in the fire, when you walked off the cliff, and when you lay down a while ago."

I stuffed *Inferno* back into my inside and damnable pocket; one more layer of insulation. "That doesn't make any sense, Virgil. You pulled the four-wheeler off me."

"Yes, and you were dead."

"At the fire?"

"I found your body." He dropped his shaggy head to look at me again. "You keep dying, but you keep coming back. It is all very strange, but I think the Old Ones have sent you back all these times to guide me."

"No, I had a conversation with the agent, Pfaff."

"I had a conversation with her as well, down in the over-hang; I told her how you had died and that I was going after the man with the bag because it was what you would've wished."

I brought my hand up and felt my forehead for a tempera-ture as my headache attempted to come back.

"I told her how you had burned up in the fire." His posture softened a little. "I'm sorry, it's disrespectful to talk of these things, but I thought it was something you should know."

"That I'm dead?"

He nodded and then was still, like a lizard on a rock; he didn't even blink, but I swear the bear did. "Yes."

"Thanks for enlightening me."

He didn't catch the sarcasm in my voice or chose not to acknowledge it. "You're welcome."

I guessed it wasn't that outrageous; I was sure that Virgil had been killed, but it seemed as if he was just as certain that

I had died, and numerous times. He had me, four deaths to one. "Well, whichever one of us is dead, we'd better get going. I'd hate to think that the Old Ones went to all the trouble of bringing us back and that we couldn't get the job done." Turning, I tacked against the wind that struck the ridge with six-pound sledgehammer blows.

"With the four-wheeler, the handlebars had driven into your chest, and your eyes were bugged out; you had frozen to death." Over the wind, I could hear his trudging footsteps behind me along with the rattling of the teeth and hooves, striking in rhythm with the words. "I didn't see you when you fell off the cliff and into the pass, but I heard the yelling—not very dignified."

We were on the steep incline, following the path that Raynaud Shade had left behind, even stopping at the collection of boulders where he'd thrown the few shots to slow me down. "Uh huh."

"When I found you on the Knife's Edge back there you were frozen the second time, but you looked more comfortable. You know, like you had died in your sleep?"

I stopped and rested an arm on the boulder. I was feeling pretty strong, but my breath continued to remain short.

"The fire was the worst one; you were floating in the pond like barbecued chicken, only with really white teeth."

It was silent, except for the noise of the wind and the accoutrement of Virgil's lance. It was another couple of hundred yards to the top, but then what? What was Shade doing up there? How many people had he killed to get here and why?

My mind, with the appearance of Virgil and his chatter, had become clear—but my body was another matter. The last reserves of energy were petering from my tank, and I didn't know how useful I was going to be once we got to the top. Virgil, aside from the fact that he'd had bullets pass through his body and appeared to have a living lance and cloak, seemed to be in fine fettle. If it came down to a fight, which I was sure it would, Virgil might have to be our man. "Virgil?"

"Yes."

"I've got to tell you." I took a few breaths just to steady my voice. "I'm not so sure how much help I'm going to be topside."

"You will be fine."

I leaned my head against the rock to try to steady myself in the endless, vertically sloped world. As I leaned there, I could feel my legs giving out beneath me.

I was about to crumple when two powerful hands grasped me and sat me on the lee side of the boulder. He took the Sharps from my shoulder and rested it against the granite. "You need to sit, Lawman."

I was numb; my headache was gone, and I couldn't feel anything, even the cold. "I don't think I'm going to make it." I watched as the brows on the bear headdress furrowed and narrowed as they looked down at me. "Hey Virgil, I don't mean to sound crazy, but are you sure that that headdress and cloak you're wearing is dead?"

The big Indian stared at me. And the bear winked.

Subconsciously, I pulled a little away. "Virgil, that damn thing is alive."

He studied me a few moments more and then began laughing. It was like a seismic event, slow and low at first but then roaring from his mouth. "That is why they sent you, Lawman. I thought it was because you never stop; you never quit. That first time we met in the long road culvert, you fought me to a standstill and no one has ever done that. I thought that was why the Old Ones had sent you, but it is because you make me laugh. No one tickles me the way you do—you say some of the craziest shit."

The bear winked at me again and then rolled its eyes.

"Virgil, I'm not joking."

He shook his oversize head at me and then leaned in close. "Did I ever tell you how I killed this bear?" I started to speak, but the headdress raised an eyebrow above his face, placing the upcoming story in a dubious light. "It was a tremendous fight, epic in nature. I was very tired, but I'll tell you how I defeated him."

"Virgil, there's something I have t-to tell you."

He ignored me and with one swirling movement, the giant Crow heaved himself up from where he crouched and whirled. His cloak flew off, and the wind filled it. The billowing headdress turned of its own accord and towered over Virgil with its claws outstretched, ready to knock my friend senseless with forepaws powerful enough to break a full-grown moose's neck. It froze there in the incline of Cloud Peak with its ferocious mouth hanging open, bellowing the wind into submission. Even the fog and snow were frightened, and everything stopped almost as if we were in a self-contained snow globe.

Virgil whipped his face back to me and spoke in a hurried whisper, as if the medicine that held the wind-bear might not last long enough. "I was busy and not paying attention when he came on me." He raised the war lance, and I watched it dance again; this time, the teeth of the coyote skull gnashed, and the elk teeth and deer hooves clacked. The horse tails swished, and the ermines slinked up and down the elongated shaft covered with felt trading cloth and sinew.

The giant bear continued to hover over Virgil as he spoke. "I could not see him, but I could feel him there."

I fell forward but kept my face up where I could watch the spectacle. "Virgil, you've got to let me tell you something."

"I grasped the lance in two hands and then rolled it back, rotating it." He swung the broad, obsidian spearhead toward the heavens in the opposite direction as a strange St. Elmo's fire flickered on its edge, growing and cracking until it sparked like metal in a microwave oven. Virgil then grabbed it firmly and thrust it into the floating bear behind him. The grizzly collapsed onto the point of the spear, and all at once the wind began blowing again and the snow continued to fall.

Plucking the headdress from the end of his war lance, Virgil swung the cloak around and enveloped himself, the bear's head once again shrouding his own. He laid the lance on the snow between us.

He stared at me, his face only inches from mine. "You must remember how I did this."

I nodded; it seemed so important to him. "I will . . . but Virgil, I'm not going to make it—and I need to tell you something." His face had a patient look, but there was no inquisitiveness there. I lowered my head so that all I could see was the spear in the snow. "The man up there, he's the one who took your grandson—the one who killed him." The words spilled from my mouth like broken teeth. "He took Owen's remains, and he's got them up there with him."

I stopped speaking and took a few deep breaths in an attempt to regain my wind, but it didn't seem to be working. I rolled my weight back onto the rock, slouching to the side enough to elevate my view. I'm not sure how long I leaned there like that before opening my eyes again. When I did, the lance was on the ground but Virgil was gone.

And so was the rifle.

17

I listened to myself breathing and thought about whether or not I was dead—it felt like it.

My breath was ragged, and no matter how fast I thought I was, I couldn't catch it. When I tried to stand the first time, my kneecaps had sounded like heads of iceberg lettuce being twisted apart, and I'd fallen. This is how it ends with everyone. You fall—you don't get back up. I wondered if Henry and Joe would find me, or if some unfortunate alpinist would stumble across me. If I was as off the main ascent routes as I thought I was, then it was possible that no one would find me for years. Like the man who disappeared into Lake Marion, I wouldn't come home and people would say, "Hey, do you remember that sheriff of Absaroka County that up and disappeared?"

Dumb ass. Yep, that'd be me.

I crouched a little lower against the boulder and tried to concentrate, but my head was killing me again, if I wasn't dead already. Thinking had become more and more difficult since Virgil had left.

I'd never given up on anything in my life when I was alive. I hadn't always won, I hadn't always been right, but I'd never given up. Not till now. Now that I was dead.

So, was that my purpose, to lead Virgil to this point? Maybe this was what it was like to be dead, going through the motions until you came to a grinding halt thinking about all the things that you still had to do. It certainly didn't seem so different from being alive.

Who would they send for me—the same individuals who had saved me before on this mountain and who had haunted Shade throughout his lifetime? Maybe it was like Virgil's statements about the *Inferno*, that all horrors are horrors of the mind. We summon up the devils we need to punish us for the things that we've done. If that was the case, then why had they sent me for Virgil?

Cady.

I wanted to talk to her about Virgil's prophecy. I thought about the cell phone and what the chances were that it still had battery power—*Slim to None: The Walt Longmire Story*.

I moved my hand up the length of the lance and could feel the horsehair wrapping around my hands with the wind, almost as if it was gripping me back. The deer hooves clacked together like chimes and the elk teeth mimicked them. In that small darkness with my eyes closed, I thought specifically of the things that I had to do, and the order in which I had to do them. I had to move, dead or alive. I couldn't allow Virgil to face Raynaud Shade alone. It was his responsibility, but it was my duty.

You have haunting to do.

I decided to put Virgil's beliefs to the test. My back felt like it was going to snap, but I hoisted the ascent pack onto my shoulder and used the lance to stand, my knees once again doing the vegetable melody.

I stood there in the blowing snow feeling like some

mountain sentry, but it helped to stand, not to fall down, not to concede, not to die—not again. I readjusted the balaclava back over my face, pulled the collar of the jacket up, the Gore-Tex encrusted with iced condensation and frozen mucus from my runny nose.

I growled in my throat, just to give my body a warning, and then turned to let my eyes follow Virgil's footprints as they angled up. I could see only two steps before they vanished into the low-flying clouds and blowing snow.

Two steps.

"Two steps."

I smiled at my cracking voice sounding back the words of my mind like the echoes from the rock walls below. I knew they were my words because ghosts' teeth didn't chatter—or did they?

Just two.

"Just two."

Swallowing what moisture there was left in my mouth, I turned and looked up the boulder field toward the summit, or where the summit should've been—and started up.

My right leg had become weaker than my left, probably because it was my dominant side and I had used it more strenuously. The strain on the tops of my thighs was excruciating, and my ankles moved like nineteenth-century hinges connected to my lead-encased feet. I kept my head down, dragging the snowshoes and concentrating on the rapidly disappearing prints, using the lance as a walking staff the same way the big Crow had.

I remembered that there was still a water bottle in the ascent pack, so I rested the lance against my shoulder and fumbled to get the container out. I found the thing and took no comfort in the fact that it felt like an anvil encased in plastic. I used my teeth to unscrew the top and then stuck the mouth of the bottle into my own. There was no residual water so I put the cap on as best I could and tucked the frozen bottle inside my coat next to the paperback of *Inferno*. The second the bottle got inside, I realized I'd made a mistake and plunged a hand in to get it away from me. My core body temperature was fighting a battle of its own, and I'd just dropped a thermal bomb on it for its trouble. I yanked the bottle from the neck opening in my coat and watched as it arced through the air like a mortar and disappeared into the darkness.

"Well done."

I took the spear back in my hands and looked at it. Why had he taken my rifle? It was the one of the two weapons that I would've chosen, but not the one I would've suspected for Virgil. Even with only one round left, maybe he wanted to make sure.

"Vengeance is mine."

Maybe so, but maybe it's only the living that can kill the living.

"And the dead that can kill the dead."

At least I still had my .45, and for close work it would do just as well.

"You just have to get to the top."

I stumbled and almost fell, catching myself with the lance and pressing it against my face, the coyote skull against my own. The decorations on the staff were acting as wind chimes, but I could hear something overlying the rhythm—a pattern that was staccato and sharp. A sound from my past.

I took another couple of deep breaths and listened, but it didn't repeat itself.

Vertigo slipped my perception just a little, and I almost felt as if I was falling again. I swallowed, but there was nothing there. I tried to remember what it was that I was doing, why I was leaning against a war lance. The top, I had to make it to the top of this mountain—something about Virgil and his grandson, Owen.

"Raynaud Shade."

I kicked off again, and this time headed straight up the incline. The big Indian's steps were rapidly disappearing, and if I didn't get moving and fast, I'd never catch up with him. He had angled his ascent, possibly to lessen the climb, but more likely in order to reach the top in some other direction than the one Shade might anticipate. There wasn't much room to maneuver with the cliffs on all sides, but Virgil was highly motivated. The only problem was that I'd seen Virgil die by Raynaud Shade's hands once, if not twice, already.

The rhythm repeated itself, more sharply this time, and it felt as if something flew by me, something small that sparked off of one of the larger boulders to my right, ricocheting deep into my memory. Gunfire. It was the Armalite set on automatic, and then the single, thundering shot of the Sharps.

I pushed off with a great deal more urgency, actually finding the momentum easier to sustain. I switched the war lance to my left hand and dropped my right one down to my holster—and felt nothing.

I panicked and yanked at my jacket with stony fingers, but the holster was most assuredly empty.

My eyes blinked in the safely encased goggles as a full-blown gust traveled from the center of my body. I could not remember holstering the Colt on the Knife's Edge. I'd been so startled by Virgil's appearance, the .45 must have slid from my chest when I stood.

There's no feeling like the one you have when you realize you are desperately in need of a gun and, in one of the few times in your life, don't have one. That short-circuited, spasmodic split second shot through me as I tried to think of what else I had in the way of firearms, but there was nothing. I couldn't go back; I barely had the energy to make it the twenty yards to the top, let alone a round-trip close to two hundred.

Never find it.

"Never make it."

The spear.

"For heaven's sake."

Dropping my head like a buffalo bull, I charged up the hill as if I was in slow motion, and the only thing I was conscious of hearing was my breathing. My lungs felt like they were going to burst from my mouth as I continued to push in a direct line for the top. It took forever, and I was sure I was going to stumble into a firefight, but when I did stumble it was because I had reached a flat spot.

I stopped and looked around, breathing so hard I was afraid I might swallow the balaclava. The wind was even stronger near the summit where there was nothing between the North Pole and me, the blowing snow enough to prove it; streaming diagonally, the flakes looked like meteors.

"Hell, they might as well be meteors for as high as I am."

I was at the apex of the Bighorn range. There was a down-grade to my right and a large outcropping at the center, but the entire summit was no larger than the size of a basketball court, a basketball court with out-of-bounds lines that plunged in a sheer vertical drop of a mile.

I stepped to the left and could feel the platform of granite rising another three feet against my leg. I didn't move but listened for something, anything that would give me an indication of where Virgil or Shade might be. I could only see maybe three feet ahead of me. I stretched out an arm and watched as my hand disintegrated and disappeared.

I drew it back, afraid that it might not still be there.

There was movement to my left, and I yanked my head around to see nothing except a few Tibetan prayer flags that someone had placed there. There were capsules lodged in the cracks of the rock as well, some of them evident and others half covered with snow.

They had to be here, unless they had already shot each other. I grazed my hand along the granite platform, leaned forward, and picked up the end of a tail.

Carefully, I lowered my goggles and, lifting and brushing the snow aside, could see that it was the painted buffalo hide that Hector had mentioned had been hanging on the wall at Deer Haven. Why in the world would Shade have dragged that all the way up here?

I sat and pulled my legs up after me, effectively joining the buffalo hide as if I were at a picnic. I sat there for a minute before noticing there was a lump at the center of the ceremonial robe that was now in the center of the Crow and Cheyenne world.

I laid the spear on the snow and leveraged an elbow to get closer, passing my hand over the surface and clearing the portion that read DEPARTMENT OF JUSTICE EVIDENCE.

I pulled the black, rubberized duffel toward me, the yellow letters looming large like passing a billboard on the highway. I lay there for a second, then snagged the large zipper pull and drew it back a little. I could see bones, so I reached into my coat pocket, pulled the femur from the protective Gore Tex, and poked it into the bag.

Owen was whole again.

I rested my face against the rubber and felt like I had accomplished something—that even if I was dead I had finished the job.

"You just won't die, will you?"

At the sound of his voice, I rose on one elbow and rolled away with the duffel still in my hands. There were no more words from the darkness, and unless his one eye was better than my two, he couldn't see me any better than I could see him. I tried to come up with something pithy but then decided that remaining silent might be a pretty good idea since the range of my weapon was only about six feet.

I grazed back across the buffalo hide and grabbed the war lance, dragging it back to me.

"I'm glad to see you."

The direction of the voice had changed, and he was now to my right.

"We're the only ones that they speak to, you and I."

To the left.

I raised myself up, aiming the head of the spear into the gloom.

"I can't believe you're still alive after all the times I've killed you."

Continuing left.

"You must be dead."

Right.

"Hell, I don't even have any bullets left. No bullets. Do you believe that?"

No.

"You probably have bullets left in that rifle of yours, even if I shot you a few minutes ago, huh?"

Maybe.

"No blood though. That concerns me; no blood."

It was quiet for a moment, and I took the opportunity to slip the goggles back up over my eyes. The way he had positioned himself, I was looking directly into the storm and the barrage of darting flakes.

"Are you a ghost now, Sheriff?"

I struggled onto my knees with the duffel between my legs.

"I sometimes think that I'm a ghost; that I wasn't really meant for this world. It's been that way ever since I was young and especially since I killed the boy. I think I knew what I was at that point, and what it was that I would become. There is no shame in it, becoming what your nature says you must be."

The spear in my hands felt like a telephone pole as I swung it slowly to where the voice continued speaking.

"Why are you here? I would have thought that you would've given up, but I suppose these same demons chase you. What is it you have done, Sheriff?"

I didn't move and still could see nothing except the shifting shadows of wave after wave of the snow in the air. It seemed as if the wind was lessening again and the flakes were now taking advantage of the situation to move in the air in patterns of their own, making it even more impossible to see.

"I think they answer to a terrible need—what is your terrible need?"

This time his voice came from my left and sounded closer. I planted my knees so that I could move quickly to the side.

"I have not finished my work. I must bury this boy here among the forever snow and ice, leaving his spirit behind so that mine may continue onward. It is like that; sometimes you must cut a part of yourself away so that you may grow. I was not sure if I needed blood sacrifice for this medicine, but I brought the woman along for that purpose. When I saw that you were determined to follow me, I changed my plan. I could see that the demons wanted you here, or why else would they keep dragging you back from the grave?"

"Maybe I've just got friends in high places." As I said the words, I pivoted to the right and dragged the duffel with me; the .223 fired high but still sliced through the sleeve of my jacket.

One shot, and then I heard the telltale click of the empty magazine; unless he had others for this particular weapon, he was out. He could still have one of the semiautomatics from the Feds, but to be honest, I was beyond caring.

Maybe I was beyond everything.

I raised myself up on my feet as silently as I could, propped my legs against each other, and prepared for whatever was coming next. Teetering there like a tree ready to fall, I held out my lone branch in an attempt to keep the demon at bay.

I stood like that, breathing the air through my collar and listening for anything. He'd gotten quiet, having played his main gambit, and now it was just going to be a battle of his nerve against mine.

My breathing was taking a toll on my equilibrium, and I found myself billowing back and forth with each breath, almost in a hypnotic state.

I was looking north, ever north at the house. It was as if I were the house, shuddering in the arctic wind. I felt the broken dishes in the sink and the emptiness of the exploded canning jars in the cellar. There were shoes by the bed, large, steel-toed workboots with the toes curled where they have sat for almost a year. There was a bottle there, empty and broken at the neck. It was lying on the floor, the glass shrouded by dust.

His last thoughts are of him, the boy; of what will become of his son.

There is no firewood left, no food, no water, nothing, just winter sunshine.

The touch of the white man's Indian woman clung in the floral design of the paper peeling away from the bedroom walls like dried leaves and the oilcloth-covered shelves. Tattered dishcloths and rags were stuffed in the cracks of the windows, frozen solid with the seeping moisture and dreadful cold.

The Indian woman left him and the child.

What will become of the boy?

This far from the lodges, the powwows, the meeting places, and the warmth of human interaction, a fire glowed in the darkness of an open closet door; a small set of eyes peered over the pulled-in knees at the warmest spot in the otherwise abandoned house.

What will become of the boy?

In a place near the arctic tundra all those silent months, the psychologists said that he spoke to him, keeping a running monologue that had mirrored the conversations that they had had when the man was alive and troubled in his mind.

What will become of the boy?

The mummified body of the old man did not smell any longer, a blessing that he died in the winter, holding off the creatures that would return him to the earth. The boy did not allow that when they came, fighting them till his fingers bled from the nails that he dug into the doorjambs. He had become one of those animals, and the social services people commented on the butcher knife that rose from the father's chest and how ferocious were the two eyes that would someday become one.

I stared at the flourishes on Virgil's weapon moving with the wind. The small, delicate feathers hidden among the brass beads were owl and, according to both the Cheyenne and the Crow, the messengers of the dead. Transfixed, I watched the tiny feathers. They were the only things on the spear that didn't move.

It arrived slowly, that finger-up-the-spine feeling, but when it struck me, I became completely alert with a shudder that took what little breath I had. My lungs constricted, and I twisted the war lance the way Virgil had shown me. It had seemed so important to him then, and I hadn't understood—but now I did.

Rolling the heavy lance over my shoulder, flipping it, and then wrapping my hands around it like rawhide sinew, I arched back and careered it with my entire weight.

It struck something solid with a liquid thump. It was good that it did because otherwise the momentum would've carried me over the east face. The end of the spear disappeared into the whiteout.

I could see the coyote jaws at the base and the leather wrapping, the red felt, the deer toes, the elk teeth, and the wisps of horsehair that were swinging with the wind and the momentum like the tails of an entire remuda. The painted decorations on the coyote skull were somehow more vibrant in the darkness and snow. The owl feathers remained motionless.

Hand over hand I pulled it back to me like a fisherman pulling in his catch and, emerging from the mist, there he was. The force of the blow must've cracked his sternum like a chicken bone, and the lance had driven all the way in to the hilt. His head was hanging down, the long hair hiding his face completely.

With each pull, he took unsteady steps toward me, and it was only when I got him within four feet that I could see the blood that spilled like an open spigot. His arm started to rise, and I saw the steak knife in his hand. He swung it faster than I would've thought possible, and the blade missed me by the closest of fractions.

It was all he had, and his next move was a groping, loose-limbed gesture that I caught with my open hand. I fastened what little grip I had left on his forearm and held him there. Slowly his head began to rise, and it took so long, I was sure that he wouldn't make it, but he did.

That frightening lone living eye stared at me through the hair, and he choked the words through the freezing strings of blood that hung from his mouth. "Are—you—dead?"

I kept my eyes on him through the amber plastic and tried to tell him the truth even though I wasn't sure what that was anymore. I owed him that much. "No."

He breathed out a sigh of surprise, and I felt him grow heavy on the end of the lance as we both kneeled to the ground. Our faces were only a few inches apart. I moved my hand farther up the length of the spear, thinking I might be able to jimmy the thing from his chest, but when I did, he used his free hand to stop me. "No." The hand, slippery with blood, fell away.

I watched as the shine in the one eye dimmed. He slumped forward, and only leaning against the length of the lance kept him partially erect. I reached across with a clumsy hand and closed the eye.

I don't know how long we both sat there, but I began to lose consciousness after a while. They say that one of the more unpleasant aspects of stage three hypothermia is that along with decreased cellular activity, your body actually takes longer to undergo brain death.

I had a lot of time to think.

The shaking had completely subsided now, a sure sign that my body had given up trying to warm itself. I suppose my pulse and respiration rates would slow as well and before long my major organs would fail—including my heart.

I really didn't think that there was any way Henry and Joe were going to be able to find me in time, and if they did, what could they do? The bag containing the remains of Owen White Buffalo lay on the ground between my knees, but my eyes refused to budge from Raynaud Shade. It was a horrifying yet compelling display; the strands of saliva and blood had solidified and, even if I could've gotten the spear loose, he would've remained locked in the same position.

Maybe that was what was happening to me; I was solidifying along with Shade and the mountain itself. It was almost as if even my breathing had stopped. I tried to blink and was shocked when I did. Closing my eyes felt good, and I thought about just leaving them closed but I had one more thing to try to do.

I shrugged, attempting to get my hand to rise up and unzip my inside pocket. No luck. I couldn't get the zipper pulled with my glove on my hand, so I dropped my chin, trapped a few fingers against my chest, and pulled the glove loose. I yanked on the small tab and it unzipped, the gymnastics of which threw off my balance. I fell against the lance, only inches away from Shade.

I sat there for longer than I thought, then pushed my hand up to where I could feel Saizarbitoria's cell phone and something else in the pocket, and started working whatever it was out from the bottom. The paperback of the *Inferno* fell onto my lap. I stared at it and watched as it slipped onto the bag containing Owen.

My attention slowly returned to the phone. I turned it over, stared at the buttons a few more seconds, and then hit the red one.

Nothing.

I gasped one of the last warm breaths I had in utter desolation but then watched as the device flickered green with letters that read LOW BATTERY. With a facility I wasn't aware that my thumb still had, I punched in the 215 area code and then the rest of the number. I pulled at the elastic band of the goggles that had guarded my ears and pressed the phone to my face.

The phone rang and then rang again in agonizing slowness. It rang one more time, and then my daughter's recorded voice began speaking. "This is Cady Longmire. I'm unable to answer your call right now, but if you'll leave a message I'll get right back to you."

"Cady—it's . . . it's Dad." The beep I was supposed to wait for interrupted me and I started again. "Cady, it's Dad. I'm a long way from home. I just . . . I wanted to tell you that I love you, and that I'm sorry. I'm just so sorry that I'm not going to get to meet her . . ." I could feel my eyes watering. "I heard some news; a little bird told me—well, a big one actually." I swallowed and tried to come up with some more words but before I could, I heard another beep and the phone disconnected. When I shifted it around, the screen was dead. I had no idea how much of my last message had gotten through.

I would have thrown it if I'd had enough energy, but instead, I simply let it slip from my hand. Crouched against the diagonal shaft of the war lance and turned away from the wind, I clawed the bag containing Owen a little closer—if they found me, they were damn well going to find Owen.

I'd make sure of it.

I couldn't raise my arms any longer, and I couldn't feel my legs. The effort of making that phone call was my last. It was all I could do to continue breathing, and my head dropped against the trade cloth on the lance.

The pin feathers were clogged with ice and were higher than any owl would've ever carried them. They were curled with the absolute cold but still did not move. Taking that as a sign, I used what energy the core of my body had left and closed myself in with the bones of the boy, the book, and the dead man.

As I lay there looking over his shoulder, I could see something in the snow and frozen fog.

I smiled as best I could and waited.

He leaned into the wind and spoke to me, and I was amazed to feel it die down with his voice. "How are you, Lawman?" He came closer, and it was as if he clouded the unsheltered sky. "Do you know how this place really got its name? There was an Absaalooke boy hunting these mountains who was pushed from a cliff by an evil man. The boy fell but was able to reach a cedar branch. As he hung there he was spoken to by seven bighorn sheep led by a great ram by the name of Big Iron. Big Iron saved the boy and gave him the gift of many powers—wisdom, alertness, agility, and a brave heart. Big Iron told the boy that the seven ruled the Bighorn Mountains and that the Absaalooke must never change the name or they would become as nothing."

The only air that I could feel moving was from his breath; strangely warm with a vague scent of cedar, and his features began to change; first the signature scar healed itself, then the wrinkles softened and stretched away as if the years were melting. The girth of the man folded into himself and became smaller, like a child.

"It was fun being big."

I tried to raise a hand, but it wouldn't cooperate. Instead the boy reached out, clasped my shoulder in a surprisingly strong grip, and leaned forward to whisper. "Aho."

My head lolled back, and as I looked into the sky, the vaporous trails and darting meteorites of snow subsided.

At first the view streaked like a dirty windshield, but gradually, small specks of starlight began filtering through and I was sure I was seeing the night sky. The fog and snow was level with the top of the mountain, and it was as if I were resting on a plain of clouds stretching out forever.

I thought about the thirty-fourth canto and could actually remember all the words of the closing passage. Perhaps it was because it had been specifically final, perhaps it was the relief of finishing the thing, or perhaps it was that last gasp of hope when Dante followed Virgil from that dismal underworld.

> We climbed, he going first and I behind,
> until through some small aperture I saw
> the lovely things the skies above us bear.
>   Now we came out, and once more saw the stars.

The waxing moon tossed a dull glow on the surface of the clouds, but it was the scattered layers of stars that held my attention. I looked at them and tried to feel the courageous heat of their battle as they fought against the natural state of all things in the universe: dead cold.

I could see the thick band of the Milky Way leading back through the galaxy. I tried to raise my head, but it fell to the side. Someone placed a hand on my face, and I looked up as best I could; it was like looking out of a well. "Owen."

The face came close but the breath was colder this time, and I could've sworn he was chewing gum. "Hey, hey—he's alive."

I could see something—they were Indians the way they always were. Two now, but closer, backlit by the thick stripe of the Milky Way running the distance from horizon to horizon; Virgil's Hanging Road—the direct path to the Beyond-Country.

Muffled and strained, I could hear someone speaking with more urgency than I thought the situation deserved. "What did he say?"

"A name, I think."

I wanted to laugh. If I could have formed the words, if my lips could have moved or my tongue cooperated, I would have laughed and told them that sometimes it helps to be dead to confront your demons, and that I had been dead a long time.

EPILOGUE

I was lying on my steamer chair swaddled in my battered sheepskin coat, the tactical jacket I'd grown fond of, and a few quilts, despite the direct rays of sunshine cascading down. The only part of me that was free to move was my right arm, which I was exercising by doing twelve-ounce curls in an attempt to balance my electrolytes. Cady thought I was balancing my electrolytes too much and wouldn't allow me to have a cooler on the deck anymore, but she had been discussing wedding arrangements with Vic when my accomplice had sneaked me another from the refrigerator in the kitchen.

There were a few pronghorn antelope grazing in the pasture behind my cabin that were taking advantage of the tender seedling grass that was pushing up through the darkened soil at the confluence of Clear and Piney creeks. A solo eagle drifted over the ridge and hovered there before plummeting earthward and out of sight—one less black-tailed prairie dog.

It was a beautiful June day, warm with a gentle breeze blowing from the Cheyenne and Crow reservations and, like the high plains summer to come, it stretched with hope. The hills were green, and the grandfather sage shimmered with that ethereal silver that made the Powder River country look burnished.

Just above the aforementioned ridge and the rippling foothills that led to the plains proper, I could see the very tip of the snow-covered peaks of the Bighorn range—and Cloud Peak.

I lowered my eyes from the mountains and looked at the hills instead.

Lying there in direct sunlight in the middle of the afternoon with the temperature hovering at seventy-five, I shuddered. The Cheyenne Nation watched me and took the beer bottle from my hand.

Cady and Vic were attempting to find lodging for the forty-some Morettis that would be attending my daughter's marriage to Vic's little brother in a little more than a month. As near as I understood from the threads of conversation that were drifting from the kitchen window, some of the more adventurous Philadelphians were going to be sleeping in teepees.

A few of the hazy clouds parted, and a full blast of sunshine struck my face from ninety-three million miles away. I closed my eyes and soaked in warmth; I could see why sunflowers did this all day. Dog panted but refused to seek the relative cool of the crab apple tree my daughter and Henry had planted in the middle of the deck in an attempt to get my little cabin up to nuptial standards. Everybody, including Dog, seemed to be hovering about me as if they were afraid I might drift away and be gone again.

It was possible they were right.

I glanced at the Indian; nobody did silence like the Cheyenne Nation.

We were both dealing with feelings of déjà vu, this scene seeming remarkably similar to the one after my last adventure on the mountain a year and a half ago. We had both sat here, drunk beer, and stared off into the distance as I'd re-collected myself from what had been one of the most harrowing experiences in my life—up to now.

I hadn't been talking much in the last few weeks; there just didn't seem to be that much to say. I had been gone—now I was back but having a hard time getting all the way back. I studied finished, man-made surfaces with distrust and couldn't seem to operate the simplest technological devices like television remotes or phones.

It was like a part of me was still up there. I pulled my hand up to finger the sensitive part of my ear that had been refrozen; I hadn't lost any more of it, even though the in-office raffle had sprung up again, complete with a chart and buy-in squares. My old boss and the now-retired sheriff of Absaroka County was still pulling for full amputation, but so far Vic was in the lead with "tenderness and an increased inability to hear things not wanting to hear," the last part having been written into the square on the chart hanging on my vacant office door. This had all the earmarks, no pun intended, of being something like what had happened to me eighteen months ago.

Henry had turned and was watching me, and I was sure he was having the same thoughts.

I closed and then opened my eyes when the clouds blocked the sun, and the first thing they rested on was the very tip of that hulking massif. I'd lived in the shadow of that mountain my whole life and had summited it numerous times—never again.

Henry and Joe Iron Cloud had gotten me down to the western cirque on the borrowed buffalo hide. Vic had taken over from Saizarbitoria at Meadowlark Lodge after returning from Deer Haven, which allowed Tommy Wayman and Sancho to clean up my messes as they came: first Hector, who was relieved to see somebody who wasn't an Indian or Vic; then Beatrice Linwood and Marcel Popp, then Moser, Borland in the Thiokol, the dead Ameri-Trans guard, and Agent Pfaff. Saizarbitoria, being the mountaineer, had stayed on the peak until Omar and his multi-million-dollar Neiman Marcus helicopter flew me straight to Billings for treatment, and I'd had tubes stuck in me for the better part of a week before they transferred me down to Durant.

I had spent the majority of my time in a place in Memorial Hospital that not many people knew about, a tiny little patio in the back that was built for the doctors so that they could have a place to go smoke before they all got healthy and stopped doing such things. It was there that I'd developed the pattern of allowing people to speak to me before talking to them, just to make sure they were really there.

Then I had come home and spent most of my time on the deck.

I was having trouble being indoors.

I'd also been having trouble concentrating, and that was another reason I'd stopped talking; I was getting tired of the strange looks people were giving me when I opened my mouth. I guess the things I was saying didn't make much sense.

I listened to the few house wrens and goldfinches in the new crab apple and a meadowlark in the pasture a little away. The sun cast its warmth through the hazy clouds, and my eyes slowly closed again as my head slipped sideways; maybe it was the sun, maybe it was the beer, maybe it was just that I'd thought that I'd never get warm again.

"Just because he was not there does not mean he was not there."

I opened my eyes and wobbled them over to where he sat in the adjacent steamer chair; we might as well have been on a cruise. This was the first thing he'd said today, other than "How is the patient," but I think that was meant for Cady more than me. He didn't say anything else but sipped his own beer—and then mine.

"Hey."

"WYDOT discovered the Jeep you mentioned on the slope leading down to Tensleep Canyon; they must've rolled it. The man and the woman were both dead." He studied my wrapped hand that I tucked into my coverings like a mummy returning to the tomb and then handed me back the half-bottle of Rainier. It shadowed the blown-out, spine-ripped paperback of Dante's *Inferno* that I'd decided to read again; something light for summer.

His dark eyes came up, and I suppose the period for silence had ended, but with Indians you never knew. I balanced my electrolytes again, without wiping off the bottle, just to show him that I valued our friendship over personal hygiene, and continued the running argument that we'd been having for weeks. "He was there."

The Bear nodded and watched the birds as they skimmed back and forth between the crab apple and a struggling cotton-wood at the corner of my cabin and said nothing. Like I said, with Indians it's hard to tell.

"What about the location of Moser's body and the four-wheeler?"

He blinked, pleased at having waited me out. "They were recovered along with the Thiokol and the other prisoner—and the one you left at Deer Haven."

"Hector."

"Hector." He took a deep breath and exhaled from his nose like a shotgun blast, something more playing on his face. "You know, I do not think he liked the idea of being alone on the mountain surrounded by Indians."

Vic joined the conversation from the open doorway behind me with the phone in her hand. "Speak of the devil." She walked over to my chair and absconded with my beer, just as the Cheyenne Nation had, and handed me the phone. "Pancho Visa."

She took a sip.

"Hey."

"Tough."

The gangbanger had been calling me sometimes twice a day to check on my progress. I brought the phone up to my undamaged ear. "Hector, you've got to stop calling."

"No, wait. I'm jus' sayin'. This is important. How you doin', Sheriff?"

I watched as Vic lowered the bottle, and I was amazed and aroused by the way she could drink from the thing without allowing the slightest bit of lipstick to remain. "Hanging in there. Hector, is this a legal call?"

"Umm . . . Yeah. Was that that hot deputy of yours on the phone?"

"What do you want, Hector."

"Oh yeah. The public defender here in Houston, David Thompson, wants to know if you'll write a letter to the judge requesting a leave of absence . . ."

"Requesting leniency."

"Yeah, that's it. Leniency. Do you think you could do that?"

"Yep."

"I mean, it's pretty important. It would get me off the chair."

"I'll have Ruby write it up and I'll sign it." I reached for my beer but was denied.

"Cool. I don't have the address, but I'll get it and call you back."

"You don't have to, I can get . . ." The phone went dead in my hand. "Expect another call from the BankAmericard Bandit." I gave the receiver back to Vic and looked at Henry. "What about the Ameri-Trans guard?"

He took my beer from Vic and drank. "The dead one?"

I nodded and tried not to think too much about the confrontation in the overhang. "The dead one."

Vic walked past me, then turned and sat on the leg rest by my feet. "He had a criminal record that had gone undiscovered by Ameri-Trans. A chronic gambler, he was more than a quarter of a million dollars in debt. He had made a deal with Shade, but as everybody suspected, the money turned out to be bullshit."

"You left quite a trail of prisoners and weapons the whole way."

It had been like this, everyone asking me questions and then not being satisfied with my answers. Most had given up, but giving up was not in the Cheyenne or the Philly/Italian lexicon— there were only tactical retreats and then reattacks. If we were going to get past this, then I was going to have to ask some questions, which was something I didn't want to do. I looked back at the mountain. "They didn't look for the cave hard enough."

The Cheyenne Nation was dressed for spring in worn jeans, moccasins, and a tan work shirt rolled at the cuff. He wore his hair loose because that was the way my daughter liked it. "It was a solid rock face, Walter. There were no ledges, caves, or crevices large enough to hold a marmot, never mind men the size of Virgil and you."

"What about the hand?"

He took a deep breath and pointed. "There was no hand in that coat when the medical personnel removed it from you. I was there."

I couldn't help but put my own hand into the pocket of the tactical jacket. "I told you I lost it."

Vic sipped my bottle of beer, a luxurious token to my recovery. "There wasn't enough time to examine the area in and around Lake Marion in detail, but the rangers said they found a branch sticking out of the ice where you said you found the hand with the ring on it."

It was quiet again, and I was thinking about not talking.

Henry gazed at the mountains and one in particular. "I brought the lance to the state archeologist, Bill Matthews, and he confirmed that it is over a hundred and fifty years old and in remarkable shape." He grew silent for a moment, and we listened to the birds making their bright, life-affirming sounds. "Matthews got curious when I told him the story Virgil supposedly told you about the drowned elk hunter who confronted the bear. He said he had heard this same story, researched it, and discovered that it did, indeed, occur."

"There you go."

His face slowly turned to mine. "Walter, it happened in 1898."

I sat there, feeling as if I were sinking into the deck chair, falling away from everything and everybody I knew. I had fought so hard on the heights of the mountains to get back to them, and it seemed as if no matter how hard I scrambled to hold on, I was slipping away. "When was the last time Virgil picked up his supplies on the mountain?"

His eyes remained steady on mine. "More than five months ago."

I fiddled with the lint in my pocket—I suppose still looking for a hand other than my own. "No one but me has seen him or heard of him or anything?"

"No."

I returned to silence.

He stood, and I watched as he walked across the deck and looked at the mountains.

Kasey Pfaff had suffered from a few of my symptoms but to a lesser degree, and it looked as if McGroder was also going to be fine. Beatrice was awaiting sentencing by the Feds and being held in the Big Horn County jail, and Tommy Wayman gave Ruby a call periodically to let us know how she was doing.

My attention was drawn back to Vic as she turned and looked at Dog, spread out on the deck like a Kodiak, reminding me even more of Virgil. I hadn't told anybody about Virgil's living coat—hell, things were bad enough with everybody thinking I was a nut.

The Cheyenne Nation's voice broke my reverie. "The memorial for Owen White Buffalo is to be held on Thursday. Will you be able to go? I think Eli delayed the services until you were better. He would like to speak with you."

I nodded my head. "Is that what this is all about, me getting my story straight before meeting the family?"

The silence hung around the two of them like the clouds on the mountain, and just as majestic.

"Joe Iron Cloud discovered your .45 on the Knife's Edge, and I found Omar's rifle standing next to the boulder where you rested before the final ascent. It was propped up where we couldn't miss it."

I should've stopped playing with my ear before somebody yelled at me again, but it was itching. "Did it have any rounds left?"

"One."

I glanced at Vic and reached out for my beer, which she started to hand back to me but then pulled away. "You think I'm crazy?"

She smiled a saddened smile. "Hey, you say Les Brown and his Band of Renown, Cy Young, and Harvey the six-foot rabbit were up there—I'm okay with it."

Henry returned his gaze to the mountains. "Just because he was not there, does not mean he was not there."

"I wish you would stop saying that."

I felt a warm arm slip across my shoulder from behind and encircle my neck as Cady pulled my hand away from my ear. She smelled good as she propped her pointed chin on top of my head, strands of her red hair slipping down beside my face and covering my wounded feature. "I think insanity runs in the family. Hell, it practically gallops."

To keep my hand away from my ear, I stuffed it back in my pocket. "Thanks a lot."

Her voice vibrated through my head, and I was reminded of the echoes on the mountain. "I think . . ." She paused, and I noticed Henry had turned to look at us—for the first time he was smiling that flat, barely detectable smile of his. "That your brain produced what you needed to keep going, kind of a psychological enabler. Your mind realized your body was running out and that you needed help, so it summoned up Virgil.

He'd already been on your mind because of Owen, and your greatest concern became your greatest need."

Vic continued to sip my beer. "You were about to die, and you needed help."

I didn't respond.

"Is it that hard to believe?" Cady swung around looking at me with those frank, gray eyes of hers and sat on the arm of my chair. "Or would you rather believe in ghosts?"

I brushed a glance at Vic and then at the Cheyenne Nation. "I believe that he was there."

"There was no cave, there were no prints."

"The wind could've blown . . ."

"No, there were spots where they would have still been there, but the only tracks everybody found were yours." She turned to look at Vic and then Henry, who could've nodded but spared me that. Cady turned back and kissed my ear. "I don't know why it is you're dwelling on this—you're home, and you're safe." Her eyes started to well. "I'm just so glad. It was horrible to get that phone message. I couldn't hear a lot of the words, but I knew it was you."

My own eyes filled a little, too. "I just wanted to talk to you, hear your voice."

She sobbed a little and then stifled it with her serious look. "I think you should stop doing things like this. You're no spring chicken, you know."

I pushed my fingers through the torn bottom of my pocket and into the lining of the Gore-Tex jacket. I thought about the things Virgil had said but tried not to dwell on the prophecy of upcoming sadness. "I know."

She smiled bravely, and I watched as all at once the tears

sprang in her eyes and wet her face, her whole body swelling. "No more mountains."

I punched my fingers down to the bottom seam of the jacket. "No."

Vic joined in. "No more falling off cars."

My fingers closed on something. "No."

Henry's turn. "No more getting shot."

A circle trapped in the corner. "No."

"Good." She swallowed and sniffed. "Because I've got something important to tell you."

My fingers closed on the metallic object in the lining of my jacket, and I thought about what Virgil had said about the horrors of the *Inferno*, that they were the horrors of the mind and the only ones we need truly fear. "You're pregnant."

Cady inhaled and looked at both Henry and Vic, and then they all stared at me with more than startled expressions.

"And it's a girl."

Cady swiped at the tears streaking her face, and I wanted to say something more to her, something fine. It seemed that on the tip of my tongue was something it had taken me more than a half-century to learn, something wise, beautiful, and brave. They were words that my daughter and granddaughter would especially need to know now, about everything that would hold Virgil's other prophecies at bay.

I pulled Cady off the armrest and into my lap, holding her close. I gasped a little in my happiness of having both of them in my arms, and lost the words, unable to hear them in the rushing sound of our blood—all three of us.

I kept her on my lap with one hand and continued to twist the fingers of the other into my pocket. I fished the piece of jewelry out of the lining. Wolves circled the silver background in turquoise and coral, chasing each other around the enormous band. Angled sideways, I could read the inscription: ICHISSHE, SANDRA—BACHEEISAA VIRGIL.

"With love for my husband Virgil, Sandra." I held the ring up where they could all see it and then turned it sideways so that I could look through it and focus on the platinum strip of dying light at the very top of Cloud Peak.

APPENDIX

The folks who have read advance reader's copies of the novel now in your hands were disappointed that I didn't include the book lists that the extended members of the Absaroka County Sheriff's Department made up for Saizarbitoria. I was concerned that it might slow the narrative, so I have included them, with their comments, here.

From Walt: *The Grapes of Wrath, Les Misérables, To Kill a Mockingbird, Moby-Dick, The Ox-Bow Incident, A Tale of Two Cities, The Adventures of Huckleberry Finn, The Three Musketeers, Don Quixote* (where your nickname came from), *The Complete Works of William Shakespeare,* and anything by Anton Chekhov.

From Henry: *Bury My Heart at Wounded Knee, Cheyenne Autumn, War and Peace, The Things They Carried, Catch-22, The Sun Also Rises, The Blessing Way, Beyond Good and Evil, The Teachings of Don Juan, Heart of Darkness, The Human Comedy, The Art of War.*

From Vic: *Justine, Concrete Charlie: The Story of Philadelphia Football Legend Chuck Bednarik, Medea* (you'll love it; it's got a great ending), *The Kama Sutra, Henry* *and June, The Onion Field, Fear and Loathing in Las Vegas, Zorba the Greek, Madame Bovary, Richie Ashburn's Phillies Trivia* (fuck you, it's a great book).

From Ruby: *The Holy Bible (New Testament), The Pilgrim's Progress, Inferno, Paradise Lost, My Ántonia, The Scarlet Letter, Walden, Poems of Emily Dickinson, My Friend Flicka, Our Town.*

From Dorothy: *The Gastronomical Me, The French Chef Cookbook* (you don't eat, you don't read), *Last Suppers: Famous Final Meals From Death Row, The Bonfire of the Vanities, The Scarlet Pimpernel, Something Fresh, The Sound and the Fury, The Maltese Falcon, Pride and Prejudice, Brideshead Revisited.*

From Lucian: *Thirty Seconds over Tokyo, Band of Brothers, All Quiet on the Western Front, The Virginian, The Basque History of the World* (so you can learn about your heritage you illiterate bastard), *Hondo, Sackett, The Man Who Shot Liberty Valance, Bobby Fischer: My 60 Memorable Games, The Rise and Fall of the Third Reich, Quartered Safe Out Here.*

From Ferg: *Riders of the Purple Sage, Kiss Me Deadly, Lonesome Dove, White Fang, A River Runs Through It* (I saw the movie, but I heard the book was good, too), *Kip Carey's Official Wyoming Fishing Guide* (sorry, kid, I couldn't come up with ten but this ought to do).